THE FAI

'A great book of suspense, intrigue, lies, lust, power, and murder ... a story that you just have to read.'
Sue Hartigan, All About Murder Reviews

'Rennick has created a fast-paced thriller in which you will figure out who the killer is several times, only to find out it is someone you never suspected.'
Kathy Thomason, Murder Express

'Rennick's characters are delightfully human ... truly original – a real departure from the normal, run-of-the-mill crime thriller.'
Nicola Sly, Phoenix Book Reviews

'The Fallen is an engrossing read where nothing can be taken at face value.'
Karen Meek, newBOOKS.mag

'A new voice has emerged on the British mystery writing scene ... *The Fallen* reminds the reader of some of the novels by the great British writer Peter Lovesey.'
Tom Mayes, iloveamysterynewsletter

'Robert Rennick is a newcomer to the whodunnit scene, but *The Fallen* immediately places him among la crème de le crime.'
Alexander James, Infinity Plus

About the author

Robert Rennick was born in East Yorkshire and was educated in Hull, York and Bristol. A journalist for more than twenty years, he's reported for regional newspapers in Berkshire, South Wales, and South Yorkshire. He now works as a news editor in a leading international newsroom. Robert is married with two children and lives in Middlesex and, when he can, the family's chalet on the Isle of Wight. *The Fallen* is his first novel.

More information from www.robertrennick.co.uk

THE FALLEN

An Iain Hogan crime thriller

by

Robert Rennick

First Published in Great Britain by Eyelevel Books

The author asserts the moral right to be identified as the author of
this work

ISBN 1 902528 29 8

Acknowledgements

Special thanks to my editor Paul Barnett. I was very fortunate to secure the services of a Hugo Award-winner. Any mistakes in this book are ones I've re-introduced after he excised them.

A big thank you to Sue Hartigan of the All About Murder group on Yahoo. Sue was the first to show faith in this book, and has done so much to promote it. Many thanks to Jon Moore at Eyelevel Books for permitting this new large-format paperback and hardback edition. I'm also indebted to Steve Warne and Peter Elliston for featuring the book on their first edition websites, and to everyone on the Isle of Wight and elsewhere who has bought the book, read it, or stocked it in their shops. Thanks too to Louise Webb for correcting some hospital details.

Also thanks to Phyllis Taylor Pianka, Toni Bellin, Stefani Catenzaro, Trish Cook, Melissa Gould and Andrea Hensher for their comments and suggestions.

1

The siren, then the blue lights, galvanised him. Sound and vision triggered some basic instinct, something atavistic. Hogan thrust the gearstick forward, and slammed his foot down on the accelerator.

Out of the corner of his eye he saw an old woman turn in shock at the side of the road, the village peace disturbed.

The moaning siren and flashing lights of the police squad car disappeared past him over the brow of the hill, towards the coast, down to the Undercliff. He aimed the Peugeot dead straight and followed, straddling the broken white in the centre of the road. It flashed strobe-like beneath the car.

His body lurched against the seat belt as the Peugeot dipped down the hill. The police car was still there, ahead of him, further towards the sea, diving into a one-way street.

He followed, swerving past the No Entry signs without braking, the car's tyres screaming for mercy. And he prayed no one was coming the other way.

The eerie pulsing of the siren's call was still loud and clear as he took the next corner, almost losing control. But then the road opened out.

It was clear ahead. He'd lost them.

He braked to a halt and scanned the horizon, the southern shore of the Isle of Wight, stretching to east and west. No sign until . . .

Yes! There! By the lighthouse.

The white lighthouse and its slowly rotating beam, piercing the daylight. And the blue police lights alongside, manically flashing.

Hogan parked the Peugeot next to the squad car. He saw the figures of two policemen over by the bottom of the upper cliff, and approached quietly. They still hadn't seen him. He watched as one officer hunched over a shape and examined it without touching.

'Poor lass,' the policeman said. Then he stood straight again, and peered upwards at the cliff, before turning to his colleague. Hogan was behind them, out of their vision.

'What do you think, Pete?' Hogan heard him say.

Hogan watched the policeman called Pete bend down and take his turn peering at the shape. Now that Hogan was closer he could see it was a body, and from the reactions of the two police officers it seemed it was a dead body.

'Dunno. Could be anything. Suicide – jumped off. Accident – fell off. Or . . . or something else,' said Pete. He scratched his head. 'CID should be along soon.'

Hogan coughed and moved forward into their line of sight.

Pete turned round. 'Bloody hell, you lot got a move on didn't you? We've only just arrived.'

Hogan didn't reply. He just nodded and walked towards the body.

'So are you the new guy, then?' Pete said.

For a fraction of a moment Hogan paused. Then he turned towards the policeman and fought back a smile.

'Yes, that's right,' he said. It was true. He was the new guy. No need for any lying there. Which new guy? Well, that was another question, and it hadn't been asked.

Pete looked him in the eyes. 'What do you want us to do then, sir?'

Hogan pulled his best exasperated look. 'Oh, come on,' he said. 'Surely you know the drill by now?'

Pete's face fell. Hogan even began to feel a little guilty. But the policeman immediately recovered himself.

'Yes, sir, of course. Gav – get the tape out of the boot. We'd better seal the area off. We don't want any sightseers.'

Hogan approached the body. He knew he didn't have much time.

It was a girl, quite young. Late teens, maybe. Her skin looked remarkably healthy for someone who was dead. Long thick black hair, but blood on one side of the forehead, and bruising. She looked so vulnerable, Hogan had to fight the urge to stroke her, comfort her. And her left arm. So sad and grotesque. The way the elbow bent the wrong way under her anorak. He shuddered and pulled away.

2

Someone else was approaching. Hogan moved back towards the two policemen.

'Who's this, then?' said Pete, looking at the newcomer.

'Dunno. Maybe it's the fucking press,' said the one called Gav.

Hogan watched as Pete's face creased in puzzlement.

'Hang on. That's Dudfield!' Pete eyeballed Hogan more thoroughly now. 'Detective Sergeant fucking Dudfield. So who the hell are *you?*'

Hogan just shrugged as Dudfield got still nearer.

'Birkitt,' Dudfield barked at the one known as Pete. 'What's going on?'

Pete looked shamefaced again. 'Bit of a problem, Sarge.'

'What?' said Dudfield grumpily.

'This geezer here. Claims he's from CID.'

Hogan's face reddened. 'I did nothing of the sort,' he insisted angrily.

'OK, that's enough,' Dudfield shouted. 'You two, get on with your work. As for you, sir' – Dudfield had come right up to Hogan's face, and was jabbing a finger into his chest – 'who are you? And what do you think you're frigging doing?'

Hogan sighed. 'Iain Hogan, *Wight Evening Star.*'

Dudfield raised his eyebrows and snorted. 'Might have known. Shitty little rag. Have you got any ID? How about your driving licence?'

Hogan reached into the pocket of his black waxed jacket and pulled his wallet out. He handed the licence to Dudfield.

The detective frowned.

'Says here your name's *Benjamin* Hogan. How do you explain that?'

'I don't particularly like my first name. So I use my second. Why? It's not suddenly a crime is it?' Hogan asked sarcastically.

For a moment he thought he might have pushed Dudfield too far.

'Don't get lippy with me, sunshine. Whatever your name is, impersonating a police officer is a serious offence. You are in the shit, matey. Deep, deep shit.'

Dudfield looked as though he might arrest him, but a cry from Pete Birkitt interrupted them.

3

'Sarge! Quickly! Over here! I just saw her leg move. It sort of spasmed, like. I think she's alive.'

Hogan cut the rasher of bacon and smeared it into the egg. Saliva pumping in his mouth in expectation, he brought the forkful up towards his lips.

Just then his mobile phone rang. He could see the other guests in the small hotel's dining room giving him disapproving looks.

'Yes,' he said, reluctantly answering. Never identify yourself to a caller, that had always been his way. You never knew what you might find out.

'Benjamin!' the voice at the other end barked. It was Richard Howze, the man who had been his mentor when he'd started out as a cub reporter more than two decades earlier. And now his new boss as well, the editor of the newly launched *Wight Evening Star*. Hogan was about to join the paper as its chief reporter.

'What?' said Hogan. 'I'm in the middle of my breakfast.'

'I don't care about your frigging breakfast,' said Howze. 'I've just had mine interrupted, too – by Superintendent Reilly of the Isle of Wight Police.'

Hogan groaned. He knew what it was about. He'd hoped the detective might have been distracted by the fact that the girl who'd fallen from the cliff had turned out to be alive. No such luck. Howze was so angry, and shouting so loud, that Hogan had to move the earpiece of the phone a few inches away from his ear. But he could still hear Howze clearly as he ranted on.

'The Superintendent claims you interfered with one of his men's investigations by pretending to be a police officer. What the effing hell do you think you're doing? You're not some broadcasting hotshot now, you know. I gave you this job to help you out – but remember you're only on trial. I'm beginning to see why they got rid of you, Benjamin.'

'Fuck off,' said Hogan into the phone. Hogan hated it when Howze used his first name, as he invariably did. Hogan preferred his middle name – Iain – or better still just his surname. 'Benjamin' had been his

4

father's idea, after his idol, Ben Hogan, the American golfer. It reminded Hogan of a part of his life best forgotten. Hothoused by his dad into a boy golf prodigy in such a way that by his late teens Hogan had come to hate the game.

'Look, I can explain,' he told Howze, 'but not now. I'll ring you back. I'm not really supposed to use the mobile in the hotel dining room.'

He stared at an elderly woman who was giving him the evil eye, and shot her a sickly smile.

Lee Hughes was, as always, precisely on time as he left the grounds of the chalet park at Reeth to take his golden labrador dog Lucy for her usual evening walk. As he set out there was nothing unusual to tell him that this time his walk would be different, that this day would change his life. It seemed like a normal late-September day, though somewhat hot for the time of year. The blaring police and ambulance sirens eighteen hours later would be the first sign, for most of the village, that anything was wrong.

Lee started to sweat profusely as he climbed the cliff path out of Reeth, being pulled along by Lucy.

'Easy girl, easy,' he said, trying to get the dog to slow down.

Lee didn't like the heat – it made him feel uncomfortable. He was overweight. Too many sweets, too many carbohydrates. But Lee was very fixed about what foods he did and didn't like.

Hot days brought visitors to the island, holidaymakers, surfers, walkers.

Walkers. They caused Lee the most grief, because they used his and Lucy's path. In the depths of winter, he and Lucy could walk the mile and a half to the Blackgang Chine theme park without encountering anyone else at all. The only exception would be the odd rabbit or red squirrel.

Now, with high summer over, there were a few less visitors, and the consolation for Lee was that most of the island's many tourist attractions were still open. He loved to spend time at the island's two model railways. They had the precision and certainty that Lee craved

5

– and therefore they held no fears for him.

But what Lee loved best was being out here on the coastal path, taking Lucy for her daily walks. It was an uncomplicated life when he didn't encounter anyone else. When he did, those who met him found him almost weirdly over-friendly, extremely polite, with a very deliberate manner. Almost as though someone at some time had carefully tutored him in the art of meeting and greeting. Which they had.

Up ahead, Lee saw a figure kneeling on the cliff edge. He braced himself, knowing he should say hello, that he should be polite. It was what good boys did. Boys who were naughty were rude, but Lee wanted to be good. All his life he had wanted to be good – yet so often at school, at work before he lost his job at the supermarket, so often he'd been told he was naughty.

As Lee approached he realised the figure was a woman, and that she wasn't looking at him. She was shrieking and crying. Lee became frightened.

'Hello. How are you? It's a lovely day, isn't it?'

He thought that was right. He'd been good; he'd tried to be polite.

The woman turned round. She looked terribly angry, or frightened, or something – Lee wasn't sure. There were black streaks below her eyes, as if she'd stepped out of some kind of monster movie. Her red fleece hung open; the shirt below was torn; her breasts were partly exposed.

'Help me, please help me!' she yelled at him.

Lee didn't know what to do. The conversation wasn't going the way it should be. And now Lucy was leaping at the woman, licking and sniffing her hands and face.

'Get it off, get it off! Revolting animal! Help! Help! Help!'

Lee firmly ordered Lucy to sit. The dog obeyed. But now he was frightened. The situation was outside his normal experience.

He reached into his breast pocket.

'Here,' he said to the woman, offering her his mobile phone. 'When I need help I ring Mummy. I'm sure she'll help you, too.'

The woman took the phone and began dialling, her hands shaking all the time. Lee couldn't understand why she was touching so many

6

buttons – when he dialled Mummy he needed just to hit the star button twice and then the number one.

He tried to grab the phone back to show the woman. He wanted to be good. He wanted to be polite.

But she pushed him away – pushed him away so hard that he fell, landing awkwardly and hitting his head on a rock. It hurt. He felt groggy, confused. He'd been trying to help, hadn't he? What was the woman doing?

He pretended to be asleep, hoping she wouldn't hit him again.

Then he heard her talking. 'Hello, hello. It's me. Me! Please help me. Come quickly. Something terrible's happened.

'N . . . n . . . no, no I c . . . c . . . can't tell you. I can't.'

Lee heard the woman sobbing.

'No, she isn't. Don't ask. Please don't ask – just come and help quickly. Otherwise I'm going to jump. Where am I? St Rhadegund's Cliff. Near the radio mast. Oh please don't be so horrible. I need you. You know that, don't you?'

Lee struggled to understand what was going on. Why was this woman saying all these things to Mummy? It didn't make sense. He'd have to ring her himself to make sure she hadn't been frightened by this madwoman. But the woman had his phone – and Lee was too frightened to try to get it back.

Lucy was licking his face all over, whimpering. He looked up, his hands over his face, peeking through his fingers in the way he did when there was something frightening on the television. He noticed the woman had once more turned to the cliff edge, sitting with her feet over the drop. Maybe she was going to jump.

But Lee wanted his phone back, so he could ring his Mummy.

He slowly got up, and crept towards the woman. She was still holding his phone in her hand. Perhaps he should ask her to give it back? But what would happen if she said no?

She'd already hit him once. Lee was frightened.

He moved slowly alongside her and made a grab for the phone.

* * *

7

Hogan managed to cut a deal with Howze. His new boss would sweet-talk the police if he filed copy on the cliff incident straight away, in time for that evening's edition of the paper. Hogan had intended to do that in any case. The story was already half-written on his laptop, even though he wasn't officially joining the paper until the middle of the week. Today he was supposed to be looking for somewhere to live – he couldn't afford hotels for the full four months of his trial contract. But the accommodation hunting would have to wait.

The second part of Howze's deal was that, after Hogan had e-mailed in the story, he was honour-bound to join his new editor in the pub for lunch. Following lunch, Howze would introduce him to the rest of the staff at the *Star*'s new offices. Hogan knew from past experience that, as far as Howze was concerned, 'lunch' in the pub meant precious little eating but plenty of drinking.

Writing the story proved harder than Hogan imagined. He was rusty. Too used to relying on news agencies to produce the facts and do the donkeywork. The girl had survived – PC Birkitt had been right – but she was in a coma on a life-support machine in Yarwater General Hospital. Hogan found that when he rang the police to get further details they were surprisingly helpful. Either news of his alleged 'impersonation' hadn't filtered down to the press office or Howze was over-dramatising things. Most probably though, it was because the police had no idea who the girl was – she had been carrying no identifying documents at all, and no one had been reported missing – so they needed the help of the press. There were fears over the stability of that part of the cliff. The police wanted that section of the Coastal Path closed, but a women's rambling group had voiced its opposition . . .

Eventually Hogan knocked something into shape, pressed the 'send' button on his computer, and fired the story off to the *Star*.

Hogan's B&B was in Reeth, close to St Rhadegund's Cliff, where the girl had fallen. Howze had said he'd meet him in the Red Lion – halfway to Yarwater, one of the island's main towns. The Peugeot struggled with the journey, and Hogan immediately regretted his attempts to keep up with the police car the day before. He cursed his wife Lynn. Her affair with an American businessman had led to their trial separation. Somehow she'd managed to be the one to keep the new people-carrier, leaving Hogan with the 15-year-old Peugeot GTI. He parked the car and entered the lounge bar of the pub.

He saw Howze propped against the bar, enjoying some rumbustious joke with another similarly hirsute and even more rotund character. Hogan remembered the first time he'd seen the man, some twenty years ago, at the *West Surrey Sentinel*. Howze had been full of bonhomie – enjoying being let loose during his spell as acting editor of the local weekly newspaper. Hogan had been a nervous trainee on his first day in the office.

Looking at Howze now, Hogan felt that, despite the broken blood vessels on the man's face and the slightly bulbous purple nose, it was himself rather than Howze who'd weathered the years less well. Howze at nearly fifty years of age looked remarkably like he'd done in his late twenties. Then, his appearance, thoughts and actions were for the most part those of a middle-aged man. Now Howze's age had finally caught up with the rest of him.

As Hogan approached the bar, Howze turned round and saw his one-time protégé. 'Aha – the one and only Benjamin Hogan at last. How are you, my fine fellow?'

The slightly over-the-top greeting was accompanied by both a bear hug and a hearty backslap.

'Hello, Richard. Good to see you again.'

'Benjamin,' said Howze, turning now to his drinking partner, 'let me introduce you to the Beast – the most fearsome character on the Isle of Wight.'

The Beast, who, when Hogan had first walked into the bar, had been perched on a stool, when standing towered over the other two men, even though they were both around six feet tall. The Beast must have been approaching seven foot, and was heavily built with it.

The giant of a man crushed, rather than shook, Hogan's proffered hand as Howze continued the introductions.

'This man,' said Howze, referring to the Beast, 'is going to be the saviour of investigative journalism on the Isle of Wight. He is the person to thank for allowing me to offer you one of the best jobs in

British journalism – that of chief reporter of Britain's newest and most fearless evening newspaper.'

Hogan could see the Beast – he didn't yet know his real name – was as embarrassed by Howze's outrageous bullshit as Hogan himself had regularly been twenty years ago.

'And this, Mister Beasty, is one of the country's foremost investigative journalists, Benjamin Hogan. At great expense I've recruited him from a top broadcasting organisation to bring him back to his true home, the wonderful world of print journalism.'

Hogan managed to restrain himself from laughing out aloud – in case the Beast really did think he was some crack journalist hired on an inflated salary rather than an average hack who was taking the job as a desperate escape from redundancy.

Howze handed Hogan a pint of locally brewed beer, the enticingly named Wight Spirit. He'd ordered it despite knowing full well that Hogan – himself a prodigious drinker in schoolboy and student days – was for medical reasons supposed not to drink.

Hogan tried to refuse, but Howze was having none of it. 'If you're working on my paper . . .'

'*Our* paper,' said the Beast.

'Of course, Beasty, apologies. *Our* paper. If you're working on *our* paper, then you have to drink, I'm afraid, Benjamin, my old buddy. And you have to drink our beer! And so, a toast. To a great team – and to the *Wight Evening Star* and all who sail in her!'

The Beast, Hogan and Howze together raised their glasses and drank. Hogan spluttered slightly, the strength of the brew and the unfamiliar taste after so many years without drinking alcohol overcoming him for a moment.

The Beast and Howze had no such problems. As Hogan looked up from his glass after his struggle with the first mouthful he realised the other two men had both almost emptied their glasses already – matching each other gulp for enormous gulp.

* * *

Three weeks earlier, the hooded figure had clambered over the farm gate, swearing as something dropped from the rucksack.

It was a small half-length spade. A fresh pile of cow dung cushioned its landing. Its owner picked the spade up gingerly, and began wiping it clean on the long grass with gloved hands.

It wasn't put back in the rucksack but carried as the figure walked swiftly across the field towards the cliff edge.

There was another fence here to negotiate, a tangle of barbed wire, most of it rusting and dull, but occasional newer replacement sections sparkling like Christmas-tree lights under the moon's glow.

Now the rucksack was on the floor. The figure knelt and began to use the spade.

Digging, cutting, through the springy downland turf. Marking a shallow trench, starting at the cliff edge, slowly moving across where the land jutted out slightly from the path.

The turf a couple of feet nearer the edge was worn. The ground held its secrets closely, but countless events had happened here. Walkers had rested, families had picnicked, lovers had kissed.

Soon erosion – and its insatiable hunger – would be fed. Weeks, months, years – how long did this ancient piece of land have left?

But timescales can be changed. A little encouragement, a little bit of digging.

The trench was soon complete, making a quasi-island of the tiny cliff promontory. Now the figure opened the rucksack and lifted out tiny packets and a tangle of wire.

Then more digging, this time in a pattern along the trench. Small holes dug with a trowel.

The figure arranged the wires and packets and placed them in the holes along the trench, then pressed a button on the box to which the wires led. The earth shuddered, but for now held firm.

The grass was long by the trench – it was only worn away a little nearer to the sea. Here by the trench the grass could be swept like a fringe over a wound, and this was exactly what was being done to it right now – very carefully. Cosmetically, the wound appeared healed. But, inside, the ground was hurting.

Something had changed. Nature had been challenged. Man had

interfered again. And Nature would take its revenge in time.
Just give it a little time.

After their liquid lunch, Hogan, Howze and the Beast set off in convoy for the *Star*'s new offices in Bolbrooke, on the outskirts of Yarwater. Following Howze's job offer, Hogan had read up a little on the island and its towns and villages. Bolbrooke, the location of the *Star*'s premises, got high ratings in the various guides – a pretty village of Victorian houses, with a magnificent and historic castle.

But Hogan saw Howze and the Beast had parked their car near some monolithic warehouse blocks. They were just getting out of Howze's Discovery next to a discount warehouse and furniture store.

His mood of optimism, probably induced by the lunchtime beer, dissipated.

'Here we are, Benjamin,' called Howze. 'I said our new offices were impressive.' He seemed to be half-laughing at the younger man.

Hogan grunted, and followed the other two round the back of the furniture store, noticing a scrappily but newly painted sign pointing the direction to the *Wight Evening Star*. Impressive my arse, he thought bitterly.

He walked quickly to catch up with Howze and hissed in his ear, so that the Beast wouldn't hear: 'I thought you said the office was in the pretty village of Bolbrooke. I was expecting a view of the castle. And perhaps some old-world charm – not this.'

Howze whispered back: 'As you well know, Benjamin, you must always follow the two most important rules of journalism. Never assume anything, otherwise you make an ass out of 'u' and 'me'. And the second rule, of course' – Howze winked – 'is never to let the facts get in the way of a good story. Don't tell me you've forgotten those two rules! You've obviously been away too long.'

Hogan followed the Beast and Howze through the back entrance of the furniture warehouse, which again had a hastily erected temporary nameplate overhead for the *Wight Evening Star*, and up a narrow staircase.

At least this bit's nicely decorated, thought Hogan.

As they reached the top of the stairs, the ambience suddenly changed again.

Hogan looked around, and was surprisingly impressed by the open-plan office, which looked to have been interior-designed to a high standard. It was bathed in glorious natural light through roof windows, and everywhere seemed to be a glint of glass and stainless steel, with modern minimalist furniture. Clearly a lot of money had been spent on kitting it out – a lot of the Beast's money.

'Hope you like it.' This came from the Beast, who until now had been remarkably quiet.

'Yes, I like it,' Hogan replied. 'Very, very impressive.'

Howze waved his arm around in a grand gesture. 'Just look around you. Good, isn't it? All very attractive – and not just the furniture!'

Howze winked again in his leery style, and just then Hogan realised what he meant. He looked around and could see several very pretty young women.

'I can see you're impressed by your future colleagues, Benjamin,' Howze whispered. 'Your eyes are almost popping out of your head. I'll introduce you to them in a minute, but just one word of warning. You are their chief reporter, their mentor – I don't want you leading any of them astray. So no trouser trouble, OK?'

Hogan found that he was deployed on the mystery of the cliff girl virtually full-time. It was the biggest story on the island. Despite their initial reluctance, Hogan eventually persuaded the walking group opposing closure of the Coastal Path to let him sit in on their emergency meeting discussing the incident.

He sat at the back of the hall, watched the members arrive, and studied the agenda.

WIGHT WOMEN'S RAMBLERS
Extraordinary Meeting
Godshill Village Hall
8pm (prompt!)

Consider response to proposed closure of Coastal Path
Consider motion to admit male members
Any other business

'Order, Order! Shall we get underway? It does say we start the meeting at 8pm prompt – and it's already seven minutes past! Jenny, please!'

Hogan had checked the names of the main officials in the group before the meeting began. The woman speaking was the Chairwoman, Clara Forbes. He consulted his list of officials and members. The Jenny she was referring to was, he assumed, Jenny Hintlesham, the Treasurer.

Clara Forbes appeared particularly angry that Hintlesham was still whispering to one of her friends, with her hand up to cover her mouth.

The room finally quietened.

'OK. Thank you. Let's start, then. The first item on the agenda is South Wight Council's decision to close the Coastal Path at Reeth, following an incident there five days ago. Maria, perhaps you could fill in the meeting with . . .'

'Excuse me, Madam Chairwoman.' Hogan saw that it was Jenny Hintlesham who interrupted. 'As you know, I am a councillor as well as a member of this walking group . . .'

'Ramblers' group, please,' said Clara. 'There *is* a difference.'

'Well, ramblers' group, then, if you prefer . . .'

'It's not a question of which I prefer. This is a group for women ramblers – not walkers. Anyway, get on with it.'

'With respect, Madam Chairwoman, I *was* getting on with it until you interrupted me. Anyway, as you know, I am a councillor . . .'

'How could we forget?' said Clara sarcastically.

'Clara, *please*,' hissed the woman sitting next to her at the top table. 'Let Jenny speak.'

'Thank you, Maria,' said Hintlesham. 'At least *you* have a proper grasp of procedure. To get back to the point I was making, I am a councillor and I was on the committee in question which recommended that the path should be closed. We didn't arrive at the decision lightly. If the members would permit me, I could give a full account of our reasoning.'

'That's all well and good,' said Clara Forbes, 'but the person who should speak first to outline the issue is, as you know, our Secretary. And that's Maria. So can we please not waste any more time? Maria . . .'

'Th . . . th . . . thank you, M . . . M . . . Madam Chairwoman.'

At the back of the room, Hogan finally started to take some notes. The pathetic exchanges between the various committee members had re-awakened best-forgotten memories of covering parish council meetings for the *Sentinel* all those years ago. For Hogan, it represented the worst side of local journalism.

He could tell that Maria, whose surname was also Forbes, was unnerved by the arguing. She took ages to gather herself, and when she did begin speaking she was nervous and stuttering. He wondered if the two Forbes women were sisters – they didn't look particularly similar.

'As I'm s . . . s . . . sure you all know, the g . . . g . . . geology of the Isle of Wight near its southernmost tip is extremely unstable, and the coastline is receding on average by 3.5 metres per year . . .'

Hogan began to take more interest. The detailed explanation of the geology of the cliffs seemed to have a direct bearing on the story about the girl. Much more interesting than what a women's walking group thinks about closing a path, he thought. But it was obvious Maria Forbes was not a natural public speaker.

She continued, explaining how the gault or slipper clay moved under chalk rock like a jelly, and how it occasionally tumbled down towards the sea in spectacular cliff falls which over thousands of years had created a sheltered, quasi-Mediterranean area, known as the Undercliff.

As Maria began to talk about the incident on the cliff where the girl fell, Hogan noticed her stammering start to increase again. He saw she'd gone very white in the face.

Moments later, she slumped to the ground.

Jenny Hintlesham jumped up to help her. Hogan himself leapt up and moved to the front. As he did so, he noticed that Clara Forbes was remaining rooted to the spot, staring straight ahead. Her face too had turned deathly pale.

Hintlesham lifted Maria's head, cradling it gently. 'Water, please! Has somebody got some water?'

Hogan grabbed a carafe of water from the table and handed it to her. He saw that Clara Forbes had now snapped out of her trance-like state and was moving to kneel down by Maria, full of concern.

'Oh, dear. She does occasionally have these fainting fits,' Clara explained to Hintlesham. 'It's her blood pressure, and unfortunately she sometimes forgets to take her pills.'

Hogan realised from the intimate nature of what Clara Forbes was saying that the two women must, indeed, be sisters. But her explanation of her sister's fainting made him suspicious. Someone with high blood pressure wasn't likely to faint from taking too few pills. It was the other way round.

Hintlesham dabbed some of the water on Maria Forbes's forehead. Clara's sister started to come round.

'W . . . W . . . We c . . . c . . . can't go on with this . . . We can't . . .'

Hogan wasn't sure what she was talking about or who she was talking to.

Clara intervened. 'It's all right, baby. You don't have to go on with it. Jenny can take the rest of the meeting, can't you, Jenny? I'll drive you home, Maria.'

Hintlesham reassured Clara Forbes. 'Of course. Don't worry. Are you sure you still want us to go on with it? We could always hold it another day, when Maria's feeling better.'

'No, I insist,' said Clara. 'I'm sorry about earlier . . . at the beginning of the meeting . . . I was acting like the big bully . . . I should have let you have your say.'

'Don't worry,' said Hintlesham. 'It was just as much my fault. You get off and take Maria home to bed safely. I'll look after things here.'

Clara looked at Hogan. 'Can you help me pull her up, please? If we could get her fully conscious I'm sure she'd know what to do herself – she's a part-time nurse.'

She looked angry when Hogan refused.

'Not a good idea,' he said. 'She needs to stay lying down for at least ten minutes. Here, pass me those cushions.'

He put the proffered cushions under Maria's feet, elevating her legs.

'It helps the blood get to her brain,' he said. 'When she does get up, make sure she does it slowly, and get her to sit in a chair for a few minutes.'

'How do you know all this?' asked Clara, suspiciously.

'Suffer from high blood pressure myself,' he said. 'If you take too many pills accidentally, this is what can happen.'

As Hogan looked closely at Maria, he noticed something odd. There was a circular bruise around her left wrist. He glanced at her right wrist. The same there. They were strange bruises, but fading and yellowing – he didn't think they were as a result of her fainting fit. So if the faint hadn't caused them, what the hell had?

'You shouldn't have done that, you know. Especially in front of the reporter. You must keep control of yourself.'

Clara was almost shouting at her sister as they drove home to Bonchurch from the Wight Women's Ramblers meeting in Godshill.

'I . . . I . . . c . . . c . . . c . . . couldn't help it. You know how I feel about everything. We have to tell someone and get it all out in the open now . . . before it's too late. The girl is in a coma, but when she comes round . . .'

'*If* she comes round,' Clara corrected her sister, a note of cruelty in her voice.

'Oh, don't! Please don't say that! That would be too awful.'

'Come off it! Get real for a moment. The girl is in a critical condition on a life-support machine. It says in the paper she's unlikely to pull out of it, and even if she did she's expected to have severe brain damage.'

Maria started crying uncontrollably. They were nearly at the detached Victorian house they shared – the family home left to them by their dear mother when she'd died five years before. Maria was the one who'd been looking after their mother on the island while Clara worked up in London at a leading stockbrokers – occasionally coming down at weekends, though in the last few years of their mother's life, as she battled a terminal cancer, Clara's visits dried up.

Maria had pleaded with her to come home more often. But Clara was enjoying the Bohemian life she led in London. She'd got in with a rather upper-class set of lesbians. Clara was the only ex-grammar schoolgirl amongst them. And her looks would never grace the front cover of *Vogue*. But it was the severity of her features, her muscularity from all the walking and exercise, which kept her very much in demand.

In any case, since she'd 'come out' some two years before her mother's death, about the time the cancer was discovered, she had been *persona non grata* as far as her mother was concerned. Little did their mother know that Maria had secrets too – dark secrets that only Clara herself was privy to.

Their Volvo estate drew up outside the ivy-covered limestone house. Clara heard the dogs start barking. She got out of the driver's door, went round to the passenger door, and dragged her sister out.

'Ouch! Stop it – you're hurting me,' Maria complained, between sobs.

Clara bundled her sister through the door, shooed away the dogs as they leapt up trying to lick the pair, and manoeuvred Maria to the seat by the telephone in the hall.

'Look, listen to me,' Clara said, this time more gently. 'You must pull yourself together. We can't go on like this, with you breaking down every five minutes. We have to maintain an air of normality. So far no one suspects anything. We have to keep it that way.'

Maria seemed to have calmed down, her sobs subsiding. But suddenly she grabbed the phone and started to dial 999.

Clara reached across in an instant and cut the line dead. She screamed at her younger sister, 'What the hell do you think you're doing? You're *mad!* Do you want to be caught up in all this?'

'I d . . . d . . . don't care. I j . . . j . . . just want it all to end.'

Clara finally lost it. She slapped Maria hard across the face, then grabbed her sister's ponytail and yanked her to the bottom of the stairs.

'Get up to the bedroom now!' Clara shouted. 'And get ready. You know what I mean.'

Maria shuffled her pain-racked body up the stairs, still in floods of tears.

Clara went to the storage cupboard under the stairs, opened it, and took out a metal-tipped walnut walking stick.

Brandishing the stick, she climbed the stairs.

If her sister couldn't see sense, then Clara would have to teach it to her.

2

Police Constable Emma Thomas smoothed her skirt, adjusted her blonde bob, checked her make-up in her vanity mirror, and then knocked on Detective Chief Inspector Hale's door.

'Come in. Ah, Emma, thanks for coming. Sit down over there, please.'

Hale, who was half-perched on her own desk, gestured to the low fake-leather sofa opposite. To one side, in another chair, was Detective Sergeant Warren Dudfield. Thomas found it slightly unnerving that, from her low position, her eye-line was well below both of theirs, making her feel ill-at-ease from the outset.

'How are you settling in, Emma?'

'Very well thank you, ma'am. I'd say I was pretty much fully up to speed now. Three months is a long time in a job these days.'

Thomas heard DS Dudfield snort slightly to one side, but she avoided looking at him.

'Yes, but isn't this a bit early in your career to be looking at new opportunities?' asked Hale.

'Well, I don't want to seem pushy, ma'am, but when I joined the force through the graduate fast-track scheme. . .' Thomas paused as she heard Dudfield snort again, this time more loudly. 'When I joined the force,' she repeated, 'I made it clear it was detective work I was primarily interested in, and this seemed a good opportunity to show what I'm capable of. And it won't commit yourself, ma'am, to giving me a substantive detective's job straightway.'

Thomas knew CID was desperate to recruit someone, anyone, half-decent. A new detective sergeant was supposed to have arrived the day before the girl fell off the cliff at Reeth, but at the last minute had opted to take a promotion with his current force on the mainland instead. Usually, CID had to fight off would-be applicants, but Hale's reputation for politically correct policing went before her – and put many of the old-school off.

She met Sergeant Dudfield's eyes. He was very much old-school. And rumoured not to get on too well with Hale.

Now he leant forward, towards her.

'You fast-trackers have clearly defined training attachments carefully planned out for you in advance, don't you? Surely you're supposed to stay in uniform, on the beat, for six months' induction?'

He sat back, looking pleased with himself. Warren Dudfield didn't care much for the graduate fast-track scheme, or for most of the fast-trackers themselves.

'Six months is the normal period, of course, you're right, Sergeant.' Thomas smiled sweetly at him while thinking, What a jerk! 'But I believe I've worked hard, had a lot of incidents to deal with in my three months. I've already been commended for my liaison work over the problem of youths fighting and drinking in Shanklin at pub chucking-out time. The locals were getting pretty agitated. I helped to keep a lid on things. Now I want to move onto crime detection. Like the cliff-fall case.'

'Well, of course, we don't know that any crime is involved there,' said Hale. She turned to Dudfield. 'How is the girl involved, Warren?'

'In a pretty bad way, ma'am.'

'And we still think it was an accident?'

Hale had turned her gaze back to Thomas. The policewoman thought the question was meant for her.

'That's the situation at the moment,' she said. 'But I'm not so sure that . . .'

Dudfield interjected: 'Of course it was an accident! That bit of the cliff's been dodgy for years. What we need to do is stamp down hard on those people who are insisting they have the right to walk along an unsafe path. Especially that lesbian walking group . . .'

Hale's face darkened. 'Warren! That comment is totally unacceptable. Their sexual preference has nothing to do with it.'

Dudfield's face reddened visibly, and he raised his eyebrows in exasperation.

That'll shut him up, thought WPC Thomas.

Hale turned back to her. 'Emma, I'd be interested in hearing more of your thoughts about the cliff incident another time. But for now let's talk about why you want to do this attachment and what you will bring to it.'

Thomas got into her stride and, with DS Dudfield silenced and embarrassed, started to impose herself on the interview. It went so well, at least in terms of her dialogue with DCI Hale, that she wasn't surprised to get an e-mail less than an hour after the interview ended saying she'd got the job.

What surprised her more was that, a couple of days later, Hale announced that DS Dudfield had more important cases to deal with. The DCI asked Thomas if she could take over the case of the coma girl – under her own direct supervision.

Acting Detective Constable. It had a nice ring to it, thought Emma Thomas. A small step on the way to what she was determined would be a stellar career. She wanted to prove herself, but not just for her own satisfaction. Emma had a need for recognition from her own father, her natural father. It clutched at her stomach, twisted her insides, and invaded every thought in her head. She'd tried to cleanse her brain and bleach the memories through therapy. But they were always there, ready to leap out at her from behind the next corner.

Assistant Chief Constable Eurig Thomas, rising through the ranks, his smiling face, his sickening platitudes, all delivered in syrupy Welsh Valley tones. How often had Emma seen him on the TV as the latest big Midlands murder hit the headlines? And the newspaper features on his happy family life, his beautiful wife, his two perfect sons. Tipped for the top, the insiders' favourite for the next Commissioner at the Yard. Only there was a part of his life the feature writers never seemed to uncover. How he'd left his first wife and young daughter – Emma and her mother – after discovering Mum in bed with her latest boyfriend. You couldn't blame him for leaving Mum in some ways. After all it wasn't her first. Even Emma had known that, though she was only nine.

It was the way he did it that angered her. Still. Cut them off. Both of them. As though Emma was some reincarnation of her mother, equally inclusive in bestowing her affections. How could he do that to her, to his Emma? It was a betrayal so intense that she almost hated him. Her only revenge, to mirror his spectacular rise. With no-one knowing the significance of her surname. And then, one day, one day she would confront him and expose him.

She opened the wrought-iron gate which separated the two symmetrical halves of the limestone garden wall. Nice house. Ivy spreading like capillaries underneath the stately white sash windows. The shape of a figure outlined in one of them, then moving away. A solid figure, female – but muscular and manly.

Emma rang the doorbell.

It opened, and the woman she'd seen at the window greeted her.

'Constable Thomas, thanks for arriving so promptly. I'm Clara . . .Clara Forbes.'

Emma reached out her hand, and winced. The grip of the other woman was fierce, almost painful.

'Pleased to meet you, Ms Forbes. It's good of you to take time to see me.'

Clara showed Emma through to the drawing room and gestured to a two-seater sofa on the far side of the room.

'Let's sit over here. I've got some of my paperwork out on the table so that we can take you through our side of the story regarding the cliff path.'

'OK. Good idea. Nice place you've got here.' Emma's flattery was genuine: it was the sort of house she'd love to own.

Clara sat next to her. The sofa had only just enough room for two. To Emma, it was strangely intimate.

'We love it. This has always been the family home. Anyway, shall we get down to business?'

'Sure,' said Emma. 'All I wanted really was a quick chat – but I thought it would be nicer if we could do it face-to-face like this, rather than over the phone.'

Emma simply wanted to discuss the Women Ramblers' opposition to the path closure. She wanted to get Clara to persuade the group to change their minds about lodging an objection. She needed this case to proceed as smoothly as possible, to be solved in the shortest time, and without anything which might embarrass the Isle of Wight

Constabulary. That way, Emma would get the credit, and the 'acting' prefix to her rank could be eased out of the way – as quickly as possible. Persuasion was one of Emma's strong points. She didn't know if Dudfield's rather pathetic reference to the sexuality of some members of the walking group had any basis in truth. Probably not, knowing him. More likely just another of his prejudices. But if there were any truth to it, Emma would just have to try to turn it to her advantage. She looked straight into Clara's eyes, and pressed her leg up against the other woman's, as she tried to win her round.

'So what do you think?' Emma asked finally, hoping she'd been persuasive enough. 'Would you reconsider your group's resolution over the path. The council will re-route it anyway. They'll have to. If you insist on a formal objection and on taking it to a higher level, all you'll do is just delay things. Couldn't you change your minds, just for me?'

As she said this, Thomas placed her hand on Clara's thigh and squeezed gently.

But Clara shifted, uncomfortably, into the far corner of the sofa – trying unsuccessfully to open up some space between their bodies.

'I . . . I'll think about it,' she said. Emma noticed Clara's voice catch slightly in her throat. What was it – excitement or fear? 'Why don't we talk about it some more over tea and cakes? I made some earlier. I'll just go and get them from the kitchen.'

A few moments later, and Clara was back with a trolley of sandwiches and cakes. Emma felt like she'd been transported to another age, it all seemed so formal and English. But before Clara could sit down again, there was a knock on the drawing room door.

As it opened, Clara leapt up, and moved towards the doorway.

'I said we didn't want to be disturbed . . .'

'Sorry Ms Forbes, it's just . . .'

Emma looked up, startled by the foreign lilt to the voice. There was a girl, a teenager, at the doorway. Almost Mediterranean looks. And very pretty. Who was she? But Clara had placed her body in Emma's eyeline, obscuring the view.

'What?' Clara sounded angry, almost bullying.

'The tea, Ms Forbes. You forgot the tea.'

24

Clara reached out and roughly grabbed the pot of tea, and at the same time kicked the door closed on the girl.

'I am sorry Constable Thomas . . .'

'Please! Call me Emma.'

'Emma – I hadn't wanted us to be disturbed. I do apologise.'

'It's no problem.' Emma frowned. 'But who is she?'

'Who? Oh that girl? Just the au pair.'

'Ah . . .'

An au-pair? Why do they need an au pair? Hale had reckoned it was just the two sisters living together. But Emma didn't voice her thoughts out loud. Something in the Forbes household seemed odd, but Emma couldn't place her finger on it. Maybe it might be worth spending a bit of time trying to get to know Clara Forbes, her sister, and her intriguing and rather young-looking au pair.

Michael Alexander wasn't a great lover of newspapers. He preferred to get his news from the BBC, preferably Radio 4. But this story, in this newspaper, he couldn't miss.

Pages of the local paper were wrapped round his evening meal of fish and chips, keeping it warm, and the report was on the outside – staring up at him.

He was mildly surprised to find it was a paper from earlier that week, rather than some ancient one. But then he remembered that the new local evening rag had been giving away free copies to try to build a readership base. The fish and chip shop had obviously found a better use for their free copies of the paper than simply giving them to customers to read.

The headline about a mystery cliff fall caught his eye.

A girl had fallen from the path that crossed his land. She'd survived, but was in a coma in intensive care.

Should he be pleased? Perhaps. It would mean for certain he would get what he wanted: the diversion of the cliff path away from his farm. His plan for it to run alongside the main road permanently would finally, and almost certainly, become reality.

No need to worry any more about where to put the bull.

No more costly fencing to keep livestock in, and the public out.

The coast could now form a natural barrier to his farm. And as erosion ate it away he wouldn't always have to rebuild the fencing and walling which at the moment separated the coast path from his pasture. Over the years, doing that had cost him thousands and thousands of pounds.

He was surprised, given where the girl had fallen, that the police hadn't already come knocking on the farm door. No doubt they would be here soon. He'd seen the squad cars on Sunday racing through Reeth, but had thought no more about them at the time. Now, reading the report, he felt uneasy. Everything pointed to an accident. But he was still worried that the police might come sniffing around the farm. Causing trouble.

The best thing, he decided, was a pre-emptive phone call.

He looked in the phone book for Yarwater police station, dialled, and got the force's central switchboard.

'I'd like to talk to the detectives investigating the cliff fall,' he told the operator.

'Hang on a moment, please, sir. I'm not sure it is CID in charge of that one – I'll just check.'

Alexander waited, rehearsing his story in his head.

After a couple of minutes, the operator was back on the line.

'Yes, it's just been passed to CID. Sorry to have kept you waiting, sir. I'll put you through right now. What did you say your name was again?'

'I didn't,' said Alexander curtly, 'but it's Michael Alexander.'

'OK, Mr Alexander. Putting you through now.'

The line went dead for a moment.

Another girl's voice came on the line. 'Hello. Can I help you?'

'I hope you bloody well can!' It didn't take much for Alexander to lose his temper. 'I asked to be put through to the detective in charge of the Reeth cliff case, and all that happens is I get you bloody phone operators.'

'No need to swear, sir.'

The girl sounded like she was laughing at him. It made Alexander even angrier.

'Look – just put me through to CID. Now!'

'This *is* CID, sir.'

'Well, get me onto a bloody detective! I don't want to be talking to secretaries all day!'

'Ooh, dear. Who's got out of the wrong side of bed this morning, then?'

This made Alexander livid. He was just about to put the phone down in frustration when the woman continued. 'I am the detective in charge of the cliff-fall case.'

'What . . .?' spluttered Alexander.

'You heard me. This is the twenty-first century, you know. Women are *allowed* to do jobs like this.'

'OK. I'm sorry.'

'Apologies accepted.' The girl – the detective – still seemed to be laughing at him.

Chastened, Alexander went on, 'The reason I'm ringing is because I have some information which may help you.'

'Yes, go on.' She sounded more interested now.

'I believe I may have witnessed the incident.'

'How do you mean, witnessed?' The detective was now businesslike, taking him seriously at last.

'Well, I didn't see anyone actually fall. But I did see what looked like a fight on the cliff path on Saturday. Late afternoon, evening it must have been. Nearly six o'clock. At about the same point where the girl must have fallen – or was pushed.'

'"Pushed"?'

'Yes. I don't know for sure, but certainly there was pushing and shoving going on. I was over the other side of the field, checking the fencing, about two hundred yards away, so I couldn't see everything clearly.'

'And why are you telling us this now?'

'How do you mean?'

'Why now? It's five days since it happened.' The woman sounded angry.

'Sorry,' Alexander muttered. 'Only just read about it in the paper.'

'Hmm. Well, I guess we'd better repair the damage. Please come down to the station right away.'

'Now? All the way to Yarwater?'

'Look, mister, Reeth *is* the back of beyond, I know, but it's hardly Outer Mongolia. It'll take you twenty minutes to get here if you drive fast. And after the amount of police time you've wasted so far, I'd get your skates on.'

Alexander was bewildered. This woman was like no police officer he'd ever spoken to before – not that he made a habit of speaking to police officers, if he could help it. Perhaps the cops were trying to be less formal in their dealings with the public? Even so, surely the detective was taking the policy to extremes.

He was so confused by her tone that he forgot to be rude to her. 'Sorry, yes. I'll leave right away. Who do I ask for when I get there?'

'Acting Detective Constable Thomas . . . On second thoughts, just 'Detective Constable Thomas' will do. I've had enough of this 'acting' lark. And by the way . . .'

'What?' Alexander asked.

'It might be helpful if you gave me your name.' The policewoman's tone was lighter. She was almost laughing at him again.

'Alexander. Michael Alexander. I told your receptionist.'

'Right, Mr Alexander. I'll be expecting you. Make sure you get a move on.'

Hogan parked the Peugeot opposite the Buddle Inn, where he'd arranged to meet the new detective on the cliff-fall case. He turned the ignition to the 'off' position, but the motor kept running for a few seconds before finally spluttering to a halt. Hogan cursed Lynn for the thousandth time for not getting the car serviced more regularly. The delayed stopping was a sure sign the timing was out. He'd noticed too that the car was struggling with the hills on the island, as though the clutch were slipping.

A big garage bill loomed. Hogan didn't think he'd be able to afford it. He was still paying the mortgage on the family home in Twickenham until his and Lynn's lawyers could work out a settlement. Plus at the moment he had his hotel bill to pay – and he still needed to find somewhere more permanent to rent on the island.

Acting Detective Constable Emma Thomas had been the one to suggest the pub as a meeting place. It was near Reeth and the spot at St Rhadegund's Cliff where the girl had fallen, and DC Thomas was planning to show him the bit of the Coastal Path in question.

The pub was in a fantastic location, towards the bottom of the Undercliff above Castlehaven Cove, with glorious sea views. Hogan sat in the car for a couple of minutes and just drank it in, his head lighthousing from side to side to survey the panorama. By rights, with his marriage problems, money problems and the sense of dislocation he was inevitably feeling in starting a new job, his spirits should have been down. But there was something about this island that lifted him. Hogan could see his four-month trial period at the *Star* extending to half a year, if not longer. He knew the kids would love it here.

Nearby Ventnor had its famous botanical gardens, but the whole of the Undercliff was almost like a huge, naturally occurring subtropical plantation. Every private garden had palm trees. And the previous evening, when he'd gone for a short walk as a break from the claustrophobia of his room at the B&B, he'd heard scores of crickets chirruping in the hedgerows. Unusual in England at any time – but at the end of September? Unbelievable, thought Hogan. Maybe the blurb in the guidebooks hadn't been as over-the-top as he'd thought; maybe this really was the closest England got to the Mediterranean.

The Buddle Inn itself, however, was English through and through. It was an old smugglers' pub, dating back to the eighteenth century. This, the southernmost point of the Isle of Wight, had been the island's main smuggling centre.

Hogan pushed open the heavy oak front door and scanned the bar area. He was holding that day's copy of the *Wight Evening Star* prominently – the sign he'd agreed with the detective to help her to spot him. DC Thomas had joked to Hogan that he wouldn't miss her because she was a stunning and youthful Meg Ryan lookalike. At least, Hogan had thought she was joking.

But Meg Ryan – or anyone who looked even remotely like her – didn't seem to be visiting the Buddle Inn today.

29

In fact, the only woman in evidence, sitting on her own in the corner, didn't have many female characteristics at all. Yes, she was wearing a skirt – quite a short one, showing off muscular and rather manly legs. But she was – if indeed it was a she – a blonde.

I'd better make sure, thought Hogan.

'Excuse me, Detective Thomas . . .?'

'No, I'm sorry,' the man/woman replied in such a patently false falsetto that Hogan's suspicions were immediately confirmed. She was a he, or an it, or a trans- something or other. But certainly not a Meg Ryan lookalike.

He retreated to the bar, only to be confronted by another dilemma.

The Buddle Inn's magnificent range of real ales stood arrayed before him – a line of erect hand-pumps all looking horribly tempting. Howze had obviously sparked something when he'd insisted Hogan have a beer along with him and the Beast the other day.

Before his brain could compute a request for a non-alcoholic drink, such as orange juice and mineral water, temptation got the better of him. The Ventnor Brewery emblem on the hand-pump looked so inviting. He found himself demanding a pint of Wight Spirit, like a true local.

Twenty minutes later, and the detective had still failed to show. So Hogan ordered another. He was down to the last mouthful of his second pint, staring mournfully at the bottom of the glass and thinking he'd been stood up and that his scoop had gone down the pan, when there was a tap on his shoulder. He spun round on the barstool.

Standing before him, smiling slightly cheekily, was a young blonde woman, seemingly barely much more than twenty. Small features, pretty snub nose, and a thick bob of what looked like natural blonde hair.

He could feel his face redden as he realised he was gaping at her.

She held out her hand. She was smirking at him now – as though she knew what he was thinking.

'Hi. You must be Iain Hogan. I'm Emma Thomas. Sorry I'm a bit late.'

He tried to regain his composure. 'Hi, Emma. Good to meet you at last. Just call me Hogan – I prefer it. Can I get you a drink?'

'No, let me get them in, *Hogan*.' She emphasised the surname. 'The Isle of Wight Police want to keep on the right side of the local press, so buying you a drink's the least I can do. What'll you have?'

'Well normally I don't drink. . .' Hogan began to explain. Thomas raised one of her cute blonde eyebrows and looked at the nearly empty glass in front of him. 'But for you I think I can make an exception. I guess another pint of Wight Spirit.'

DC Thomas caught the barmaid's attention. 'Two pints of Wight Spirit, please, and . . .'

'It's OK. One's fine,' Hogan interrupted.

'And who said the second one's for you, Mister Reporter?' Thomas turned to the barmaid again. 'Two pints of Wight Spirit please – and can you let me see the menu?'

Hogan could tell he was going to like this woman – a lot. Perky and pretty as a picture. Only problem was, she was young enough to be his daughter. Hogan let his eyes travel down her body as she was turned towards the barmaid. He liked what he saw – but he wasn't sure he liked where his thoughts were taking him.

'I hope your legs are in good shape. The first part of the walk's quite a steep climb.'

As she said this, Thomas playfully pinched the inside back of Hogan's thigh muscle, a little too near his groin for comfort. He was already half-erect from eyeing Thomas up in the pub. Her touch, and the way it tightened the material around his crotch, completed the job.

'Nothing wrong with me,' he replied. 'I'll have you know that in my youth I was an international sportsman – well, sports boy, I suppose.'

'Tiddlywink champion or something, was it?'

'No, golf. England Boys.'

'Pah! Golf? You're kidding me! Boys shouldn't be playing golf. It's a game for old duffers. Anyway, it doesn't get you fit – look at that old fatso, Monty or whatever his name is. He looks as though he's going to have a heart attack every time anyone pulls a camera out.'

31

'Yeah, but at his peak his golf was sublime. And I'd give my eyeteeth just to have a tenth of the fortune he's accumulated down the years.'

'But he's not a real winner, is he? What's he ever won of any note?' asked Thomas.

'Oh, just the European Order of Merit seven times in a row. A cinch, really. I guess you could do it with your eyes closed.'

'No, I stick to what I'm good at,' Thomas replied.

'Which is what?'

'Aha! That's for me to know and you to find out, Mister Reporter!'

Thomas smiled meaningfully at him as she delivered this line. It's almost a come on, thought Hogan. She's flirting with me. And I like it.

They were climbing the cliff path as it rose out of Reeth, and Hogan had to admit he was starting to puff and pant. He was out of condition, badly out of condition. Golf had always been his only real exercise. In his teens, when he was playing four or five times a week, and practising constantly, it had kept his weight right down. Now, though, the golf was years behind him and Hogan took no exercise at all. Probably explains the blood pressure, he thought ruefully.

This woman detective, on the other hand, looked like she worked out all the time. She was finding the steep incline no trouble at all, striding on ahead of him, her tight denim hipsters accentuating the muscles in her legs. Hogan tried to stop himself leching at her behind and concentrate on the job, which was to try to get a story out of her. But his hormones wouldn't let him.

After a few minutes they reached the point where the path was fenced off and diverted inland. Council workmen were on the site, building the fencing up and erecting more barbed wire and clearer signage.

There was still a gap they hadn't completely closed. Once Thomas had shown them her police ID, she and Hogan clambered through and continued their walk.

After about a hundred yards the path, which until this point had been enclosed by hedges, opened out onto downland at the top of the cliff. From being just a humdrum country stroll, it suddenly became something spectacular. The view was stupendous. The lighthouse below in its crisp whiteness, picked out by the clear autumn light. The seascape extending for miles and miles. The rolling hills abutting the coast. And the magnificent chalk cliffs of the West Wight, looking like some huge sea monster had taken a vast bite of land away with its ragged teeth.

Hogan stopped, right next to Thomas, to drink it all in. They didn't speak, but Hogan could sense her powerful presence, smell her fresh scent. She had him hooked and she probably knew it.

He was startled out of his reverie by an abrupt movement. Thomas, near the cliff edge, seemed to lose her footing. All of a sudden her arms were tangled round him, so that he was holding her weight.

'Whoops a-daisy!' She laughed. 'There I go again. A pint of beer and I'm anyone's!'

'I'm not complaining,' said Hogan.

'No, I can feel that.' Thomas was pressed up against him, her breasts against his chest, her crotch against his.

Hogan didn't quite know how this situation had evolved. Embarrassed, he gently pushed her away. 'Are you OK?'

'I'll live.' Thomas was suddenly curt. Her tone had changed in an instant. She'd turned away from him, and was already walking onwards. Hogan scolded himself for the partial rejection. He'd forced her back into businesslike police-mode. The flirty girl was hidden for the moment.

About two hundred yards further on, she stopped again. "X' marks the spot! Here we are. From what we've been able to find out the girl fell, or more probably was pushed, from about this point.'

'Pushed?' asked Hogan. 'I thought the official line was that everything pointed to a fall?'

'Hmm. Some of my colleagues would like to think so. But some new information has come to light. I have a suspect. We're about to take him in for questioning. By the time your story comes out I expect this case will be close to being solved.'

He was intrigued. There hadn't been the whiff of a suspect so far.

He got out his notebook, and started to make a shorthand record of the conversation. Thomas was talking quickly, excitedly, telling the journalist much more detail than the usual police-press relationship would allow.

Hogan found his shorthand was keeping pace easily. He too was excited. The material Thomas was giving him was first-class. Hogan's report for the next day's *Wight Evening Star* was going to make a cracking good read.

Back at the *Star* offices, Hogan tried to write up his new story for the newspaper. Without much success.

The material he'd got from the woman detective, Emma Thomas, had seemed good. He'd expected the story to fall together naturally. But he couldn't get to grips with it.

He stared at the computer screen, not really knowing where to start.

It was like one of those nightmares where you're back at school – re-taking the exams you should have done better in. Those around you are still schoolchildren. You: an adult, thrown into an ugly timewarp, unable to escape.

Hogan had had enough of those sorts of dreams himself. Lots of them centred on schoolboy golf tournaments where he was supposed to be the star player but couldn't even hit the ball.

He started to tap something into the computer. But he was rusty. Both his writing skills and his knowledge of journalism law had withered over time.

After about an hour he'd finally got something written. He knew it wasn't a masterpiece, but he thought it was just about passable.

He waited for Ed Sutcliffe, the news editor and a fellow Yorkshireman, to give his verdict. Hogan had taken an immediate shine to Sutcliffe. He was gruff, blunt, but funny with it. He sat in a little glass office to the side of the open-plan newsroom, sifting through the next day's copy on his computer.

Instead of coming over to Hogan to congratulate him, Sutcliffe marched off to Richard Howze's office, brandishing a computer print-out.

A few moments later, Hogan got a top-line message from his editor on the computer, summoning him to a meeting.

He knocked on Howze's door. It was glazed and see-through.

Howze ushered him in. 'Sit down, Benjamin, mate. How are you getting on?'

'OK, Dickey. OK. Not wonderful, just OK. I must admit I found it quite a struggle to get my piece written. Ed's probably told you.'

'Yes, well, I wouldn't say Ed put it quite like that, did you, Ed?'

'No,' said Ed grumpily. He looked like he didn't want to be in the room.

'In fact, he was a bit more direct. The words 'fucking' and 'crap' were not unadjacent in one very short sentence.'

'I didn't think it was *that* bad!' protested Hogan.

'It was shite. Utter shite!' This came from Ed. He seemed quite angry.

'OK, Ed, calm down!' ordered Howze. 'Look, Benjamin, I'll be straight with you. Ed didn't really want you to join us. I think his words went along the lines of 'I don't want some failed fucking broadcasting has-been in my office'. Something like that, anyway.'

Hogan bristled at this. He was going to thump one of them in a minute. As far as he was concerned, he was doing them a favour taking their lousy job in the first place.

Howze continued, leaning back in his chair, rocking it backwards, his arms folded in proprietorial fashion. 'I went out of my way to bring you here, Benjamin, I'll make no secret of that. I had to persuade the Beast to dig deep in his pockets to fund your salary . . .'

'Yeah, so what?' Hogan had lost his temper now. 'I can tell you, the money's not that great. And it's hardly the *New York* sodding *Times*, is it! Let's face it, you're running a two-bit rag, in a two-bit town. And if you don't want me, fine. I'll fuck off. No skin off my nose.'

'Calm down, calm down, Benjamin.' Howze was at his most condescending now. 'I'm not saying that at all. I hired you because I know you're a good writer, and you were a first-class reporter . . .'

'Twenty fucking years ago!' said Sutcliffe.

Howze turned angrily to his news editor. 'Shut it, Ed! You're not always so bloody wonderful either.'

Hogan spoke out again, still livid. 'So what are you both trying to say, then? That I can't hack it any more?'

'No,' Howze replied. 'But you may need a bit of help to get rid of some of the rustiness. That's understandable. I don't see why it has to be a problem. What I suggest is that you and Ed get your heads together over this piece, maybe over a pint at the pub. Come back to it a bit later. Knock it into shape. It's the front-page lead, after all. The deadline's not till 10am tomorrow.'

'OK,' said Hogan, breathing heavily. 'I'll give it a go. But from what Ed was saying he doesn't seem so keen.' He gave the news editor a questioning look.

'Ah, fuck it. It's been a bad day. A pint sounds like a good idea.' Sutcliffe picked up Hogan's report. 'It's probably not as bad as I made it out to be. But there are a couple of legal howlers in it.'

Hogan looked shamefaced. 'Sorry. I meant to gen up on the legal side of things. But what with the divorce looming, the possibility that my wife might take the kids to the States . . . It's all been a bit much.'

'Don't worry,' said Sutcliffe. He was all smiles and friendly now. He'd made his point. 'Come on. I'll buy you a pint at the Coach and Horses. We can sort it out there.'

3

Hogan felt guilty and on the verge of crying as he heard the voice of his eight-year-old daughter Tamara for the first time in a week.

He'd tried phoning repeatedly, but Lynn kept on putting the phone down. Now she'd finally relented, letting him have a few minutes to talk to his children.

He was sitting in the tiny chalet in Reeth he'd rented on a winter let.

'We miss you Dad. It's been horrible here without you.'

'Miss you too, sweetheart. But you knew Daddy had to move to get a new job . . . and you know Mummy and Daddy haven't been getting on.'

'Yes, but it's not fair. We've got our school fireworks party this week, and I can't go because you can't take me.'

'When is it, darling?'

'Saturday night. William doesn't want to go because he hates the noise, and Mummy says she can't get a babysitter, so we've all got to stay at home.'

Hogan felt as though the frog in his throat had just doubled in size. 'Well, I've got an idea, sweetheart.'

'What, Daddy?'

'How about you both come and stay with me for the weekend, Princess, and we can all go to a fireworks party here?'

'Wow! Can we? That would be great. Mum too?'

Tears were stinging his eyes now. His feelings for Lynn might have turned to near hatred – but that didn't stop the memories of the good times.

'No. Well . . . maybe. I just don't think she'd want to.'

Hogan and Lynn hadn't fully explained to their kids about the background to the split. They were trying to let them down gently by saying he'd had to get a new job – and that because Mummy and Daddy hadn't been getting on they were going to try living separately for a while. There would be no way Lynn would want to stay with him for the weekend, or vice versa. Everything was still too raw.

But then Hogan had an idea. 'I tell you what, Tamara. Maybe Mummy could stay with Nan and Grandad while you and William stayed with me. How about that?'

Lynn's parents had retired to Bournemouth, which was near enough to the ferry ports for the island to make the plan feasible.

'Cool! That'd be great,' said Tamara. 'But William still wouldn't want to go to see the fireworks.'

'Let me have a word and see if I can persuade him.'

'OK, Dad. William! William!' she shouted. 'Daddy's on the phone!'

Hogan managed to convince his son that fireworks parties on the Isle of Wight were much smaller affairs and had far fewer loud bangs. He knew it was these that William hated. Since his son had been a toddler, the time around November the Fifth had always been a nightmare. William would hold his hands up to his ears each evening, and keep them there all night as the intensity of the explosions ratcheted ever higher. Hogan had no idea what Guy Fawkes Night was like on the island, but he guessed it would be gentler. He didn't really know, though.

William passed the phone to Lynn. Now the trouble would begin, thought Hogan.

'Hi there,' he said, as neutrally as possible.

'Hello.' Lynn sounded grumpy, but that was nothing new.

'Has Tamara told you what I was suggesting?'

'Yes.'

'And?'

'And what?' Lynn seemed angry now. 'What the hell do you think you're doing? Trying to arrange a visit from the kids without consulting me first!'

'Sorry, it's just that Tamara said . . .'

'Don't go trying to blame your daughter. How pathetic!'

'Look!' Hogan was angry now too. 'I'm their father and I have a right to see them. I'm not blaming Tamara. She just said she was upset she couldn't go the school fireworks party.'

'Yes, well, who's to blame for that? You're the one who walked out on us all.'

'Oh, for heaven's sake. Talk about people in glasshouses. You're the one who broke up our marriage by shagging some American dickhead behind my back!'

'And you think that's all my fault, do you? Do you actually think you've been any fun to live with these past few years? At least Grant can make me laugh. At least he *tries*.'

Hogan was just about to retort when he realised he couldn't. The line had gone dead. Lynn had put the phone down on him again.

He stared through the window of the chalet. Until the phone call, he'd been a little happier now he'd got a temporary home of his own: living out of a suitcase at the hotel had been getting him down.

Outside the window the weather had taken a serious turn for the worse, just like his mood. The trunk of the palm tree in the communal garden was being bent, its leaves at the top almost horizontal, as the gale-force wind howled across the chalet park. It looked like a head of hair in the path of a huge hairdryer. Except this wasn't dry hot air. It was cold. And now it was accompanied by rain. Miserable grey rain. Hammering against the chalet's windows, gradually obscuring Hogan's view.

His mobile phone rang.

'Iain?'

'Yes.'

It was Lynn again, sounding more conciliatory.

'Sorry about that. Shouldn't have put the phone down.'

'It's OK. I guess I shouldn't have suggested anything to the kids without asking you first.'

'Look, I was angry. I got the wrong end of the stick from Tamara. I thought I was going to actually have to bring them over. I didn't realise the plan was I go to my parents, and you meet me at the ferry.'

'If that's OK.'

Hogan realised they were both fed up – not just him. At least a truce seemed to have been declared, and now they were tentatively meeting halfway in no-man's-land.

'I'll have to ask Mum and Dad. It's a bit late notice . . .'

'Sorry . . .'

'I'll see what I can do. In some ways it'd be nice to have a weekend off from the childcare.'

'OK. Understood. I'll wait to hear from you – but I do think the kids will love it here.'

The conversation ended, this time amicably, although still warily.

The rain had eased. The wind had died slightly. Hogan had a new home, and a life that was starting, slowly, to get back into shape.

Howze had given Hogan the morning off to sort out his domestic arrangements.

'I'll expect you midafternoonish,' he'd told his chief reporter. 'There's no point arriving early. Ed, the Beast and I are all going out for a spot of liquid lunch. Just bring us a lead story for tomorrow, there's a good chap.'

Oh yeah, Hogan had thought. Conjure one out of thin air, bibbety-bobbity-boo style. Fat chance. But he guessed there was more to be said about Lee Hughes, the autistic man who was chief suspect in the cliff case. That would have to do. He'd contact DC Thomas – or Emma, as he'd come to think of her – and see if she had anything new for him.

He was making himself a cup of tea and a sandwich when he heard the police sirens. The weather had improved slightly, and from the chalet window Hogan could now see a number of blue flashing lights in the holiday site's car park.

He put on his raincoat and went to investigate.

A uniformed officer was stationed outside one of the chalets. Hogan suddenly put two and two together. Emma had mentioned that Lee Hughes lived in a holiday chalet. Hogan hadn't had any idea it was on the same site as where he was now living, but he guessed that had to be why the police were here in force. He tried to peer round the officer to the inside, to see if he could attract Emma's attention, assuming she was there.

The policeman at the door barred his path. 'Can I help you, sir?'

'I just wanted to speak to DC Thomas, if that'd be possible.'

'Well, now's not a good time to bother them, sir. I think you can see they're busy. Now, if you don't mind, could you just move along, please?'

'I'm a reporter on the local paper. Hogan. She knows me.'

'She may do, sir. But now's not the time to be bothering her, is it? I'm sure if you ring the press office at Yarwater later they'll be able to tell you anything we want the press to know.'

'Look, can I just have a quick word? Then I'll leave you alone.'

The constable sighed, turned, and went inside the chalet, after telling Hogan not to follow him.

A few moments later DC Emma Thomas came out. 'Sorry, Hogan, but this is a bad time.'

'What are you up to, though? Can't you just tell me that?'

'Well, I don't think it needs an Albert Einstein to work it out.' Hogan blushed at the put-down. 'We're searching Hughes's chalet. And to be honest' – Thomas lowered her voice – 'it doesn't look terribly good that, almost as soon as we arrive, we get the press on the doorstep. I could land in deep shit.'

'Sorry,' said Hogan. 'I heard the sirens and thought I'd come and take a look.'

'You were quick.'

'I've moved in here, to the site. So it only took me a few seconds to walk.' Emma's face momentarily darkened as he said this. He wondered why.

'You have? God, why? Do you like living among the low-life?'

Hogan bristled slightly. 'Nothing wrong with it here. Nice and quiet – and where else would you get your own place for sixty quid a week?'

'Yuk. Well, I wouldn't live here if they paid me. Anyway, I've got to get back, otherwise I'll be dead meat. Tell you what. Once we've finished here I'll pop round to your chalet. Which number is it?'

'Fifty-two. Top row.' Hogan pointed to the flight of steps.

'OK. See you in a mo. Be good!' With that, she turned to go. As she did so she winked and blew him a kiss.

Hogan could feel his face heat up. The PC standing guard had witnessed the exchange, and raised a quizzical eyebrow.

Getting his mobile phone out of his pocket, Hogan started to go back to his own chalet. He dialled Howze's number as he walked.

'Richard?'

'Benjamin, my good fellow. Speak up! I can hardly hear you.'

'That's because you're always in the frigging pub. No wonder!'

'Now, now. Don't get frisky with me. What can I do you for?'

'The detective on the cliff inquiry. She wants to see me this afternoon. Only down here in Reeth – not back at Yarwater. So I may work from home this afternoon and e-mail the copy in later.'

'Hmph!' Howze's affability sounded like it was evaporating fast. 'We don't pay you your inflated salary just to sit at home all day, you know.'

'Richard, we've been over that before. It's not an inflated salary at all. It's a pittance. Anyway, I'm not going to get the best stories for your paper sat on my arse in that fucking trading estate, am I?'

'Oh, yes, yes. Whatever. Do it your way, then. But I'm warning you' – Howze sounded serious for once – 'if you don't give us a lead story by close of play tonight you're history. Understand?'

'OK. Thanks, Richard. Don't work too hard yourself, will you?' Having delivered the sarcastic send-off, Hogan shut the call down just as Howze was starting to splutter a reply through his pint of beer.

A spring in his step now, remembering Emma's wink and wondering what might be in store, Hogan leapt the remaining steps to reach the second row of chalets. As he opened his front door he was pleased to smell fresh air. The disgusting mustiness had disappeared.

He set about tidying up the chalet and making himself ready for his visitor.

Hogan had two aims.

First, he had to get a new lead story out of Emma – just to shut whinging Richard Howze up.

Second, he had his own agenda with the detective. He got the distinct impression she wasn't averse to a few extra-curricular activities. There had been the hints on the cliff. The way she'd lost her footing and fallen into him. The wink just now outside Lee Hughes' chalet. Sex and Hogan had not exactly been bosom buddies over the past

42

year. Even before her affair had been revealed, Lynn had frozen him out to the extent that they'd been sleeping in separate bedrooms,

He was hoping that, over the space of the next few hours, he could maybe redress the balance a bit.

After the search of Lee Hughes's chalet was over, the knock came on the chalet door.

Hogan let Emma in.

'Find anything to pin on him?'

'Would I tell you if we had?' she said.

'Dunno. Depends. I guess, if it was in your interests, yes. If not, then probably no, you wouldn't.'

'Let's just say the guy's seriously weird – that much is obvious from what we found there.'

Hogan was trying to concentrate on her answers. But he found himself almost being sucked into her deep blue eyes. She was sexy, seriously sexy.

'But there are plenty of weirdos in the world. They're not all murderers.'

Emma Thomas smiled at him. It was a 'you're kind of cute in a stupid sort of a way' smile. 'You know very well I can't tell you exactly what evidence we may or may not have found.'

'You could give me a clue.' Hogan felt slightly hurt. Their relationship was getting to be a closer and closer one, he sensed. Didn't that give him some rights to extra information? Crucial information to help his stories that the other local journalists wouldn't get?

'Duh. I *have* given you a clue. The guy's a weirdo. Doo-lally. It was like an Aladdin's cave in there.'

'What, stolen gear?'

'Nah! Loads and loads of miniature models and railway engines. Stacks and stacks of model railway brochures and other crap like that.'

'A real criminal's lair, then.' Hogan's sarcasm was undisguised.

'We found other stuff, too. Enough for us to hold him a bit longer until we can charge him.'

'Which will be when?'

43

'None of your business.'

'You can't hold him indefinitely, you know that. You'll have to charge him soon or let him go.'

Thomas stiffened, as though she didn't need reminding. Hogan got the impression the case against Hughes might not be as strong as she was trying to make out. 'I hope you didn't invite me up here just to talk shop all day. I get enough of that in CID. I need a break. Something a bit more exciting.'

She gave him a cheeky smile.

Hogan blushed. 'Like what?'

'Jesus!' Thomas pushed him playfully. 'You're almost as thick as that dolt we've taken in. I've always had this thing about older men, you know.'

She pulled Hogan by his belt, closer to her. He felt like an awkward schoolboy on his first date. He wasn't used to this. Lust? Love? Whatever it was, it felt good.

Thomas tugged his dark head of hair down towards her. Their lips met. He was reticent, embarrassed. She took charge.

Her tongue forced his mouth open, then pushed between his teeth. She locked on, and fiercely sucked the air from him. One of her hands was behind his head, preventing him from pulling back. The other dropped from his belt, feeling the bulge in the front of his black canvas jeans.

Detective Chief Inspector Jane Hale was sitting on top of her desk again. In another meeting, this time with Warren Dudfield. He was on the low sofa where Emma Thomas had been weeks earlier. And Hale could see he looked uncomfortable there.

Hale was sick of his sullen attitude. Ever since she'd snubbed his views in the interview with Thomas, Dudfield had been in a sulk.

Now she was trying to draw him out of his moody shell by engaging him over the cliff case. With the arrest of Hughes, she'd brought Dudfield back as an experienced hand to try to make any charges stick.

'It's a different ball game now, Warren. Now we've got someone

44

under arrest.'

'It is, ma'am. It is.'

'You were always convinced it was just a fall, though. Are you so sure now?'

'Well, ma'am, with respect, it's easy to be wise after the event, isn't it? But what I deal in is evidence. Hard evidence.'

'What are you trying to say?'

'Well, you might not want to hear it, ma'am . . .'

'What do you mean?'

'I just mean what I have to say might not be what you want to hear. You don't like your little favourites being criticised.'

Hale bristled. 'If you mean DC Thomas, then no. I don't think she deserves criticism. She's doing a good job. She's got the right attitude. She puts her job first.'

Dudfield's tone hardened. 'What are you fucking saying – that I don't?'

Hale's locked her eyes angrily onto Dudfield's. But her tone remained calm.

'Do not, ever, ever, swear at me, Sergeant.' She enunciated each word carefully, emphasising the message. 'Otherwise I'll have you out of CID lickety spit. Back to uniform. Got it?'

'Sorry, ma'am.'

Dudfield's face had gone bright red. Hale sensed he realised full well he had overstepped the mark.

'Now, if you've got something useful to say about the case, say it. But I don't want just petty jealousy. Emma Thomas is doing a good job, and I would be very careful about your own position if I were you.'

'Yes, ma'am.'

'So. Have you anything useful to say?'

Dudfield appeared chastened. 'Well, ma'am, first off, I think it's worth putting out a picture of the girl – to try to identify her. All our inquiries have failed so far.'

'Yes, but she's in a coma with serious head injuries and probable brain damage. We can't ask her for permission, and we don't know who the next of kin is.'

'So there's no one going to be complaining, is there?'

'Hmm . . . doesn't sound quite right, does it, Warren?'

'Ma'am, if it helps to solve this case it's right. Sometimes the end justifies the means. We just need to get the nod from the hospital chief exec, dress her up with a bit of make-up and a hairdo, and Bob's your uncle.'

'I'm going to have to refer it up, Warren, but it might – I stress, *might* – be a way forward. I'm not promising anything at this stage. And what if the hospital chief says no?'

'He won't, ma'am. He owes me a favour.'

Hale had her suspicions about Dudfield's 'favours', but kept them in check.

'What does Emma Thomas think about it?' she said.

'Not keen, ma'am. Says we have to play it by the book.' Then Hale heard him mumble as an aside: 'She always does when it suits her, bends the rules when it doesn't.'

'I heard that, Warren.' Hale would have been more concerned had it been Dudfield himself bending the rules. At least Thomas knew the rulebook. Hale often wasn't sure if Dudfield did.

'So we try to get a photo of her out. If we can. What else?'

'Well, ma'am, I don't think we should jump to conclusions. We need to look at the evidence. And the evidence still points to an accident. There's nothing to say otherwise.'

Hale nodded, listening carefully now that Dudfield seemed to be making a reasoned argument. 'Yes, but forensics may turn up something else.'

'True. But at the moment we have to work with what we've got. I'm just uneasy at the way we seem to be leaping to conclusions about this suspect, Lee Hughes.'

'I wouldn't call a witness statement, one that puts him in an argument with a female on the clifftop on the day the girl fell, leaping to conclusions.'

'Yes, but just listen to yourself, ma'am, with respect. You said 'female', not 'girl'. 'Female.' This guy reckoned he could positively identify the man as being Lee Hughes?'

'That's right. He picked him out of an identity parade.'

'So he managed that yet couldn't even tell if the female on the cliff was a girl or a woman? Doesn't that worry you, ma'am?'

Hale stood up, turned, and went round the back of the desk to sit at her chair. She put her hands to her forehead as she thought for a moment. Dudfield, she had to admit, had a point. A very good point. But still she felt there was something else there, something else motivating him.

'OK, Warren, let's assume your reservations are correct. Why have we taken Hughes into custody? You were in the interview room when Thomas was talking with the witness . . .'

'I was brought into it late, ma'am. Thomas had already interviewed him informally.'

'I can't believe that. It would be against procedure . . .'

'That's what happened, ma'am,' Dudfield stated flatly.

'I'll look into it. But, leaving that aside for the moment, why was Hughes taken in unless both you and Thomas believed it was the right course of action?'

'She went over my head, ma'am.'

'How do you mean?'

'What I say. I didn't want us to rush into anything. She went over my head to Inspector Phillips.'

Hell, thought Hale. This gets worse. But, if Emma did really go direct to Phillips, it maybe explained Dudfield's prickliness.

'But that still doesn't explain away the ID parade, does it, Warren?'

'I just don't think Hughes did it, ma'am. He's a gentle soul, mildly autistic. It's not like him to . . .'

'Hang on a minute!' Hale found herself almost shouting now. 'You're saying you *know* Lee Hughes.'

'Yes, ma'am. I know his family. They've lived on the island for . . .'

Hale interrupted him. She was livid. 'Detective Sergeant, you are totally out of order. I brought you back onto this case as soon as it looked like foul play might be involved. But if you'd said at the beginning you knew the suspect personally . . .'

'But, ma'am . . .'

'No buts, Warren. That's it! You're off the case, period. You're lucky I'm not sending you back to uniform straight away . . .'

47

'Ma'am, I just . . .'

'Shut up! I've heard enough. You're off the case. DI Phillips and DC Thomas can deal with it now. And, if necessary, I'll take charge myself.'

Hale saw that Dudfield was angry. He stomped out of her office, slamming the door behind him, without even saying goodbye. Rude git! She would have to take him down a peg or too. Hale got the distinct impression that not only was Dudfield prejudiced against graduate fast-track entrants, he was also prejudiced against women. Hale wasn't having that. If she could pin it on him, it would give her an excuse to get rid of him.

Dudfield's type of policing was history. He was living on borrowed time.

Ed Sutcliffe took the call at the *Star*'s office. 'Hogan. It's the pigs. About the cliff case.'

He put them through to Hogan's extension.

'Hogan here.'

'You're the reporter on the cliff story, right?'

It was a woman's voice. Not Emma's, though. More serious and businesslike.

'Yes, for my sins,' he replied.

'It's Detective Chief Inspector Jane Hale here. Thanks for your help in giving publicity to the case so far.'

'Only doing my job.'

'Well, it's helped, so thanks. We thought we'd give you something in return. On the understanding you try to give it a good spread.'

'I'll do my best, Chief Inspector. But I can't give any guarantees. I just write the stories – I don't have any say over how prominently they're used. Anyway, I normally deal with DC Thomas. She's not been taken off the case, has she?'

'No, no. Far from it. She's doing very well. It was a great breakthrough to make an arrest. We've had to release the suspect on police bail for the time being. But at the moment we're not looking for anyone else. We just need to make sure of our evidence.'

'So what can I do for you, then?'

'We want to release a photo.'

'Of what?' Hogan asked.

'The girl in hospital. The one in a coma. We've taken the photo already. It looks a bit odd – after all she's still unconscious. But it's the best we can do.'

'But there must be tubes and stuff coming out of her. I'm not sure we're going to want to publish that, however important it is to you.'

'Don't worry. We've brushed it up on a computer. Taken pixels from one part of her face to cover the tubes as best as possible. We think it's a good likeness.'

'Hang on a minute, though. How have you got her permission for this?'

'We haven't.'

'So have her parents or next of kin agreed?'

'No. How could they? We don't know who they are. That's why we want to release the photo. Obviously.' She sounded angry now.

'OK, OK. Don't lose your rag. So has anyone given you permission?'

'The hospital has. But, look, I haven't got all day. If you're not going to agree to this, maybe I ought to talk directly to your editor.'

'No necessity for that,' Hogan said quickly. He didn't need Howze sticking his nose into this; he just wanted to be sure that the *Star*, and the police, weren't going to get the Press Complaints Commission stirring up trouble. But, if it helped some desperate family find their missing daughter, then it was obviously worth it.

'Can you e-mail me the picture? It's too late for today's final edition. But this story is big news on the island. I'm sure it will make tomorrow's lead story.'

'That would be helpful,' said Hale, friendlier now. 'I'll send it to you right away.'

Hogan was intrigued as to why Emma hadn't told him this was what the police were planning. 'Does DC Thomas know about this?'

'Sorry, Mr Hogan. I fail to see that that's any business of yours, is it?'

'Just wondering.'

'Mr Hogan, I am the senior officer in charge of this case. DC Thomas is a very good policewoman. But if I make a decision it's up to me, don't you think? Not her. And not you.'

The phone clicked dead. Hogan wondered why she was being so frosty. He hadn't even had time to give her his e-mail address. Maybe he didn't need to. Emma had probably already compiled a file on him at CID headquarters which would tell Hale all she needed to know.

Within thirty minutes the 'mail received' signal sounded on his computer. There was a formal press release, written in stilted police-speak. And an attachment with it, which he opened. The picture started to fill his screen. Slowly. One area where Howze seemed to have skimped with the Beast's money was with the office's computers. They're seriously underpowered, thought Hogan.

The face came into view. He recognised it straight away, of course. Hale probably didn't realise that he'd got a good look at the girl when the body was discovered, before the police realised who he was. But she looked different now in this weird photograph. Her eyes were closed, which was not going to help identify her. What struck Hogan, as it had before, was her beauty. That same lustrous dark hair framed her face. He noticed things in the photograph he hadn't spotted before. Her skin was tanned, but not with a British tan. This looked Mediterranean. Almost classic Italian looks. But there was something else there too. Something that looked slightly East European. She also seemed young – and very vulnerable.

Hogan was normally hard-nosed, cynical. Too many years in TV journalism had desensitised him. The bloated bodies floating on rivers after the latest Central African massacre. Blood, guts and limbs scattered by bombs in the Middle East or Latin America. When you'd seen all that, time after time, it took a lot to move you.

But this photograph moved him. He wondered about who her parents were, her brothers, sisters. Someone must care for her. Yet here she was, isolated and close to death in an intensive care unit.

Hogan knew he had to try to help her.

4

Emma Thomas took the hairpin bend leading into St Boniface Road without braking fully, so there was a screech of burning rubber from the Mercedes convertible's expensive tyres. The car was, of course, completely outside her earning bracket. Hell's bells – most police trainees like her would probably struggle to own a car at all, never mind a luxury open-topped sports car.

It was a present from her stepfather, to try to, as he put it 'make it up to her'. What a tosser, thought Emma. If Mum had ever found out what had been going on she'd have kicked him out. At least, I hope she would have. Maybe she wouldn't. Shit, that's a nasty thought, Emma baby. Maybe Mum knew what was going on all along, but either didn't care or didn't want to admit it for fear of losing her meal ticket. But Mum wouldn't have done that, would she? Not her own Mum?

Emma had spurned the chance to go into his business. He'd have been pawing her all the time, the fucking pervert. No way. I am good enough to make it on my own! That had been the thought that had kept her going. Driving her on. The next step – get there quickly. Win. Always put yourself first. Yeah, maybe have a little fun along the way, but don't get distracted from the big goal.

A little fun was what she was heading for tonight. But play it right and it could help win her some Brownie points in her handling of the cliff case – perhaps even open the way to early promotion. She needed to persuade the Women's Ramblers to drop their calls for a public inquiry over the closure of the coastal path.

So she was going out to play. Dinner with the freak sisters and their 'au pair'. Plenty of possibilities there. The elder sister, Clara, has the hots for me, thought Emma. I'll just have to use my usual powers of persuasion to win her round.

* * *

The next day Emma woke with a start, as something crashed to the floor in the kitchen.

It felt like an ice pick had shattered her forehead. Well, maybe it didn't quite feel like that. Otherwise she'd be a goner, like Leon Trotsky. But there was acute pain concentrated in a small area at the front of her head. Tongue like sandpaper stuck against the roof of her parched-dry mouth. And a feeling of uncontrolled nausea. A hangover – a bad one. It hadn't been a particularly late night – Emma had been too aware she had to work today – but it had ended abruptly.

Oh shit, oh shit, oh shit! She staggered past the flat's kitchen – noticing through bleary eyes that the cat had knocked off last night's dinner plate, scattering chicken bones over the floor.

She couldn't stop to clear up the mess. Get to the toilet, and fast – that was her only thought. Saliva collecting in her mouth, the puke already rising. She got her head in the right place just in time. Being sick neatly – one of my many skills, she thought to herself.

Another of Emma's principal skills was the way she could use her sexual power to get what she wanted. It had worked last night on Clara Forbes. She'd forced Clara to sign a statement there and then dropping her group's opposition to the path closure. Emma was still dressed in the clothes she'd gone to bed in, and even as she knelt in front of the toilet she patted the pocket of her jeans to make sure the statement was still safely there.

So far, so good. But then, Emma recalled, the effects of the booze had kicked in. Had the sisters spiked what she was drinking? Whatever, she had lost control – badly. She had vague recollections of being with Romana, and then Clara whispering in her ear. Much of the evening was a drink-fuelled blurry haze. But she remembered Clara's words all too well. The few words that had brought Emma Thomas's world crashing down.

'Fifteen,' Clara had said. 'She's only fifteen.'

Emma Thomas knew what it meant. The girl was underage. Just a child. Shit, she didn't look it. She was like a young woman. They'd told her she was their au pair. The lying perverts.

And now they'd caught Emma in their web. If the truth ever got out, not only would her career be ruined but likely as not she'd be

52

facing charges of indecent assault.

As the previous night's events flashed through her aching brain, Emma felt the bile rising in her throat once more. This time the nausea wasn't all a consequence of her hangover. It was also a product of disgust.

At herself.

'So you're offering me a deal?' said Emma Thomas.

'I wouldn't put it that way, exactly,' Clara Forbes replied.

The two women were sitting next to each other again in Clara's drawing room on the two-seater sofa that wasn't quite big enough.

'More like a mutually beneficial arrangement. 'Deal' sounds so grubby and underhand, doesn't it?'

Clara was dressed in just a large white towelling robe tied loosely at the front. It was flapping open slightly, the swell of her breasts visible to the younger woman. Clara knew the display had not gone unnoticed. She was enjoying the fact that the tables were turned. The secret she shared with Maria had been a heavy burden over the past few weeks, particularly for her sister. Now they had some leverage over the policewoman sitting next to her.

Revenge. Yes, there was an element of revenge. Emma had seemed so in control, so confident. She'd taken advantage of Clara's and Maria's hospitality, and Clara had been quite conscious that the policewoman had simply used her sexuality to get the ramblers' group to drop objections to the path closure.

There was no doubt Emma was attractive. Devastatingly so. But today the good looks were a little tarnished. The bob of blonde hair looked lank, greasy, unkempt. The mascara was smudged. Traces of yesterday's lipstick were still there, even though Clara knew those lips had been kissing all manner of things the night before. And her face was pale. Not fresh, unblemished pale – but pallid: sickly and unhealthy.

Clara felt a surge of power as she realised yet again that she had the upper hand. The previous night she'd deliberately drunk very little. Sex was enough of a high for her; she didn't need any help from drink or drugs.

'The thing is, if the details of our little party ever got out it could become a bit awkward for you, couldn't it?' She stared into DC Thomas's eyes as she said this, half mocking her.

'Perhaps. But I'd get over it.'

'Would you? Would you really? Somehow I don't think so. I get the impression your career is very important to you. And, if this became public knowledge, your career would be over, no doubt about that.'

Clara reached out to stroke Emma's face. The young policewoman flinched away. To Clara, she had the look of a cornered animal, waiting for the predator to move in for the kill.

'Bollocks,' said Ed Sutcliffe to Howze. 'That was Aziz. Phoned in sick. We haven't anyone to cover the magistrates' court this morning.'

Howze glanced up only briefly from his desk. 'I'm sure you can sort something out, Ed.'

'Oh, sure. Thanks for being so helpful. Might be a bit more useful if you actually employed enough staff.'

'Productivity, Ed. That's what it's all about. We need to get more out of our existing people. Put the squeeze on a bit.'

Sutcliffe noticed that Howze seemed to be saying all this almost on autopilot while trying to complete the *Guardian* crossword at the same time. Pretentious tosser!

'Maybe we could get more out of your highly paid chief reporter?' said Sutcliffe. 'He seems to do the cliff-fall case all day and every day, and nothing else.'

'Up to you, Ed, up to you. Not my problem. You deal with it how you see fit.' Howze still didn't look up from his crossword.

'Well, you hired him,' said Sutcliffe.

Howze sighed and put down the paper. 'Can't you see I'm busy, Ed? Anyway, I thought you two were getting on better now?'

'He's a decent enough bloke. And his stories on the cliff case have been good – we've had a few exclusives out of it.'

'So what's the problem, then?'

'The fucking problem is we don't have anyone to do the magistrates' court this morning.'

Howze sighed again and turned back to the crossword.

There was a long silence.

'Is that all then, Ed?' Howze eventually asked. 'Covering dung with people is reasonable?'

'What the fuck are you on about?'

'One down. Two words, each six letters. 'C', something, 'M', something, 'O', something, 'M', something, 'N', something, 'I', something. It's the last clue. I've done all the rest,' said Howze.

Sutcliffe realised he wasn't going to get any help from or sense out of his editor. He turned angrily, and was just about to slam the door on his way out when Howze spoke again.

'I tell you what, why don't you ask Hogan?'

Sutcliffe groaned in exasperation. 'That's just what I was suggesting.'

'No, stupid. Not about the bloody magistrates. I don't care how you sort that out – just make sure it gets covered. No, ask Hogan about one down. He'll know the answer. He's good at crosswords and stuff.'

Sutcliffe rolled his eyes skywards and gave his boss a two-fingered salute. He stormed from the glass-fronted office and marched towards Hogan's desk. 'What are you up to?'

'Doing a few background calls on the cliff-fall case.'

'Can't you leave it, just for this morning? Aziz has gone sick. I need someone to cover Yarwater magistrates. There's supposed to be a good porn case coming up.'

'Suppose so,' said Hogan, grumpily. 'I need to meet someone at half-four, though. So it better be finished by then.'

'Should be,' said Sutcliffe. 'If not, just leave it unless there's a really juicy case going on. Oh, and Howze wants to see you.'

'What about?'

'I'll let him tell you that. It's something vitally important,' he said sarcastically.

Hogan gathered up his notebook and put on his black leather jacket. It was a classic, suit-jacket style. Hogan had seen a forty-something minor celebrity wearing one in a photo in one of the red-tops, and had decided to buy one. He'd laughed when, a few days later, a columnist in the same paper had described the celebrity as looking like mutton dressed as lamb. He saw Howze was busy reading something and knocked on the door.

'You wanted to see me?'

'Ah, Benjamin. What a pleasure. There's something you can do to help me.'

'Oh yes?' Hogan asked warily. 'What is it now?'

'The bloody *Guardian* crossword. I finished all but one of the clues an hour ago. I just can't work it out. It's sending me mental.'

'I think you reached that state some time ago, Dickey.'

'Oh, ha bloody ha, Mister Comedian. Just for that you'd better give me the answer. 'Covering dung with people is reasonable."

'Is that your motto, Dickey? Never slow to dump people in the shit, are you?'

'Fuck off, clever-clogs. Just give me the answer. It's two words, six and six. 'C', something, 'M', something, 'O', something, 'M', something, 'N', something, 'I', something.'

Hogan thought about it for just a moment. 'Easy peasy, Dickey. I'd have thought even you could have got that one.'

'Ha bloody ha. So what's the answer then?'

'Well, let's put it this way. It's Latin, and it's something you're not.'

Howze was getting angry. His already florid face was becoming redder and blotchy. 'Don't give me frigging riddles! I want the answer, otherwise I'm taking you off the cliff-fall story and putting you on court reporting for the day.'

'It's OK. Ed's already persuaded me to do that.'

'Oh.' Howze sounded deflated. 'Well, go on, be a mate. 'Something I'm not', eh? Well, I still can't work it out.'

"Compos mentis', Dickey,' said Hogan. "Compos mentis' is your answer – a state that eludes you, I'm afraid.'

Howze was about to deliver some retort.

But he was too slow. Hogan had turned and left before Howze could think of a suitable insult.

* * *

Yarwater Magistrates' Court was an ornate Victorian building, built in neo-Roman style. Doric columns at the porch entrance, holding up an ornate triangular white-stone façade.

The porn case was due in Court Two. A drink-driving case was just coming to an end as Hogan arrived there.

When the next defendant entered the dock, Hogan knew straight away that this was the case he'd been sent to cover. The defendant looked the part: unkempt greasy grey hair, thick black-rimmed spectacles, and a stained white shirt straining tightly over a beer-belly. Hogan studied him with distaste.

The court clerk began to speak.

'Scott Kavanagh, you are charged that sometime between April and June this year you knowingly received through the postal service obscene material, namely two computer CD-ROMs containing images of lewd and obscene acts. How do you plead?'

'Guilty, your worships.'

The plea was mumbled. Hogan only just managed to make it out.

'Speak up, man!' said the chairman of the bench.

'I said I'm guilty, OK?' Kavanagh's tone had turned angry. Silly man, thought Hogan.

Sentencing was deferred for social reports. It wasn't a first offence, and the magistrates said they were therefore considering a custodial sentence.

Kavanagh was freed on unconditional bail.

Hogan shut his notebook and put his pen back in the inside pocket of his jacket. It was hardly lead-story material.

As he left the courthouse, he felt someone grip his shoulder from behind.

He turned and was confronted by Kavanagh's revolting fat face and disgusting bad breath.

'I want a word with you,' Kavanagh said. His features looked threatening. His hand was still grabbing Hogan's shoulder.

Hogan shrugged him off and turned away again without replying.

A few paces later, and the hand was back on his shoulder.

'Oi! You deaf or something? I said I wanted a word, OK?'

'What?' Hogan was impatient. He knew what was coming next.

'You're from the papers, aren't you? I don't want you writing about this, understand?'

'I hope you're not threatening me,' warned Hogan.

'What if I am?'

'It's not a very good idea, that's all. Once you've approached me, asking me not to put something in the paper, I have to inform my editor. And he will almost certainly decide the report should go in. So you're doing yourself no favours.'

'What about if I offer you a deal?'

Hogan's ears pricked up. This was dangerous territory. He decided to pretend to play along with the man, even though any sort of deal was totally out of the question. Just the fact that this conversation had happened meant the court report would have to go in the paper. If Kavanagh had left him alone, there would have been a chance the story might have ended up on the spike – it wasn't exactly thrilling.

'What sort of a deal?'

'Aha! You're interested now, aren't you? All you fucking reporters are the same. Low-life shits.'

'Mr Kavanagh' – Hogan spat out the man's name – 'you're hardly in a position to be accusing anyone else of being low-life. You're down there scumming around with single-cell organisms.'

'What the fuck are you on about?'

'Nothing. Nothing. Just get to your point, whatever it is.'

'I want to speak to that Iain Hogan bloke, the one who's been writing the reports on the cliff-fall girl.'

'Well, you're in luck. That's me.'

'Oh, right. I didn't know.'

'So what have you got to tell me that's so thrilling you're keeping me from getting back to work?'

'Something about the cliff case.'

'Really?' Hogan was genuinely interested now. Excited. Wanting to keep the man talking, despite the horrific odour of his bad breath. 'What, exactly?'

'Ain't going to tell you yet, mate. If you keep this case out of today's paper, then maybe we can do a deal.'

Hogan smiled inwardly. He would be duty-bound to report the

case whatever. No deal was possible. But equally there was no way it was going to make today's issue of the *Star*, which was already being printed. The court case would make the next day's paper at the earliest – it might even be held over longer if there wasn't enough space.

The man was writing down a telephone number now, his fat hands struggling to make the ballpoint pen work on a greasy scrap of paper dug from the pocket of his trousers.

'That's my mobile.'

He handed Hogan the bit of paper. The number was just about legible. Hogan had to recite it aloud to Kavanagh to make sure he was reading it correctly.

'Ring me after four o'clock. If nothing's gone in the paper about this case, then I might have something of interest to you.'

Kavanagh put out his hand for Hogan to shake. Reluctantly, Hogan took it. It was limp, sweaty, podgy.

Just like Kavanagh himself.

Hogan nodded a goodbye, holding his breath. He had to get away, and quickly, before the man and his halitosis made him puke.

Hogan knew Kavanagh thought he had his deal. There was nothing about the man's grubby activities in that day's issue of the *Wight Evening Star*.

So when Hogan rang the mobile number at quarter-past four, Kavanagh sounded relieved.

He gave Hogan the address of his bedsit in Shanklin, and told him to come round straight away.

Hogan was intrigued. Was this the breakthrough in the cliff-fall case, being handed to him on a plate?

The address was in a run-down area of the town. Cheap bed and breakfasts, all with vacancies. At the height of the summer, even the lower end of the market like this would probably get booked up, but, with autumn ending and winter beginning, the street was deserted.

Hogan drove slowly along in the Peugeot. It was juddering and sputtering – he still hadn't got round to getting it serviced.

The block containing Kavanagh's bedsit was towards the end of the road. A once grand Victorian seaside mansion, now it had some windows cracked, others boarded up. The render had broken off in places, with damp patches showing through. Fallen leaves swirled around the forecourt in the wind.

Hogan pressed the button on the entryphone by Kavanagh's name. After a brief conversation with a crackling version of Kavanagh's voice, he was signalled in by the buzzing of the front-door release.

The hall of the building was dark and unwelcoming. The first thing that struck Hogan was the smell. Halfway between cat's piss and rotten apples. Sharp, sweet and sickly all at the same time. Even worse than Kavanagh's breath. Perhaps the smell travelled with him, thought Hogan.

The stairs creaked as he started to climb them in virtual blackness. Third floor, number 15. Hogan was out of breath by the time he reached the door, his heart pounding. Kavanagh opened it just as he arrived. The man was still wearing that revoltingly stained white shirt. Didn't he know? Or didn't he care?

Kavanagh ushered him inside. The place was tiny. Just one room, about three paces in each direction, with a small kitchen area to one side piled high with dirty dishes and half-consumed cans of baked beans and strewn with discarded tea bags.

Kavanagh could see Hogan examining it.

'I've been meaning to have a tidy up. Just haven't got round to it, what with the court case and everything.'

Hogan didn't answer. He didn't want to open his mouth, because he was trying to hold his breath again.

The bedsit stank even more than the hall of the house. Hogan was trying to identify the odour when he saw the cat-litter tray in the corner. It obviously hadn't been cleaned for weeks.

Hogan felt himself begin to retch. He rushed to the window, opened it, and breathed in deeply.

'Oi! Don't let the bloody cold in!' shouted Kavanagh.

'Sorry. Felt a bit faint. Must have been the climb up the stairs.'

Hogan closed the window most of the way, leaving it still open enough to let some air circulate.

'So what have you got for me? I hope it's been worth my while coming all the way to Shanklin.'

'I think you'll find it worth it. You did me a favour. And I'm a man of my word. Come over here to the computer. I'll show you.'

Hogan saw that the PC was switched on. About twenty small pictures of naked girls filled the screen.

'Sit down here.' Kavanagh gestured to the seat next to him. Hogan was reluctant to get too near, but didn't really have a choice.

Kavanagh clicked on one of the smaller pictures. It was just a head and upper body shot, so the face was fairly clear. As the larger, full-screen image started to download, Hogan immediately knew he'd seen the face before.

'See, look!' Kavanagh was brandishing the previous day's copy of the *Star* in Hogan's face. 'It's her, isn't it? The cliff-fall girl? The one in the coma?'

Hogan had to admit the facial likeness was striking. But the police had said the girl in the hospital was in her mid- to late teens. This girl looked younger – early teens at the most. Her breasts were small, undeveloped.

'I'm not sure,' he said. 'She looks a lot younger.'

'Yeah, well, there are other shots. That's just the best one of her face. 'Preteen Pleasures.' That's the name of this site.' Kavanagh said it matter-of-factly, as though there was nothing in the slightest bit odd in a middle-aged man staring at digital pictures of naked preteen girls.

Hogan shuddered. The girl in the pictures could be only about four years or so older than his own daughter.

Kavanagh closed down the picture, went to a search engine and typed something in. He clicked on one of the results, and another site came up.

He clicked through a few windows until a new picture started to download.

As the photograph gradually appeared, Hogan could tell it was the same girl, older now. Her eyes were the same. But this photograph wasn't simply of her naked; she was engaged in a sexual act with a tattooed man who seemed twice her size.

'That's enough. I don't want to see any more.'

Hogan reached across, grabbed the mouse out of Kavanagh's hand and closed down the picture.

Hogan noted down the web addresses Kavanagh gave him, thanked him reluctantly, and then left the bedsit as quickly as he could.

Back outside in the autumn air, he took several deep breaths – trying to clear his lungs of the foul smell and his mind of the foul images. There was no doubt Kavanagh's information was crucial.

But Hogan was even more certain than before that the report of the court case would be going in the paper.

5

'*What?*' spluttered Howze through his beard. 'You can't be serious.'

It was the morning editorial meeting. Hogan had just told him he'd traced the website featuring the young girl to Romania. He suggested to Howze that he should fly out there to find out more.

Howze glowered at him.

'You were telling me not so long ago that this was a two-bit paper in a two-bit town. Now you want us to fund some jolly to Dracula-land. Not on your nelly, sunshine.'

Hogan looked towards the Beast. He'd arranged with Howze to let the proprietor sit in on the meeting.

The Beast spoke up right on cue, as pre-arranged with Hogan.

'I could probably fund it if it was felt to be useful.'

Hogan knew the Beast had his own reasons for the offer. He'd already taken Hogan aside to tell him that the mother of the suspect the police had taken into custody, Lee Hughes, was a friend of his, and had urged Hogan to at least treat the man fairly. Anything that could help clear Lee Hughes had to be a good thing in the Beast's book.

Howze was looking thoughtful. 'Well, that puts a different light on it. What do you think, Ed?' He turned to his news editor, the fourth man seated around the desk.

'We're already short-staffed, you know that very well.'

Hogan tried to catch Ed Sutcliffe's eye, to try to win him round. 'Come off it, Ed. You *always* say we're short-staffed.'

'That's because it's the bloody truth.'

'Yes, but the alternatives are that we publish now or we tell the police. If we did the latter we'd just be throwing the story away. But if we do a bit of digging this could be an award-winning scoop.'

Howze looked more interested now. 'So let me get this right. You're asking not only to be allowed to go to Romania but also that we conspire with you to withhold information from the police?'

'It's not a conspiracy, Dickey,' said Hogan. 'We *will* tell the police. But at the moment we haven't really got any hard information. All we've found is a website with a picture which looks very like the girl in the hospital.'

'But you're convinced it actually is the girl?' asked Howze.

'Yes. So was Kavanagh.'

Howze grimaced. 'Well, I wouldn't trust that revolting little man. Why did he give you the information, anyway?'

'He thought he was getting a deal to keep his court case out of the paper.'

'But you asked me specifically to put the report in.'

'Yes, Dickey. He *thought* he was getting a deal. I never agreed to one.'

Ed Sutcliffe grinned at this. 'So you stitched him up?'

'As the saying goes, I was economical with the truth. But I didn't lie.'

Howze sat back and pulled at his beard. 'OK, let's do it. Nothing ventured. But I'm warning you, Benjamin' – he leaned forward now, eyeballing Hogan – 'if you fuck this up it's your head on the block, not mine. I don't want to be falling out with the great and the good on this island because of a middle-aged reporter's ego trip.'

Hogan felt like answering the jibe. But he'd got what he wanted from the meeting. Now was the time to swallow his pride – and check on flight arrangements to Bucharest.

The ferry to Lymington rocked from side to side. The channel between Yarmouth and the mainland was sheltered, but as the gale-force southwesterly howled in the swell grew. Hogan hoped the kids wouldn't be too scared.

He spotted them before they spotted him, huddled together on the quay. All three – Lynn, Tamara and William – looked cold and a bit sad, standing in a circle with the children's bags. Hogan was filled with regret about the marriage and the way everything had turned out. A once happy family blown apart.

But when they saw him, coming down the passenger gangway, it

64

was smiles all round. Even Lynn. Hogan tried to remember the last time he'd seen her smiling. It made her look years younger.

William rushed towards him.

'Dad, dad, we're all ready. When does the boat go?'

'Don't worry, don't worry,' said Hogan. 'There's bags of time.'

He lifted his son up in the air, and then held him upside-down for a moment.

'Iain – don't! Not here, it's dangerous.' But Lynn laughed as she said it.

As he let William down gently to the ground, Tamara rushed up to give him a hug and a kiss. There were tears in her eyes. She was trying so hard not to cry. 'Dad, we've missed you so much.'

Now the tears came, running down her cheeks, her body heaving with sobs.

Hogan got out his handkerchief, and wiped the tears away. 'Don't cry, Princess. Daddy's missed you, too. But we've got two whole days together now.'

'Dad?' asked William. 'Is it true that on Wight island the fireworks don't have bangs. That's what Tamara said.'

Hogan ruffled his son's ginger hair. 'Some bangs.' He noticed the corners of William's mouth drop, as though he too might start crying. 'But not very big ones. Not as big as in London.'

Hogan moved towards Lynn, who was hanging back, embarrassed.

'Hello, love,' he said. He gave her a chaste kiss on the cheek, like one you might give to a dinner-party guest.

'Hi, Iain. How are you?' Lynn looked vulnerable, uncertain of herself. She had half-returned the kiss. Like him, she obviously didn't really know what was the done thing in these situations.

Tamara spoke up, an impertinent smile on her face. 'Dad? Mum said she'd quite like to come with us. Is that OK?'

'Shhsh, Tamara,' hissed Lynn. 'That's not true, I didn't.'

Hogan could tell from the way she blushed bright red that in fact it almost certainly *was* true.

'Liar, liar, pants on fire,' sang Tamara.

'Quiet, Tamara,' said Hogan. 'Maybe Mummy can come one weekend, but she wants a quiet time the next two days with Nan and

Grandad. Away from you two terrors.' He started to chase Tamara, trying to tickle her.

After a few moments' horseplay he came back to Lynn's side and whispered, so the children couldn't hear, 'Is everything OK with you? You don't seem quite your normal self.'

As he said it, Hogan could see half-formed tears glistening in her eyes. She wiped them with the back of her hand. 'You always *could* tell what I was thinking, you old rascal.' She pushed him away as she said it. 'Things are fine. I just don't know if I really want to be a single mum. Our trouble was we couldn't live together, but I'm not sure I particularly like us living apart, either.'

Hogan frowned.

'But what about Grant?' The bastard who, last time Hogan had seen him, had been talking about taking Lynn and the kids to a new life in the United States.

'Over,' Lynn mumbled.

'Over?' Hogan was genuinely shocked.

'Yup. Guess you never can trust Americans, can you?'

'That's a bit of a sweeping statement. Though I can't say I was a great fan of Grant's.'

'Mmm. Well, his attitude seemed to cool as soon as you and I splitting up became a reality. But that's not your problem, it's mine. Oddly enough, it didn't hurt nearly as much as I'd have expected it to. I'll get over it.'

The ferry terminal tannoy sounded, instructing all passengers to start boarding the ship for Yarmouth.

'Look, that's us,' said Hogan. 'But we must talk, Lynn. I'll phone you tonight.'

'OK. Don't make it too late, though. You know what Mum and Dad are like.'

He gave her another kiss on the cheek, this time with genuine affection. He bullied Tamara and William into giving their mother a goodbye kiss as well, and then the three of them set off to board the ferry.

* * *

66

The car journey to Reeth was notable only because of the way the weather was deteriorating. The children were amazed at the size of the waves that crashed against the cliffs below the Military Road, sending spray high into the air. From time to time a huge gust of wind tried to lift the Peugeot bodily off the road as Hogan fought to keep control.

An excited shout from Tamara interrupted his concentration. 'Dad, Dad! What are they doing out there in the water?'

Hogan looked to his right, down to Compton Bay. Despite the near hurricane-force winds, some people had braved the water.

'They're surfers. Why are they out on a day like this?' he wondered aloud.

'Cor. It looks cool,' said Tamara. 'Can we go surfing?'

'No, you can't.' Hogan looked in the rear-view mirror and saw Tamara's face drop. 'Well, maybe you can in a few years' time. When you're older.'

'Louise's daddy takes her surfing,' said Tamara petulantly.

'No he doesn't. He takes her body-boarding. That's different. We can maybe try that next summer. But not in this weather.'

Tamara stuck her tongue out at him in the mirror. Hogan pulled a face back.

The children had mixed feelings about the chalet. William loved it. Almost as soon as he was through the front door, he was on the bunk beds that Hogan had built from a flat-pack kit. Jumping up and down excitedly, pointing things out to Tamara. But Hogan noticed she seemed less keen, and a bit withdrawn.

'Don't you like it, sweetheart?'

'It's OK, Dad. But it's so small.' She continued in a quiet voice, 'There wouldn't be enough room for Mum, would there, if she wanted to stay here?'

Hogan knew it was true, and could hear the hurt in what Tamara was saying.

Outside, night had already fallen, even though it wasn't yet six o'clock. The blackness closed in on the little chalet, making it seem even smaller. Hogan thought it would be a good idea if they went back out straight away and arrived early at the fireworks party. He'd chosen one that was especially aimed at younger children and advertised itself as 'bang-free'.

They drove along the upper coast road. Undercliff Drive had been closed again because of another landslide. There were real fears this could be it. The road – one of the most beautiful on the island, winding its way along the coast through the lush vegetation of the Undercliff – might have to be shut permanently.

Some other families with small children were already arriving at the car park above Steephill Cove. The fireworks display was going to be down on the beachfront.

Hogan hadn't been to this bay before. It was tiny, and had to be approached by steep steps – there was no road access. He led, with William behind and Tamara bringing up the rear. Other families were already picking their way down the steps, with flasks and picnic baskets in their hands. Hogan swore under his breath – he'd forgotten to bring any food.

The wind from earlier in the day had died down, having blown away the heavy clouds. As Hogan turned a corner on the steps he caught a beautiful view of Steephill framed in the moonlight. A huddle of ancient fishermen's cottages hugged the sides of a tiny wooded bay. He could imagine the scene hadn't changed in tens or perhaps hundreds of years. Smugglers would have used these tracks, ferrying their illicit booty from the south of the island to the more populated centre and north and the mainland beyond. Probably on a moonlit night like this.

Tamara was impressed. 'Wow, Dad. It's beautiful.'

People were gathering round on the small seafront. The tide was out and a man was on the shore making the final arrangements for the fireworks display.

Glancing over to his right, Hogan noticed that the café seemed to have been opened specially for the evening.

Tamara was looking in that direction too. 'Dad, look!' she said. 'They've got hot dogs. Can we get one?'

'Not now, darling. Let's wait a bit. We don't want to miss the start of the show.'

'Aaw, Dad! Don't be so mean. I'm starving.'

Hogan knew there was no point arguing. 'Oh, well, I suppose we could get something quickly. Come on, William.'

But his son was rooted to the spot, not wanting to go anywhere. Hogan realised he was petrified. Trying to combat his fear of fireworks.

'I don't want to go,' William said. 'I want to stay here.'

'Oh, Jesus wept!' muttered Hogan, momentarily losing patience. Louder, he said: 'Tamara, if William's not going to move, we're just going to have to stay here for a while until he calms down.'

'Dad, that's not fair! I'm hungry.'

Hogan could tell his daughter was on the point of crying. He reached into his pocket to dig out some money. 'Look, here's a couple of quid. But just go there, get your hot dog, and come straight back. No running off, OK?'

The display began with a spectacular silver fountain. To start with William kept his face averted and his ears covered with his hands. Hogan tried to prise them away, reassuring William once more that there really would be no bangs. Then he let himself get caught up in the display.

It was a while before Hogan realised that Tamara hadn't returned. Shit! Where was she?

He grabbed William's hand and dragged him towards the café.

When he saw Tamara leaning against the café wall, eating her hot dog, he felt a huge wave of relief flow through him. She's safe, thank God! What the hell was I thinking? But then came a new sensation, dread mixed with anger, as he realised she was talking to a middle-aged man.

Kavanagh.

'Tamara!' he shouted. 'What the hell have you been up to? I've been worried sick.'

'Dad, stop worrying. I'm fine. This nice man bought me the hot dog, so I didn't have to use your money.'

She held out Hogan's two pounds, but he wasn't interested. Instead, he grabbed Kavanagh by his filthy shirt and pulled the other man towards him. Hogan felt like he'd lost control of his senses.

69

'What the fuck is some low-life scum like you doing here?'

'I've as much right to be here as you,' Kavanagh replied steadily, meeting Hogan's gaze.

Hogan felt Tamara pulling at his shoulder. 'Dad, let him go. He hasn't done anything wrong.'

But Hogan was jabbing his finger at Kavanagh's chest, almost spitting the words out into his face. 'Never, ever, interfere with my family. Just stay well away from us if you know what's good for you. Otherwise I'll go straight to the police.'

Kavanagh seemed unruffled.

'I'm not going to be bossed around by you,' he said levelly. 'In any case, why should I agree to anything you say? It was you who broke our little arrangement.'

Hogan shooed Tamara away to stand on the other side of the café terrace with William.

'We never had any arrangement,' he said, 'so don't try to kid yourself. And if you don't want to find yourself with a bloody nose, or worse, you'll leave here now. Not when the fireworks are over, not in ten minutes, but *now*!'

Kavanagh shrugged his shoulders and turned to go. But as he did so he leaned over to Hogan and hissed in his ear: 'Don't think I'm running scared of you, because I'm not. I gave you good info on the basis that we had a deal, then you welched on it. Don't imagine I'll forget it. I won't. I'm going to make you suffer, just like you've made me suffer.'

Hogan fished his mobile from his pocket. 'Get out of my life and stay out,' he warned. 'Otherwise I won't hesitate to use this and call the police.'

Kavanagh stuck a single finger up at him and walked off in the direction of the steps back up to the car park.

Hogan went over to the children. They were both in tears now. Tamara was set-faced and stomping her feet. 'What did you have to go and do that for? He was a nice man. He hadn't done anything wrong.'

Hogan hugged her and tried to calm her down. 'I know him, sweetheart. And, believe me, he is *not* a nice man. He's a nasty piece

70

of work through and through. And you know you're not supposed to talk to strangers.'

Tamara sobbed. 'Sorry, Dad.' She possibly even meant it.

'Look, let's all cheer up. How about a Coca Cola and an ice cream, and we can sit out here on the terrace and watch the rest of the fireworks?'

The children's faces lit up instantly, and the tears were soon forgotten.

Apart from the shadow Kavanagh had cast over the evening, in terms of the fireworks themselves it was a big success. William pronounced that he was no longer scared of them, and Tamara said it was the best fireworks party she'd ever been to. By the end of the show both of them had found friends among the other children and were arranging to meet to do some rockpooling the next day.

As they climbed back up the winding steps to the car park, Hogan persuaded Tamara she shouldn't tell her mother about the incident with the man.

'Least said, soonest mended,' he told her.

They turned the corner to the car park.

William spotted it first.

'Hey, Dad! What's happened to the car wheels?'

Hogan's mood darkened as he peered at them. The two on the side nearer him were completely flat. His anger increasing, he went to the other side of the Peugeot. Exactly the same – two more completely flat tyres. Hogan bent down to examine them. On each tyre there was a neat knife-slit. Kavanagh had warned him he would pay him back, and the bastard seemed to be doing just that. Four new tyres would set Hogan back at least two hundred pounds, two hundred quid that he could scarcely afford.

He knew, however, that the evening could have been a lot worse. Tyres could be replaced, whatever the cost. But, if Hogan hadn't interrupted Kavanagh and Tamara when he did, who could tell what might have happened?

It was a chilling thought.

Hogan hugged both his children closely to him before using his mobile to call a taxi.

6

The flight from Gatwick Airport to Bucharest Otopeni was due to take just over three and a half hours, and Hogan planned to use the time to map out a plan of action.

There was little to go on. A picture of a girl, a name for her (but who was to say it was a real name?), and an address for the website operators in Bucharest. Perhaps it wasn't enough to justify the trip. Howze had certainly blanched at the cost – nearly two hundred and fifty pounds for the airfare alone – even though it was the Beast's money that was paying for it. Ed Sutcliffe had finally given Hogan the OK to go, but only once Aziz had returned from his sickbed, and then for a maximum of three days. Not very long in which to try to find a needle in a Romanian haystack.

Howze had also put his foot down about paying for posh hotels. Hogan had booked himself a cheap one-bed apartment via the internet. The special autumn rate of forty-five dollars a night was just about within the *Star*'s budget.

As the plane took off, Hogan tried to make himself comfortable in the economy window seat of the Boeing 737 and began to read the blurb about his apartment. He'd chosen the flat because it seemed centrally located, just two minutes' walk from the Piata Romana and a Metro station. The latter would in turn give easy access to the Gara de Nord, Bucharest's main railway station and reputedly one of the main hangout points for the city's street children. Hogan hoped perhaps to get some sort of a lead there. The Piata Romana was also on the same line as the nearest Metro station to the website company's office.

The plane finished its climb away from Gatwick and Hogan began to relax. Through the window he watched the cotton wool clouds covering the English Channel. Lynn hated flying, hated it with a phobia-like intensity, and some of her nervousness had rubbed off on him. Before he'd known her, flying had never bothered him, but as he unclenched his fists from the papers he was holding and set them down on the folding table in front of him, he realised the extent of the unease he'd felt at take-off.

He reached into his bag and brought out a cropped picture of the 'coma girl'. He wondered what sort of a life she had led. The face was beautiful, unlined, tanned. She looked healthy and well nourished. How had she slipped into a life of vice?

The picture of the girl turned his thoughts to his own daughter, and her brush with Kavanagh. Luckily she seemed not to have told Lynn; had she done so Lynn would have been on the phone to him straight away, telling him off again. But relations between Hogan and his wife had improved. Perhaps they could get back together and make a go of it. One thing he knew for sure, though. He wasn't going back to London. The island was his home now. If he, Lynn and the kids had a future together then it would be there.

Customs and passport formalities were relatively painless. Romania seemed to be opening its arms to European Union citizens; Hogan hadn't even needed a visa. He gathered his bag from the luggage carousel, and went to look for a taxi. By the time he'd fought through to the front of the queue, he had almost lost his temper. There seemed to be numerous families with small children getting priority treatment, so that for a time the queue hardly moved at all.

When he finally got a taxi he scrabbled in his briefcase for his Romanian phrase book to ask the driver how much the fare into town would be. '*Cat costa biletul?*' he ventured.

'*Unde te duce?*' the driver replied.

This left Hogan stumped. He started trying to look the phrase up in his book. By the time he'd worked out that the driver was asking him where he wanted to go, the people in the queue behind were starting to shout with impatience.

One of them grabbed Hogan, and tried to shove him aside.

'*Da-te la o parte sau iti trag un sut in coaie!*' shouted a fat, peroxide-headed woman.

Hogan hadn't a clue what the insult meant. He stood his ground, but decided to take the easy way out with the taxi driver.

'*Vorbiti englezeste?*'

'Yes, I speak English,' said the driver, in a near-perfect American accent. 'Where do you want go?'

'Bucharest centre. Near the Piata Romana.'

'It will be about seven or eight thousand lei.'

Hogan was momentarily thrown by the currency numbers game – it seemed even worse than Italy.

The driver could obviously sense his confusion. 'About twenty dollars,' he said as he loaded Hogan's bags into the boot of the Mercedes. 'OK?'

Hogan nodded, climbed into the rear seat, and then asked what the peroxide blonde had been shouting at him.

'She was saying she'd kick you in the balls if you didn't get out of her way,' said the driver. 'So nothing *too* rude!'

Hogan laughed.

The driver introduced himself as Alexandru, and asked Hogan what he was doing in Romania. Hogan explained he was a reporter, searching for the girl whose picture he'd seen on the web.

Alexandru turned his head, while still driving in the direction of Bucharest, and asked to see the photo. Hogan dug it out of his briefcase and handed it to him, worrying how Alexandru was able to drive without looking at the road.

'She's pretty. But young. Why do you think you will be able to find her? There are two million people in Bucharest. It will be – how you say it? – looking for needles in hay bales.'

Hogan grinned dourly.

Alexandru had echoed his own earlier thoughts.

He had cropped the photo to just show head and shoulders. It wasn't obvious it came from a porn site. 'She is – or was – in the sex trade. She posed for nude pictures . . . and worse.'

Hogan watched Alexandru's reaction in the rear-view mirror. The man seemed shocked. 'But she is so young. Some people!' The Romanian raised his eyebrows. 'I may be able to help you, you know.'

As he said it, Alexandru swerved violently to avoid a moped. He opened the window, leaned out, and gesticulated at the rider. '*Fututi pizda mati!*

Hogan asked him what the curse meant.

'I told him to go to hell.' Alexandru laughed. 'Well, it was perhaps a bit stronger than that, Englishman.'

Hogan smiled. The only Romanian he was learning was swearing.

'So you were saying you might be able to help me. How?'

'You need a guide and a translator if you're serious about your search.'

'And you would do that for me?' asked Hogan.

Alexandru shook his head violently, smiling all the while.

'No, no. Not me. I like driving my taxi. Less hassle. Except when you get motherfuckers like that moped rider.'

'So who, then?'

'My niece. She was an English teacher. But it didn't pay enough. So now she is a guide for American and British businessmen.'

Hogan was thoughtful. It would be a help, a huge help, but could he afford it on the *Star*'s limited expense account?

'What's she charge?'

'Up to two hundred dollars a day usually. But business is slow now winter's nearly here. So I could get you a good rate.'

Hogan haggled with Alexandru as they entered Bucharest itself, and they finally agreed that he would ask his niece to be the Englishman's guide for seventy-five dollars a day, on a three-day rate. Alexandru would arrange for her to ring Hogan at his apartment within the hour.

The apartment was on the fourth floor. There was no lift. By the time he reached the flat Hogan was out of breath. Yet again, he thought wryly.

He opened the door and was pleasantly surprised. For something meant to be a budget apartment, it was surprisingly luxurious. Modern furniture, white walls and plenty of space. He dumped his overnight bag on the double bed, then walked round the corner to the lounge and looked out of the main window. Mihai Eminescu Avenue stretched into the distance, choked with what Hogan assumed was rush-hour traffic. One side of the street had cars, lorries and buses jammed solidly together, two abreast. Traffic in the other direction, to the west towards the city centre, was moving more freely, but still virtually nose-to-tail. Horns blared constantly.

Most of the architecture was uninspiring: Eastern Bloc concrete and square lines all the way. But he'd seen enough on the taxi ride through the city centre to know this wasn't typical of all of Bucharest. Some of the city had an ornate, Parisian feel to it. Then, just as he'd been beginning to get the feeling he might suddenly see a Romanian version of the Eiffel Tower round the next corner, the onion-domes of one of the many Eastern Orthodox churches had appeared instead, bringing him back to reality.

He turned away from the apartment window, sat on the black leather-look sofa, and pressed the TV remote to while away the time as he waited for the call from Alexandru's niece. He flicked through till he found something in English. CNN came first, but it was reporting some obscure domestic American story. Hogan kept on channel-hopping and finally discovered BBC World Television News. He settled for that – not really paying attention to the reports, just grateful for the familiar-sounding voices.

As he was about to drift into sleep, the unfamiliar shrill tone of the Romanian telephone made him jump.

He picked up the receiver. 'Hello?'

'Is that Iain Hogan?' It was a woman's voice. The 'Iain' was wrapped in a syrup of what sounded like an Italian accent, with tinges of something Slavic. 'It's Antoaneta here. Alexandru's niece. He asked me to be calling you. He is saying you have need of a hostess.'

Hogan couldn't help noticing that Alexandru's English had been considerably better than Antoaneta's. No wonder she didn't get paid very much as an English teacher. They debated the financial arrangements, with Hogan managing to peg her down to two hundred dollars for the three days. He gave her the address of the apartment, and she promised to be with him within thirty minutes.

Then something weird happened. It was one of those unexplained moments – thought Hogan – when you just seem to be in the right place at the right time. A 'coming up' trail in the news bulletin promised a report from Bucharest on the underworld of the sewer children.

He had to wait through the international sports section before they got to the special report.

It was actually a follow-up bulletin, centring on a return to the Gara de Nord to see what progress had been made fighting the problem since a previous visit. Apparently the main TV networks had first exposed the sewer children to the world in 1997, and now the BBC's Central Europe correspondent had come back.

Hogan was shocked as he saw filthy children inhabiting subterranean lairs. The report said that, to some extent, things had improved at the station itself, with extra policing and a platform ticketing scheme which priced the pathetic children out of the concourse. But a short distance away from the station the reporter found that the horrors continued. The children sniffed solvents from plastic bags, their expressionless faces as blank as their brains as the narcotic effects of the paint fumes hit home. The BBC's correspondent interviewed one boy who told how a foreign paedophile had lured him and two friends to a remote forest area and persuaded them for a few lei to have sex with him. The Romanian government had set up a department of child protection, but it appeared to be overwhelmed.

The doorbell rang, interrupting Hogan's viewing. He went to the door and opened it.

He wasn't sure what sort of woman he'd been expecting. Before even opening his mouth, Hogan was looking her up and down. It was a nasty habit, but one he was finding difficult to kick – the old adage of judging a book by its cover. And being a bit too obvious about it on the way. She was no beauty, facially at least. Too-prominent nose, pond water eyes slightly too close together, as though they were squinting, trying to find a way to peer round the protuberance in front of them. But as Hogan let his eyes fall, following the sweep of the woman's lustrous long black hair, he realised it framed a perfectly proportioned body. Hogan's roving eyes were drawn to her breasts, held in a tight crimson bodice, low cut, showing plenty of cleavage as her fur coat flapped open. It was obvious she wasn't wearing a bra.

He was just about to let his eyes travel further down her body when Antoaneta coughed and smiled. The smile transformed her facial features – as though it was drawing her eyes apart, and taking attention away from her nose.

'I am cold, Mr Hogan. Are you for letting me in?'

Hogan blushed, annoyed with himself. Swivel-head. That was what Lynn often called him as they drove along, and he admired various female forms along the way. Swivel-head – but in the end whose head had been turned by that American git?

Hogan took the coat Antoaneta was offering him, and finally welcomed her inside.

After Hogan had filled in Antoaneta about the details of his search for the girl, she suggested they set off straight away to see if they could find the website's office. It was dark now, nearly six o'clock in the evening, but she seemed confident there was a good chance the office would still be open.

'Should we get a taxi?' asked Hogan.

'No, there is no need. Not unless you are wanting to. The underground train is going very fast, and the station is near.'

Light snow was falling now, the snowflakes picked out under the neon glow of the streetlights and in the headlights of the cars. Hogan hunched himself inside his overcoat to try to keep out the cold. He glanced sideways at Antoaneta as they crossed the Calea Dorobantilor at the junction with Dacia Boulevard, dodging the traffic above ground rather than taking the pedestrian subway. He wished, politically incorrect or not, that he was the one with the fur coat.

A horn blared. Antoaneta grabbed him and pushed him out of the way of an onrushing car he hadn't seen.

Shit, he thought. That was close.

Antoaneta laughed. 'I think you are taking much time to get used to Romanian roads. They are busier than England, yes?'

Hogan was slightly annoyed to look a fool, but tried to smile it off.

In just a couple of minutes they were in the Piata Romana and heading down into the Metro station. Hogan gave Antoaneta some lei and she went off to buy their tickets, but to his surprise she came back with only one.

She saw his quizzical look. 'Don't worry. This is for ten *calatorii*, ten entries. We will need only four to get us there and back.'

Hogan followed her to the bright orange turnstiles. Antoaneta fed the magnetic card into a green box on top of the turnstile, went through, and then handed the card back to Hogan so he could do the same.

The passageways of the Metro system were impressive. Marble pillars held up a blue roof. Hogan and Antoaneta walked across what appeared to be a solid limestone floor.

She saw him admiring it. 'It's nice, yes? Mr Ceaucescu was an evil man, but some of his legacy has helped us.'

They were almost at platform level now, and Hogan felt a rush of cold air whistle past his face.

'Ah, we may have just missed one,' said Antoaneta. 'You can tell by the wind.' She laughed and pointed to her long black hair, which was now a dishevelled mess. Hogan looked at her as they walked the remaining steps to the platform. Not a ravishing beauty, but sexy all the same.

If they had indeed missed a train, then trains were frequent, because another quickly arrived: sleek and silver, whispering through the tunnel, the front car with its bright yellow, red and blue 'Flying M' logo and crimson stripes. Hogan thought of London's Underground, its litter-strewn dirty stations and its overcrowded platforms. There was no comparison. This was a thousand times better.

The doors whooshed open and he and Antoaneta stepped inside. Even though this was the rush hour, they still managed to get seats side by side. Functional, crimson plastic seats, and not terribly comfortable, thought Hogan, but seats nonetheless.

Antoaneta had led the way through the various pedestrian tunnels at the station, so Hogan hadn't had to struggle to read the signs, but he knew they were on line M2, heading in the direction of Depou IMGB. The acronym looked as though it stood for a trades union or something similar, but he was tired now and couldn't be bothered asking Antoaneta. In any case he wasn't sure if she would understand what a trades union was.

They sat in silence, and Hogan studied the Metro map, mentally crossing off the stations as they passed. They were heading seven stations down the line, to Aparatorii Patriei. Hogan wondered what that meant. Father's Apparatus? A vaulting horse or something more sinister? He chuckled to himself – he had absolutely no idea. The language seemed to be Latin-based, similar perhaps to Italian, but Hogan's Latin was woeful.

First stop Universitatii, and then Piata Uniril, where more people got on and off, presumably because it was a connecting station with the M1 line, which crossed the city from west to east.

After only a few minutes, they were at their destination. Antoaneta grabbed Hogan's hand and pulled him to his feet. 'Come on. This is fun. Let's get going.'

Above ground the snow was now settling, muffling the sounds of the city with its softness. Antoaneta walked quickly, and Hogan struggled to keep up. The street they were heading for was Sos. Oltenitei. As they turned into it, Hogan saw that it appeared to be a commercial and service industry area. Most of the company names he hadn't heard of, although there was the occasional multi-national.

Antoaneta stopped outside a rather grey, block-like structure. 'This is it.'

'What is?' said Hogan, perplexed.

'The address you had. It is here.' She pointed at the building. 'Bucurestnet.'

'I don't see a sign,' said Hogan, still puzzled.

Antoaneta shrugged and smiled, as if to say that that wasn't her problem.

They approached the front door of the building. There were still no signs, no bell to ring. Nothing. As though guests weren't particularly welcome. Antoaneta hung back, letting Hogan lead the way.

He pushed at the door, and was surprised when it opened. She followed him through it. There was a light at the end of a corridor, that was otherwise in complete darkness. Hogan moved towards the light, conscious that Antoaneta was just behind him. He could feel the reassuring warmth of her breath on his neck.

The door to the lit room was open, but Hogan knocked nonetheless before going inside.

There was just one man in the room. He looked to be perhaps in his late thirties, but had a pockmarked, lived-in face. He was dressed in a full-length black leather coat with the collar turned up. His most notable feature was a completely bald head. The glare from the single unshaded light bulb reflected off it.

He glanced up from his computer, apparently disinterested. '*Buna seara.*'

Hogan nodded at him and let Antoaneta do the talking. As she moved out from behind Hogan he could see the man appraise her openly, his eyes travelling up and down her body. Sizing her up, like she was a commodity. But then I'm guilty of doing that too often myself, thought Hogan.

Antoaneta and the man exchanged a few sentences in Romanian. Hogan strained to understand even a single word, but couldn't.

As Antoaneta continued her questioning the man started to become angry. He banged his fist down on the table as though he were bringing the conversation to an end. '*Nu! Noapte buna!*'

Antoaneta translated. 'He says he cannot breach client confidentiality. Bucurestnet simply provides the webspace and servers for a number of clients. He is – how do you say it? – of certainty that he is not giving to us any information.'

'But can't you tell him a young girl's life may be at stake?'

'I am telling him that already. When he banged the table that was his final word – no and goodnight.'

The man evidently understood more English than he was letting on, because when Antoaneta said this he nodded vigorously.

Hogan scowled at him, then turned back to Antoaneta. 'Ask him if money would help. How much does he want?'

Antoaneta translated, but the man shook his head. 'You Americans,' he said, seeming suddenly to discover an ability to speak English. 'You think your dollars can buy you anything.' He spat on the floor to emphasise his distaste.

Hogan didn't think it was worth explaining that actually he was British, and that there was a difference. Instead he turned back to

81

Antoaneta. 'So what can we do?'

She shrugged. 'Nothing. I'm sorry. Let us be going back to the apartment. Maybe tomorrow we can find out something else.'

They turned to go. Then Antoaneta stopped.

'Wait, Mr Hogan. I have an idea.'

She approached the man again, bent over, and whispered in his ear. Hogan noticed his eyes seem to light up, and then he gave an evil laugh, took a long drag on his cigarette, and exhaled in Antoaneta's face. Instead of coughing and backing off, she took the man's hand, brought it up to her mouth, and took a drag from the cigarette herself. What the heck's going on here? thought Hogan.

'Mr Hogan, you must please leave us alone for fifteen minutes. Wait outside the building. I may be able to be persuading him.'

The man laughed cruelly. 'Don't get too cold, American, while I'm enjoying myself. *Cacanar!*'

Hogan was dubious about leaving the two of them together, but Antoaneta signalled with her eyes and smiled, as though to say she would be all right. Hogan pulled his coat up round his neck again and went outside.

He rubbed his hands together, stamped his feet, and tried to push his neck further down into the body of the coat. But nothing could keep out the icy cold. It felt as though it was burrowing into him, inside his head, and into the very marrow of his bones. He tried to wait the full fifteen minutes, but after about ten he'd had enough and went back inside.

This time he didn't knock but marched straight into the office, even though the door had been closed since he'd departed. As he did so Antoaneta and the man broke apart. She looked embarrassed, her clothing dishevelled, her denim mini skirt high on her hips above her stocking stops. She tugged it down. The man was doing up his flies and smacking his lips.

Hogan tried to catch Antoaneta's gaze but she looked away.

The man laughed. 'You have a good woman there, American. Make sure you treat her right. Just like I did.' Smirking, he fetched a piece of paper out of the desk drawer. He wrote something on it, then brandished it at Antoaneta.

'Here. This is what you've earned. I hope to God you think it was worth it. Now, both of you, get the fuck out of here and don't come back.'

The journey back to the apartment was conducted in total silence. Hogan didn't ask what was on the piece of paper and didn't thank Antoaneta. For her part, she wouldn't meet his eyes. They sat opposite each other on the Metro as it sped under Bucharest's streets. Hogan supposed he should be grateful, but he didn't feel it. He didn't know what exactly had gone on back in the office on Sos. Olteniţei, but he was fairly certain Antoaneta had prostituted herself.

For him.

Why? That was the strange thing. Why was his mission so important to her?

They stopped off at a late-night corner store to get some supplies. Antoaneta chose them – bacon, wine, sauerkraut, a couple of other items he wasn't paying attention to. Hogan paid. Again virtually no words passed between them.

As Hogan opened the front door of the flat, Antoaneta finally smiled at him. 'I can see you are shocking?'

'You mean, I'm shocked?'

'Yes, sorry. You can see my English is not as good as it should be for a teacher. That's why I had to leave. Now I'm concentrating on what I *am* good at.'

'And what went on back there? With that bald-headed bastard. Is that what you're good at?' Hogan surprised himself by how vicious he sounded.

'You are offended. I am sorry.' Antoaneta smiled again, and brushed her hair back from her face. Hogan felt the sexual chemistry between them. 'But to answer you, yes, that is what I'm good at. Does that shock you? It is what business visitors to this city expect from a hostess. But you . . . you seem different.'

Hogan was aware of his erection now, pushing against the material of his trousers, weighed down by the heavy front of his coat.

He smiled at her. He wasn't so very different at all.

'Come on. Let's cook up that food we got at the store. I'm starving,' he said.

Antoaneta's cooking was superb. Hogan hadn't realised this was all part of his seventy-dollars-a-day service. He was famished, and the dish – 'Bigus' – filled the hole. Sour cabbage with smoked bacon, salami and hot dogs, fried and then cooked in the oven. The way her grandmother used to cook it, Antoaneta admitted, the dish took hours to prepare. That was before . . . Before what? She didn't complete the sentence, and a sad look passed in front of her eyes. She recovered herself and explained that now the supermarkets sold some of the ingredients pre-prepared – you could cheat. Cheating or not, it didn't matter to Hogan. After he'd devoured a huge helping, Antoaneta laughed as he dived into the casserole bowl to scrape out more.

The smoked meats and the piquancy of the cabbage gave the Bigus a delicious flavour. Hogan tried to put to one side the thought that all the salt would play havoc with his blood pressure. And everything was washed down with a Romanian Pinot Noir; his teetotal days seemed to have been left far behind.

By the time they had finished it was approaching eleven o'clock.

'It's getting late,' said Hogan. 'Hadn't you better be heading for home?'

Antoaneta's face fell. 'I am thinking I would like to stay here. You wanted to start early tomorrow. It is a long way for me to get home now.'

Hogan looked toward the bedroom. There was just the one bed, albeit a double. Then he turned his attention to the sofa. It seemed to be one of those designed to convert into an extra bed. He went into the bedroom and searched out some blankets, then carried them back to the living room.

'I'll sleep here.' He pressed down the foam of the sofa. 'Seems comfy enough. You take the bedroom.'

Antoaneta grabbed the blankets from him. 'No, silly man. You are a guest here in Romania. I will be sleeping out here if you do not want us to be sleeping together.'

84

Hogan suddenly realised she had been put out by his automatic assumption they wouldn't be sharing the same bed. As she told me earlier, he thought, it's all part of the standard package.

But it was too late to go back now. He helped her convert the sofa into a bed, said goodnight, and retreated to the bedroom. Alone.

He woke in the middle of the night, disoriented. At first he thought the warm near-naked body pressing against his own was Lynn's. But then he remembered they had split up, and were probably heading for the divorce courts. He switched on the bedside light and saw Antoaneta's face on the pillow. Hogan was only half-surprised. Her face looked more at peace with itself here, as though the contrasting features had declared a ceasefire, her long black hair arranged around her. He lifted the duvet, admiring her near-perfect body. She was naked from the waist up. Her breasts were bronzed like the rest of her skin, with no tan lines. God, they look so inviting, he thought. Then the sweep of her flat smooth stomach, a pierced belly button, and a high-cut black thong.

Swivel-head. Ogling again. It was almost as if Lynn was inside his head, admonishing him. He remembered the first time they'd met, during a game of 'sardines' at a party thrown by one of the *Sentinel's* reporters. Lynn had stuck her tongue in his ear – well, that was what he'd always claimed: she denied it. Lynn.

He guiltily dropped the duvet back over Antoaneta, and felt her waken with a shiver.

'Mr Hogan? Are you awake?'

'Uh huh.'

'I am being sorry for coming into your bed. It was cold. I was lonely.'

Hogan was silent.

Antoaneta reached across his naked form. Part of him wanted to return the embrace – the part between his legs. But for once he let his brain control his erectile tissue, rather than the other way round. He gently pushed Antoaneta away.

*   *   *

85

When Hogan woke in the morning Antoaneta was already up. The smell of cooked bacon wafted through to the bedroom. Then she was back, a tray of cooked breakfast for both of them.

'I'm knowing from my language lessons that you English people like bacon and eggs for breakfast.'

She smiled. Hogan grinned and wondered if he'd arrived in heaven rather than Bucharest.

The previous evening, over dinner, Hogan had been surprised to learn that the name and address given to Antoaneta by the man at Bucurestnet were not, in fact, those of the owner of the Preteen Pleasures website. They were for the go-between, a girl who liaised with Bucurestnet and brought the monthly fee, in cash, for the webhosting service. But the man had warned Antoaneta that he'd not seen the girl for more than a month. The Preteen Pleasures payments were overdue. He was just as keen to trace the owners as Hogan was; unless there was payment soon, Bucurestnet would have to remove the site.

The address, Antoaneta explained, wasn't an address as such – at least, it wasn't for a proper house. The paper simply had the name of the girl written on it, and directions to her lair, a sewer tank room under a park in the northern outskirts of the city.

More snow had fallen overnight. The pavements were icy. Hogan, unprepared, slipped into Antoaneta time and again. She thought it was hilarious. Where the snow wasn't turned to slush by the traffic or ice by the pedestrians, it was almost six inches thick.

Without warning, something hard, cold and icy struck Hogan on the side of the head. He turned, heard some boys laughing, and looked up to the apartment balcony. Half a dozen kids were gathering snow to open fire again. Hogan shook his fist at them. Antoaneta took more direct action. She bent down, formed some loose snow into a ball-shape, and then launched it up towards the boys on the balcony. It was a good shot – a great shot, in fact, striking one of the boys full in the face just as he was about to throw another snowball of his own.

As they entered the Metro station, still giggling like children, Hogan shook the snow off his upper body. Antoaneta slapped the top of his head and his back to get the rest of it off.

This time they travelled north up the blue M2 line, just one stop, and then changed at Piata Victoriei onto the yellow line, M3. Looking at the map in the trains, Hogan could see this followed a circular route under the city centre – just like London Underground's Circle Line. The map showed it as the same colour, too. But the trains were more modern, more comfortable, and more frequent.

One stop further, then another change to the green M4, taking them out to the northwest of the city.

This was a slightly longer journey, four stops to the 1 Mai station. They had time to sit, and did so, next to each other.

Antoaneta lifted one of her hands and turned Hogan's head towards hers.

He found himself looking straight into those too-close together pond water eyes. Did it matter? And who, anyway, was Hogan to be so clinically assessing another's looks? He was no male model himself.

'So, Mr Hogan. We seem to be getting nearer to your goal. What happens if we are completely solving your little mystery today? Maybe tomorrow you can treat me . . . to lunch . . . dinner . . . who knows what?'

She stroked his face and smiled. He realised he was very fond of her. He thought of Emma – so much more beautiful to look at than the girl next to him. But with a side of her that Hogan wasn't particularly sure about. And in some way, Antoaneta seemed to have qualities Emma lacked. Kindness? Loyalty? He wasn't sure Emma would score particularly highly there. In another time, another place, he might have pursued Antoaneta – but there was Lynn to think about, and the kids.

Out of the corner of his eye he saw they were already leaving Grivita station.

The next stop was theirs.

Above ground, there was more snow in this part of the city, and it was still falling, the snowflakes thicker now. They found walking difficult along Boulevard Expozitiei. The Metro stations were few and far apart here, towards the outskirts, and they had a couple of kilometres to walk along the street, near the Romexpo trade centre. They passed the luxury Hotel Sofitel, took the left fork into Boulevard Martasti, and trudged onwards towards the entrance of Herastrau Park, where the Bucurestnet man had said they would find the girl.

As they entered the park Antoaneta checked the written instructions and looked around for the park-keeper's hut, the landmark they needed to find their bearings. Twenty paces along a path directly east of the hut they found the manhole cover they were seeking.

Antoaneta picked up a broken branch from nearby and banged on the metal cover.

'Marica! Marica! We need to talk to you.'

There was no reply.

They waited a few moments, then Antoaneta tried again. This time the manhole cover slowly lifted.

Hogan was expecting a girl to appear, but this was a small boy. His head came up first, topped by a red woollen cap. Then he hauled up his body, clothed in a torn, shabby grey anorak. As the boy exhaled in the cold morning air, Hogan could smell fumes, and he flinched away.

'Aurolac,' explained Antoaneta. 'It is a cheap liquid for helping with painting. They are sniffing it and getting out of their heads.'

The boy stood rooted to the spot, shivering pathetically.

Antoaneta appeared to ask him what his name was.

'Vasile,' the boy replied.

But when she asked him about Marica he just shrugged.

Antoaneta whispered to Hogan, 'Some money may help in making his tongue loose.'

Hogan dug his wallet from his pocket and peeled off a one-thousand-lei note. The boy grabbed it but still did not say anything.

'I think you will have to be giving him another,' said Antoaneta.

Hogan reluctantly gave the boy another note, and wondered how he was going to be able to explain his mounting expense account to Howze when he got back to the Isle of Wight.

The boy grabbed the note and stuffed it into his anorak pocket. He gestured with his arm to Antoaneta and climbed back into the manhole. Antoaneta and Hogan followed.

Hogan was wary of shutting the cover behind them: the inside of the underground passageway was dark. But in the light from the opening he could see Vasile gesture angrily for him to close it. Antoaneta got out a small torch from her pocket.

'It's OK,' she said. 'He probably wants the place kept warm.'

The foetid air down here was certainly several degrees warmer than outside. Hogan felt the pipes at the side of the tunnel giving out heat. They moved along the passageway, hunched almost double because of the restricted height. After a few metres the tunnel opened out into what Hogan assumed was the tank room. A jumble of bodies covered in filthy blankets littered the floor.

Hogan noted the debris of previous solvent-sniffing sessions – empty paint-thinner cans and plastic bags.

One of the blankets started moving, and a boy's head popped out from under it. The prone boy began questioning Vasile angrily.

As always Antoaneta had to translate for Hogan's benefit. 'This boy is wanting to know what is happening. He is angry. I am thinking you will need to give him some money too.'

Hogan dug another thousand-lei note from his pocket and gave it to Vasile's colleague.

The two boys now pointed to another tunnel, speaking in hushed tones to Antoaneta.

'They say she is down there. In about thirty metres. There is another tank room.'

Hogan was getting claustrophobic as they travelled further into the tunnel network. The walls were damp. Every now and then rats scuttled from the light beam of Antoaneta's torch. He was glad she was leading the way. The smell was almost worse than in Kavanagh's flat: the same combination of excrement, decay and dirt.

The passage finally widened into the next tank room, although there was no increase in head-height. The torch picked out a human-shaped bundle underneath a blanket.

Antoaneta trained the beam on it but didn't move towards it, instead stepping aside to let Hogan go forward. As he did so he heard shouting from back down the tunnel in the direction of the first tank room.

Then a clang of metal, a shaft of natural light, and another louder metallic noise as the passage behind was plunged into darkness again.

He turned to Antoaneta and raised his eyebrows questioningly.

'Maybe those boys are getting up finally. Each day they are on the streets for begging, I am thinking.'

Hogan reached down and shook the bundle gently.

'Marica,' he whispered. 'Marica! Marica!'

No response.

He started shouting the name, and shook the body more vigorously. Still no response.

Hogan feared the worst. He turned the body over, and the lifeless grey face of the girl stared back at him, caught in the harsh light of the torch. He brought the back of his hand up against her cheek and held it there for a moment. Her skin felt cold. He stroked her matted hair gently, wondering for a moment about the pathetic life this slight girl had led. Then he pulled up the blanket and covered her face.

'I'm sorry, Mr Hogan,' said Antoaneta softly. 'Truly I am sorry. I am thinking now you are not solving your mystery, and that your journey from England is a waste.'

He knew she was almost certainly correct. The trail had gone cold.

They turned and made their way back down the passage. The other tank room was now empty. The boys had fled. Hogan wondered how much they knew about the circumstances of Marica's death. Whatever they knew, they didn't seem keen to divulge it.

As they hauled themselves up through the manhole, Bucharest felt even colder. Shielding his eyes from the light, Hogan felt his teeth chattering, his whole body shaking.

Antoaneta saw this, and obviously sensed his depression. She opened her fur coat and welcomed him against the warmth of her body. As they embraced, Hogan felt a surge of emotion, and tears filled his eyes.

They stood there cheek to cheek, Antoaneta whispering close to his ear. 'You must not be giving up,' she said, the determination clear in her voice. 'You have come too far. We still have two days left to find something. I am sure we will do it.'

Hogan pulled his head back to look into her eyes. He smiled, and was tempted to kiss her. Instead he affectionately rubbed her nose.

'Antoaneta. Wonderful Antoaneta. I hope you're right. I do hope you're right.'

7

Clara Forbes eased Emma's Mercedes through its gears as she accelerated away from Ventnor towards Reeth. Emma was organising a party to thank the Wight Women's Ramblers for withdrawing their objections to the closure of the cliff path, and to celebrate her confirmation as a Detective Constable.

She'd been insistent that Clara should borrow the car for the forty-five-minute journey to the caterers in Freshwater.

'You'll love it,' she'd said. 'You can really open it up along the straight runs on the Military Road.'

Clara intended to do just that.

Emma had gone off at the same time to catch the bus to Shanklin to finalise the evening's entertainment. They were having a jazz band on the lawn.

Before she went, Emma had been busy organising everyone. Good little policewoman that she is, thought Clara. She's been so wonderful for us, ever since that bit of nastiness back in early October. Their arrangement seemed to have worked well. The September cliff fall seemed to have dropped off the police's radar. The suspect had been released on police bail, and the girl was still in a coma, still unidentified, and Clara was confident that was the way it would stay. Emma seemed to have ensured that the police hadn't come round asking awkward questions. After all, she *was* the police, and in immediate charge of the case, so perhaps it wasn't surprising.

Now she was organising this party for the ramblers. It was a really sweet idea, thought Clara.

At the same time as sending Clara to the caterers to check final arrangements and deliver the table lists, Emma had despatched Maria to the wine warehouse in Cowes in the Volvo. Maria had made a feeble attempt to protest: she didn't like going to shops on her own. But Emma would have none of it.

'Come on,' she'd said. 'We've not got much time left. Division of labour is the only way we'll get everything done. If we all go off separately we get the final bits and bobs sorted out in about two hours each. Then we can relax.'

With the three of them gone, Romana had been left to mind the house in their absence. She was good at that, and used to it, thought Clara. After all, she'd been there ever since her arrival from Romania. The real truth of the matter was that Romana wasn't allowed to leave the house. People might see her and start asking awkward questions. Clara had taken the precaution of putting locks on all the windows. She'd made sure all the house doors were locked, too, before the three of them went their separate ways.

Of course, if Romana was minded to, she could no doubt escape, thought Clara. But Romana was a compliant little thing. And not stupid. She knew that her papers were in a false name. If she went out and about she'd face the ever-present possibility of being detained as an illegal immigrant, and then sent home to Romania; and once there it'd be back to the streets and selling sex, the only thing she'd ever known.

Even so, it was best not to put temptation in Romana's way.

Driving along the Blackgang Road towards West Wight brought back unpleasant memories for Clara. Things she didn't want to think about. Clara shivered. She glanced to her left to St Rhadegund's Cliff, but then quickly looked back, gripping the wheel more firmly. It's over now, forget it, she told herself. No one will ever know what really happened.

But she realised she was still shivering. The air conditioning was turned down low. Clara swore to herself under her breath, angrily remembering that she hadn't been able to find her favourite red fleece. The one she always wore when out walking. Red was a colour she liked. It made her feel powerful, masculine.

Emma had told her not to worry about the fleece, and had ushered her on her way, saying the car had an excellent heating system. If only I could work out how to adjust the damn thing, thought Clara.

As the road straightened past Chale, Clara hit the accelerator.

The car responded instantaneously with a rush of subtle power. The speedometer climbed quickly. Fifty, sixty, seventy. Effortlessly.

Then a double flash of light. What the heck was that?

Clara looked in the rear mirror. Now she saw the speed camera, hidden behind the tree. Sneaky. Bloody Isle of Wight Police. Didn't they have anything better to do?

She wondered if she ought to ring Emma on the mobile to warn her. Clara hoped it wouldn't get the young policewoman into trouble. This whole journey was a bit naughty because Clara didn't have the right insurance to drive the car. It meant Emma would have to take the rap for the speeding fine. God, I *do* hope it doesn't get her into trouble, she thought. Luckily neither of them had told Maria that she was taking the Mercedes, otherwise her sister would have been worrying herself senseless about Clara breaking the law.

She tried Emma's number but failed to get a reply.

She'd try her again once she reached Freshwater. There was at least one other call she had to make, too.

Why hadn't Emma warned her about the speed camera?

Surely the police would tell their own about where they were all placed? Maybe they didn't.

Clara shivered again. This bloody air-conditioning. It's too cold. Where the hell has my fleece got to? I hope Maria hasn't borrowed it again! It doesn't even fit her properly, she looks drowned in it.

What should have been an exhilarating drive along the island's finest stretch of coast was fast becoming extremely frustrating. Clara Forbes was losing her temper – rapidly. Maybe she should turn back and get the fleece? It would add only another twenty minutes to her journey.

Lee Hughes crouched behind the dry-stone wall, and stroked his dog. Trying to keep it from barking.

He had excellent eyesight and he had seen the two figures long before they had had a chance to notice him. It was the red top one of them was wearing. That was what terrified him. He'd seen it before.

She had been so nasty to him. When he had tried to be good.

He didn't want to meet her again. So he hid behind the wall.

Some of the stone was loose. There were gaps. He could see the others through the gaps, but thought they probably couldn't see him.

Was it a mother and daughter? He was never very good with ages. It looked like it was two women, and one looked younger than the other did. Maybe she was a girl. He was never very sure where being a girl ended and being a woman began.

He thought they were mother and daughter because they were holding hands as they walked along. They laughed and cuddled like a mother and daughter might.

Then they stopped at the cliff edge. Near where he had seen the nasty woman.

Now they kissed. A mother and daughter might do that too.

But they kept on kissing. The older one seemed to have her hands in the younger one's clothing. Her hands would be cold on the other's skin, he thought. But then he saw she was wearing gloves. Black gloves.

They stood still for another moment, and hugged. But only for a moment because, next thing he knew, the older one was pushing the younger one. That's what he thought he saw. Or did the younger one just stumble and lose her footing? Whichever, she had now gone. Over the cliff edge.

Now there was just the woman in the red top.

Something nasty had happened, he felt sure. Something naughty.

Should he tell someone? Perhaps. That would be the *good* thing to do. But he didn't like that woman in the red fleece. He could remember her frightening face from the last time. Whatever had happened, he didn't want to see that face again. Didn't want her to hurt him.

And anyway he wasn't really supposed to be here. He was supposed to stay with Mummy at all times. But secretly each day he took the bus to come back to the cliff – *his* cliff.

So maybe he would keep what he'd seen to himself.

He stroked the dog. It's a secret, he thought. A secret for you and me to share, my lovely.

Clara was agitated as she got back to the house from Freshwater. Her mood at the beginning of the day had been elated, with the party to look forward to. And then the thrill when Emma had lent her the

Mercedes. But on the journey to West Wight it had all started to go wrong. The speed camera, the car's unfathomable air-conditioning system, and her growing irritation over mislaying her favourite fleece. Then the trouble with her mobile. She kept it locked as a matter of course, and she was the only one who knew the password. But the first time she'd tried it today it hadn't responded. Only after a couple of attempts had it eventually sprung into life.

She unlocked the front door. The house was silent.

I must be the first back, she thought. But where are the dogs? Maybe one of the others has got back already and taken them for a walk.

'Romana!' she called. No answer.

Now she was worried. The au pair was always here – had no choice but always to be here. What had happened to her?

Clara moved quickly through the hall towards the kitchen. Maybe the girl just hadn't heard.

'Romana! Romana! Stop being silly, where are you?'

Clara was shouting now, hysteria rising.

She opened the door to the kitchen. All was still silent. The sun had finally broken through the autumn clouds and shafts of light were streaming through the window.

It was weirdly cold. Then Clara looked again at the window and realised why. The window was open. The key still dangled in the lock, tinkling lightly in the breeze.

She noticed there were stains around the window frame.

What was it? Mud?

She moved closer to examine it.

Oh my God, Clara thought, it's blood. What the hell is going on here?

Then the smell hit her. She hadn't noticed it at first, but now she realised it was overpowering. It was the unmistakable smell of dog excrement. She turned from the window, her eyes followed the bloodstains on the floor to the far corner of the L-shaped room, where the smell came from.

What she saw there made her start shaking. Then she let out a long series of howls.

'No, no, n . . . o . . . o . . .!'

It was the dogs.

Their throats slit.

Their guts sliced open, spilling out onto the limestone floor.

Her dogs. Her beloved dogs.

Maria and Mother had always hated them, suffered them. Now they had got their wish. Both dogs dead, their lovely golden fleeces matted in a bloody butchered mess. Their eyes staring madly, but unseeing. Who had done it? Who had killed her beautiful animals?

Clara reached down and, in turn, shut both the dogs' eyelids before rigor mortis could set in.

It seemed like hours passed before Clara heard the sound of the front door being opened.

She said nothing.

Just sat huddled in the kitchen, shivering, her arms hugged around herself.

'Clara, Maria! I'm back. Where are you?'

It was Emma. She would know what to do. Practical-minded Emma. She would keep cool in a crisis.

Clara heard the drawing-room door open. Emma was calling again.

Then the kitchen door opened.

'Romana? Where *is* everyone?'

Clara finally found her voice.

'Romana's not here. Just me.' It was barely more than a whisper.

She saw Emma turn the corner of the kitchen. Saw the shock on her face as she surveyed the scene

'Oh, Clara, what's wrong? Oh my god!'

Clara watched Emma's face. Saw her revulsion. Then Emma dropped to her knees, and Clara welcomed her comforting hug.

'My poor baby. My poor baby. You loved those dogs. Who could have done this?'

'Maria. It must have been Maria.' Clara was half-surprised by her own accusation. But her sister had always hated the dogs. 'She's done it to spite me. And run off with Romana – that's what's happened.'

Clara gazed into Emma's eyes. They were sparkling as usual, but the policewoman was looking dubious.

'I can't believe that,' said Emma. 'Maria's such a nervous thing. However much she hated the dogs, surely she'd never hurt you in this way.'

'Yes, she would.' Clara could hear the hatred in her own voice. But she wasn't sure if she really believed the accusation herself. 'What do we do now?' she asked.

'We'll have to clear up the mess,' said Emma. Her tone had transformed in an instant. Businesslike again now. Almost dismissive. The practical policewoman taking over.

'But shouldn't we call the police or something?' asked Clara.

'Don't be so bloody stupid.' Clara felt Emma almost spit the words out at her. 'We have to keep this very quiet. You know that as well as I do.'

Clara started crying. Emma was right. Too much had happened. 'But what about Romana?'

'You've said it yourself. As soon as anyone finds her they'll rumble that her papers are forged. She'll soon be on her way back to Romania.'

'So what can we do?'

'Nothing. I've already bloody told you.' There seemed almost to be hatred in Emma's voice now. 'Just keep quiet and all this will blow over – you'll see.'

'OK.' Clara felt shattered, too weak to disagree.

'Oh, there is *one* thing you need to do, though. Get on the phone to all your pratty walking friends. Tell them the party is off.'

Clara was ushered by Emma into the drawing room, onto their favourite sofa. Only this time there was no intimacy between the two. Emma appeared cold, practical. Clara understood there was no point arguing with her – they both knew enough about one another to bring ruination. Clara felt they both recognised the only escape from their horrors was silence.

The front door was opened again. Another greeting.

'Hello? Anyone home?'

It was Maria. She too sounded disorientated by the fact that the dogs weren't barking. In her view, it's probably a blessed relief, thought Clara.

She heard Maria walk down the hall, then stop as she saw Emma and Clara through the open drawing-room door.

'You've seen it too then?' Maria asked. Clara thought her sister seemed fearful. She was looking down at the floor as she asked the question, not wanting to meet Clara and Emma's gaze.

Silence hung awkwardly in the space between the women. Then Maria spoke again.

'It's terrible, isn't it? All our worst nightmares.'

Clara answered, her tone icy. 'I'd have thought you'd be pleased. You probably did it, didn't you?'

Maria appeared puzzled now. 'What do you mean?'

'The dogs,' said Clara. 'You've never liked them.'

'The d . . . d . . . d . . . dogs? B . . . b . . . but I don't understand.'

Clara stood up, and approached her sister. She pulled her arm back and slapped Maria across the face, her ring catching her sister's lower lip.

'You knew how much they meant to me, you bitch.'

A spot of crimson welled up, and then slowly started to drip down Maria's chin. Maria's hand moved to her face. Touching the wound. She examined the blood on her hand.

Emma intervened, holding Clara back. 'That's enough, Clara,' she said. 'This isn't helping.'

Maria seemed stunned. 'I still don't know what you're talking about.'

Emma spoke precisely, her tone clipped. 'The dogs are dead.'

Maria gasped.

'Their throats slit.' Emma sounded dispassionate. Empty.

Almost as though it didn't matter, thought Clara, sitting down again and beginning to cry once more. Maria came over to comfort her.

Emma sneered at them. 'You two are pathetic. Crying will do no one any good. More to the point is where Romana has got to.'

'What do you mean?' asked Maria.

'She's disappeared,' Emma replied flatly.

'Oh, no. What's happening to us?' cried Maria. 'You've both seen the paper, haven't you?'

Emma and Clara shook their heads. Clara watched Maria open her bag and get it out. It was the evening paper, the *Wight Evening Star*. Clara thought it was a horrible gossip sheet. She much preferred the island's weekly.

But she read the lead story Maria pointed to with mounting dread. It was labelled 'Exclusive', and headlined 'New Hope for Cliff Girl'. Maria's trembling hands tried but failed to hold the paper steady as Clara and Emma read the report. Clara instantly grasped what it meant. The girl from the cliff fall appeared to be coming out of her coma. Superintendent Stephen Reilly of Yarwater CID was hoping the girl might finally be able to tell them exactly what had happened the day she fell. That she would be able to tell them who she was. And why she was on the Isle of Wight.

Clara felt desperate. She exchanged fearful glances with Maria. Then she looked at Emma, expecting to see the same there. But what she saw instead in Emma's face and eyes was rage – pure, unadulterated rage.

'The bastard. The fucking interfering bastard,' the policewoman said.

'Who?' asked Clara. She couldn't understand Emma's reaction. It seemed so odd.

'Reilly. This is *my* fucking case. What the fuck does he thing he's doing, talking to the press?' Her pretty face was contorted with anger.

'Is that all you can think about at a time like this?' Clara shouted. 'Professional jealousy? Don't you think we've got more important things to worry about? Anyway he's a superintendent – your superior.'

'Don't start lecturing me. This is important. As long as I'm left pretty much in charge of the case, just reporting to DCI Hale, we have a chance of keeping the lid on things. If Reilly starts interfering we're in trouble.'

Clara was forced to admit she had a point. But something about Emma Thomas was beginning to concern her.

8

Despite Antoaneta's encouraging words, Hogan's mood was black as they walked south through the snow-covered park. Now that the boys had deserted the sewer tank room, there was little point in hanging around. He decided it would be best to go back to the flat, get warm, and then try to think of a new strategy.

They had come up against the proverbial brick wall. And there were just two days left before he had to fly back to England.

On their way to Herastrau Park they had followed the directions given to them by the man at Bucurestnet. But now Antoaneta led the way to a different Metro station, Aviatorilor. The walk was a similar distance, two kilometres, but this station was on the M2 line, with a direct link back to the Piata Romana.

Back in the flat, Hogan rushed to the shower. The needles of water pummelled some heat back into his body, and some hope into his heart.

As he relaxed with a hot drink after the shower, Hogan racked his brains to try to come up with a way of finding the owner of the Preteen Pleasures website. Back in England, he'd already checked the registered owner. That's what had led them to Bucurestnet in the first place. But Antoaneta was insistent that the man there was telling the truth. His company was simply the host. Their only tangible link to the owner was Marica, and she was dead.

'You are looking so sad,' said Antoaneta.

Hogan smiled at her, but it was a forced smile. 'Not sad. Just fed up. What do we do?'

'We still haven't talked to the boys about Marica. Maybe they know something about her.'

'Hmm. They didn't seem to want to hang around long enough to talk. But perhaps you're right.'

'Were you for checking her papers?'

'How do you mean?'

'Her papers. Were you checking her clothing to see if she had any in her pockets?'

Hogan groaned and held his head in his hands. It was the obvious thing to have done. Why hadn't he? Partly because he didn't want to disturb the dead girl any more than they had. Already, witnesses – the sewer boys – had seen them go towards the tank room. Marica's body had shown no signs of decay, so she had probably not been long dead. Hogan didn't want himself and Antoaneta to end up in a Romanian police cell.

But the body was their only lead.

'We're going to have to go back there again, aren't we?' he said.

'I am thinking so, yes. But let's be waiting a couple of hours until the boys come back from their day's begging. They may know more than they are letting on.'

Darkness had fallen by the time they got back to the park. A flashing blue light by the entrance nearest the park-keeper's hut caught Hogan's attention. He grabbed Antoaneta and pulled her behind a tree.

'Look, the police. We don't want to be meeting them.'

They waited and watched from behind the tree. Hogan could see figures with flashlights by the manhole cover. Then a stretcher. Then a body, presumably the girl Marica's, being lifted out and taken away.

Without warning, someone hissed at them from behind.

Hogan turned. Peeking out from behind another tree was Vasile, his face highlighted every few seconds by the ghostly blue flashing of the police car's light.

Antoaneta whispered to Hogan, 'Be staying here. I will go and talk to him. Give me some lei notes to bribe him.'

Hogan peeled off five one-thousand-lei bills. Antoaneta gestured for more. He sighed, but gave her another five notes.

He watched Antoaneta and Vasile in animated conversation. The boy looked slightly frightened. Every now and then he would drop his eyes, as though Antoaneta seemed to be threatening him. He took all the proffered notes, and then the two of them approached Hogan.

'We are in luck, Mr Hogan. When Marica was too ill to take payments to Bucurestnet, Vasile here would sometimes do it for her.'

'So does he know who owns the website?'

'No. But he can lead us to the house where Marica collected the money from. It's not far. Come on.'

Antoaneta moved swiftly to the park's perimeter wall, avoiding the entrance where the police light still flashed. Hogan and Vasile followed. They helped each other over the wall, and then Vasile took the lead. They were walking in the direction of the Sofitel Hotel, which Hogan and Antoaneta had passed that morning.

Then they turned down a side street. Hogan realised they were now in the heart of the Romexpo trade centre. Vasile, up ahead, was making another turning, walking more quickly, so that Hogan and Antoaneta were having almost to break into a half-run to keep up. Snow had stopped falling, but it was still thick underfoot, making the going difficult and absorbing the noise of their footsteps.

Hogan noticed Vasile had stopped and was pointing at a villa on the opposite side of the street. He said something to Antoaneta.

She translated. 'He says that is the house where he and Marica used to be going. He will not go any further. He says he has earned his lei and the rest is up to us.'

Hogan couldn't help thinking that the boy had done precious little for the money.

'Goodbye,' Vasile said to Hogan, using English for the first time.

Hogan nodded sourly at him.

The boy turned and walked back towards the park, heading for another night in the filthy tank room. The ten thousand lei would no doubt buy plenty of pots of paint solvent, thought Hogan.

He and Antoaneta moved silently towards the villa.

It was a modern, westernised building, standing behind a tall fence of iron railings. It wouldn't look out of place in London's commuter belt, thought Hogan, with its neo-Victorian pastiche architecture. None of the windows showed a light – the place appeared deserted. At the side of the gate was an entryphone system. Antoaneta was about to push one of the buttons when Hogan shook his head and pointed to the railings. It would be better to climb in, unannounced, and see what they could find out, rather than declare their presence straight away.

He gave Antoaneta a leg up and she hauled herself to the top of the fence, making a feline leap to land softly on the inside of the compound. Hogan immediately regretted having let her go first. She was probably fitter than him. He was struggling to reach the top of the fence – his hands slipping on the ice-cold railings. Antoaneta came back to help, forming her hands into a human step as Hogan levered himself up and finally reached the top. His jump down was less elegant than hers – he landed heavily, turning his ankle over in the process.

Antoaneta laughed softly and helped him up. 'Athletics and you are not going together, I think,' she whispered.

Hogan pulled a face at her.

As they moved towards the villa, powerful lights came on without warning. Hogan shadowed his eyes with his hand and pulled Antoaneta to the side of the compound. They edged round by the perimeter fence. The lights clicked off again – the two intruders were obviously managing to stay outside the area that triggered the automatic system.

He led Antoaneta around the side, to the back of the building. As they turned the corner, he spotted lights in a low wooden structure towards the bottom of the garden. It looked like a large summerhouse. Hogan let go of Antoaneta's hand and crouched down, inching forwards through the snow, bent almost double.

When he got to the window, he lifted his head slowly, inch by inch, above the level of the wooden sill. He immediately saw the almost blinding photographer's light – it was this that had pierced the darkness of the rear garden. Three figures were gathered round the camera. It was pointed towards the other side of the room, where a young girl reclined on a chaise longue. She had beautiful elfin features. One of the three who had been beside the camera moved out now, towards the girl. It was a tall, elegant woman – her long fur coat flapping open as she walked.

The woman opened the sheer white shirt which partly covered

the girl, exposing adolescent, half-formed breasts, then moved back behind the camera.

Hogan turned to usher Antoaneta forwards, but found she wasn't there.

Where the fuck had she gone? He was alarmed. He hissed her name as loudly as he dared.

No answer. Panic gripped him as he scanned the garden. Still no sign of her. Just the blackness of the night and the white snow picked out in the beam of the photographer's lights shining through the window.

He turned his head back towards the summerhouse. As he did so, he heard a thud, a crack.

As an unbearable pain kicked in, he just had time to realise the noise came from something hitting his head.

He felt himself fall, the snow coming up to meet his face.

Unconsciousness enveloped him.

The light, piercing still, penetrated even his closed eyelids. He didn't think he would be able to open them. He wasn't sure he wanted to. And his head. God, it hurt. Pain pulsing in waves. Worse than his worst-ever migraine.

He opened his eyes. The light was in the corner of the room, shining directly into his face. He tried to shield his eyes with his right hand but realised he couldn't move it. The same with his other hand. Both of them tied tightly behind his back.

'Welcome, Mr Benjamin Iain Hogan.'

It was a woman's voice. A slight foreign accent, but pretty much impeccable English. How did she know his name? And where was Antoaneta?

'What were you doing back there? Trying to get a free show? You like little girls, do you?'

Hogan tried to speak but his throat was dry. Partly fear, partly genuine thirst. His eyes were beginning slowly to get used to the powerful light. He could see now that the woman speaking was the same one who'd been directing events in the summerhouse.

'I don't want to appear over-dramatic, Mr Hogan,' she was continuing, 'but, unless you have a very good reason for being here, then perhaps you might like to visit somewhere else. One of our hospitals, for example.'

As she said this Hogan felt something smash down on his right knee. As he yelled in pain, his lower leg kicked out in reflex. Then he looked down and saw that what had hit him was the barrel of a gun. And the gun was joined to the hand of a rather vicious-looking Romanian thug.

The woman was leafing through some papers on her desk. Hogan strained his eyes to try to see what they were. He could see a wallet – his own wallet. That's how she knew his name.

The woman held up a piece of paper, and thrust it into his eyes.

'What's this?' she demanded angrily.

'It's a picture of a girl.'

The woman slapped him across the face. The blow jarred his already tender neck. He wanted to put up a hand to protect himself, but of course he couldn't.

'I know it's a picture of a girl. It's taken from our website. What I want to know is why you've got this picture and what you're doing sniffing around my house?'

Hogan didn't answer.

'And what's this?'

The woman was holding up another photograph now – the police publicity photo of the girl who was in hospital.

'It's the same girl,' said Hogan. 'She is fighting for her life in an English hospital.'

'And why should I care about that?'

Hogan felt more confident now. These people were in the wrong. He had the moral high ground.

'Because you were probably partly responsible for her ending up there.'

He saw his words hit home. The woman's face, just momentarily, crumpled.

'Francesca. One of our best girls,' she whispered. 'What's wrong with her?'

'She fell. Several hundred feet from a clifftop. Or maybe someone pushed her – that's what I'm trying to find out.'

Hogan, his head still thumping, now had a glimmer of hope. The woman, in her own weird way, seemed to care for the girl. Could he use this as a lever to try to get the information he wanted, to find out who the girl was?

The woman was the silent one now.

Hogan continued, 'She's in a coma. She may die. If we can find out who she is, then maybe, just maybe, we can help her.'

'You're an English doctor, then?' the woman asked, perplexed as to why Hogan had become involved.

'No. A journalist.' Hogan saw a shadow cross her face. 'But don't worry yourself. I don't approve of your website activities. But I'm not here to judge or expose you. I simply want information about the girl – Francesca, you called her.'

'Why should I help you, Mr Hogan?'

'Because it's my guess, Mrs . . .' Hogan paused. He didn't know her name.

'Miss. Miss Nadia Popescu.' She held out her hand, forgetting for a moment that Hogan's were still tied up. He gestured with his eyes to show her he couldn't return the handshake. Popescu pointed to her guard and motioned him to untie Hogan.

Hogan still didn't take her hand. 'It's my guess, Miss Popescu, that you wouldn't wish any harm to come to your girls. It wouldn't be good for business, would it?'

Nadia Popescu nodded.

'But, before we go on, where's Antoaneta?'

'Who?' Nadia Popescu seemed genuinely at a loss.

'The girl I was with.'

The woman looked at her thuggy sidekick and started questioning him in Romanian. He answered sullenly.

'We don't know what you are talking about, Mr Hogan,' Popescu said after a few moments of this. 'You were found alone, snooping outside my photographic studio. My guard was worried and decided to detain you. That is all. He says he saw no girl.'

Now it was Hogan's turn to be perplexed. What had happened to her? It didn't seem like Antoaneta was the sort to lose her bottle and flee, but in the absence of any other explanation he had to assume this was what had happened.

He tried to put it out of his mind for the moment. What was important was finding more out about Francesca.

He shrugged. 'Perhaps she'd had enough of my search. Anyway, are you prepared to help me or not?'

'Maybe, Mr Hogan,' Popescu replied. 'But you have to understand. I am doing this to help Francesca, not you. And it has to be on the strict understanding that you do not get the Romanian police involved.'

'Agreed,' said Hogan. He didn't like the woman's activities, but he needed her help.

'Shall we move somewhere a little more comfortable?' said Popescu. 'It looks like I won't be needing my interrogation chair after all.'

He stood, stretched, and winced as the pain from the back of his head shot down his neck. He felt beneath his hair gingerly. A nice bump was forming.

9

The ward sister was having a busy night. Three new admissions and a sickness bug that had ravaged her nursing rota. She'd had to bring in temporary staff – and the temps were rarely as good as her staffers. One of the relief nurses was particularly highly strung, so the sister deployed her to look after the girl in the coma – there, at least, was one patient who was in no position to give any trouble. Pretty little thing, that girl, thought the sister. Such a shame. Her almost Mediterranean looks were demeaned by all the tubes coming out of her. Still, there was some hope. She had squeezed one of the doctor's hands a few days earlier, and there had been some flickering of her eyelids. Signs that perhaps, given time, she might make some sort of recovery. The consultant neurosurgeon was certainly full of hope about the case.

A busy, stress-filled night, thought the ward sister. And now here I am confronted by this policewoman asking all these questions again. Questions I'm sure she's already asked during her many previous visits. Still, I guess she's only doing her job, just like us.

Had there been any further signs of recovery?

No, nothing more. But the consultant was very optimistic.

'You say she's been squeezing people's hands. What seems to trigger this?'

'There's no consistent pattern,' the sister replied. On one occasion it had been when a junior doctor had simply been using her as a dumb listening sponge to complain aloud about his long hours. He got the feeling the girl was empathising. But, whatever, she had certainly squeezed his hand.

'And what about the eye-flickering? When does that happen?'

The ward sister sighed at this. Were these questions really necessary? What were the police hoping to achieve by asking them?

But the policewoman persisted.

Finally, after an interminable five minutes, the detective put away her notebook, thanked the sister for her time, and left.

Left just at the wrong time, because moments later the alarm sounded. The ward sister looked up at her screen. It indicated the alarm was coming from the coma girl's bed. Oh no! And where was that blasted relief nurse? She should have been at the girl's bedside. As the ward sister rushed to get to the coma girl's side she saw from the corner of her eye the relief nurse coming out of the toilet. And the police constable who should have been on twenty-four hour duty was running back from the kitchen, trying not to spill his newly brewed cup of tea all over the corridor. Useless gits! There was going to be hell to pay for this.

They reached the girl's bedside together.

Too late.

The alarm was sounding because she had flatlined. The respirator seemed to have failed.

The ward sister grabbed the back-up hand ventilating circuit, and attached it to the girl's endotracheal tube. Then the defibrillator.

No luck. *Really* too late. The girl was dead, her lips blue.

Several hours later, Hogan was back at his Bucharest flat again. Mixed emotions coursed through him. Elation at finally establishing the girl's identity and at getting a contact address on the Isle of Wight for something called the Families for Teens Adoption Agency, and the name of its director, someone called Clare Templeman Adams. But as he slumped on the sofa he also realised he was dog-tired. And where exactly had Antoaneta gone? He'd been hoping she might have been here waiting for him when he got back, but there was no sign of her.

When they had finally sat in comfort to talk, one to one, Nadia Popescu had proved amazingly helpful. More so than Hogan could have ever have expected. She explained she had sent two girls to Families for Teens: Francesca and another girl, called Romana. Both for paid adoptions. She showed Hogan a letter from Templeman Adams, a passage about Francesca's new family not wanting her to keep in touch with her Romanian friends. Popescu claimed she had believed the letter's contents. Hogan had his doubts about that. She probably knew very well that the girls were not ending up as genuine adoptees. But equally, Hogan conceded, she did appear sincerely upset at Francesca's plight.

And what had happened to the second girl, Romana? Was she in danger too? Hogan didn't know. But what Popescu had given him were the two girls' birth certificates and their other genuine Romanian papers. For the trip to England she'd supplied both of them with false papers, keeping the real ones to be used for other girls. Armed with Francesca's and Romana's genuine documents and the address for the adoption agency in Ryde – one of the island's main towns – he hoped to make progress back home.

The ringing of his mobile brought Hogan back to the present. He had switched it off during the search for Popescu's base, but turned it on again back at the flat in the hope Antoaneta would call him.

But it wasn't her. It was Richard Howze, and he sounded angry. 'I need you back here straight away.'

'Oh, give it a rest, Dickey. I'm not due back till the day after tomorrow, and I probably won't get back to work till the day after that.'

'I don't care what your plans are. I need you back now.'

Howze for once seemed serious.

'What's the great rush? And why are you ringing me so late at night?'

'It's only fucking ten o'clock.'

Hogan sighed in exasperation. 'It might only be ten with you, but here it's midnight and I want to go to bed.'

'Ah. Sorry. Forgot about the time difference. Still, you're my employee on an assignment I'm paying for – so I'll ring you whenever I frigging well like.'

'I thought the Beast was paying?' Hogan was enjoying winding Howze up. It was the least he could do if his editor was serious about him coming home early.

'That's enough Clever Dickery, sunshine. I'm not in the mood. Just get your arse on a plane sharpish and get back here at once.'

'You still haven't told me why.'

'Two things. We've got two reporters off sick. More to the point, there's been another development in the cliff case.'

'What?'

'The girl in the coma.'

'What about her?'

'She's dead. And to cap it all another girl's fallen from the same stretch of cliff – this time fatal.'

Hogan tried to find out more, but he couldn't. For the simple reason that Howze had rung off. Hogan dialled his number back but just got a 'caller unavailable' message.

Bastard, thought Hogan. Howze did that on purpose just to prick my curiosity – he knew I wouldn't be able to resist.

He felt tiredness overwhelm him once more, but tried to fight it off. There was a lot to do. First a call to British Airways to see if he could switch his return flight to the next day. It was late, but with the two-hour time difference there was a chance that reservation staff in England would still be working. He also wanted to ring Alexandru – after all that had happened, he wanted to see a friendly face again, and a lift from Alexandru to the airport would at least help.

But the main reason for calling Alexandru was to try to find out what had happened to Antoaneta. Hogan had hoped to have all of the next day to search for her. Now there would be just a few hours.

Constable Pete Birkitt arrived in the hospital administration room with a pile of videotapes.

'Security's given me all these. It's a complete mess up there – the guy doesn't seem to know his arse from his elbow. Kept on complaining about all the financial cuts. Claimed there wasn't a proper system any more.'

He banged the pile of tapes down on the table.

'Careful. That could be important evidence,' said Emma Thomas. She was enjoying ordering Birkitt around. He'd been a git when she'd first arrived at the station months earlier. Now she was already Acting Detective Sergeant: two promotions in a matter of months, the latter at the expense of Dudfield, who'd been moved back to uniform by

DCI Hale after he had failed to reveal his connections to the prime suspect in the case, Lee Hughes.

The hospital had lent them a room and a video recorder to view the tapes.

They started their task. Thomas found it hard to believe that the hospital's security officer had no idea at all which tape was which. It didn't help that none of them were labelled. She hoped it wouldn't reflect badly on her with Hale. The DCI had clearly instructed her earlier in the case to make sure there was a closed-circuit camera trained on the girl's bed, and that a tape recorder was kept loaded at all hours of the day. It hadn't been easy - this was against all normal rules of hospital procedure. But Dudfield had swung some favour with the hospital's Chief Exec, and the ward sister had reluctantly agreed that her staff would monitor the screen.

After the fatal cliff fall, Hale and Thomas had agreed to increase security outside the ward, at least temporarily. A constable would be on guard outside almost twenty-four hours a day, although they didn't have the staff to cover meal and coffee breaks.

The tape viewing was tedious stuff. Frame after frame of hospital beds and nurses. Little of interest. Luckily the recording machine seemed to have time-coded the tapes. But they jumped about from day to day, as though someone had just loaded whichever tape they'd found lying around.

Thomas thought this was probably exactly the case.

It took them four hours of mind-numbing spooling and rewinding until they finally got to the section in question.

Thomas watched carefully. This camera was the one trained on intensive care, with a clear view of the cliff-fall girl's bed. Thomas thought how pathetically vulnerable the girl looked here in her last moments of life. It had taken so little to snuff it out.

She thought how similar this girl looked to Romana. The same Italian-like features, with just the merest hint of Slavic cheekbones. On the screen, a nurse passed by and approached the bed. She came from one side of the ward, looking over at the girl's bed, spent a few moments there and then moved off to the other side. At no time did she look towards or face the camera, so there was no way of easily identifying her.

'Stop the tape,' Emma ordered Birkitt. 'Just move it forward frame by frame from here. Nice and slowly.'

Birkitt obeyed without question.

Thomas was trying to see the life-support monitoring screen by the girl's bedside. As the nurse moved away, she could see that the girl was still breathing, still alive. She looked at the time code. This was about the time that she had been deep in conversation with the ward sister.

'Look,' she said to Birkitt. 'She's alive at this point.'

Birkitt kept on pressing the frame-advance button.

They could see the girl continuing to breathe as the tape was slowly inched forward.

Then the image disappeared. Just snow-like interference on the screen.

'What the fuck's that?' demanded Thomas.

Birkitt shrugged. 'Dunno, guv. Looks like a shite bit of tape. Doesn't really surprise me, given the mess in that security office. It was a shambles.'

'Fast forward, quickly.'

If Birkitt, an old hand in the force, resented being ordered about by a newly promoted graduate trainee, he didn't show it. He diligently shuttled the tape forward, until the picture came back again. Not gradually but all at once, noted Thomas.

'There! Freeze it there,' said Thomas.

She looked at the screen. The monitor showed a flat line.

'Move it forward. Just frame by frame again.'

The line was still flat. No sign of life. The girl must have been dead by now, thought Thomas. And the key bit of evidence was missing. Somehow she was going to have to explain this away to Hale. Not only that but the fact that, when she'd passed the ward that day, she'd given the OK for the constable on guard to go off and make himself a cup of tea.

She hoped she'd got herself entrenched enough in Hale's good books to ride this one out.

*   *   *

114

Hogan was shattered by the time his plane touched down at Gatwick. And yet Howze had insisted he get back to the island that night and report to the office. It was almost, for all his protestations, as though Dickey Howze felt Hogan had done something wrong.

Hogan flung his bags on the Gatwick Express for the train trip back to London. From there another train to Portsmouth, and then the ferry to the island. There was no way he was going to be going into work, whatever Howze said.

His mobile phone weighed heavily and temptingly against his leg. Hogan got it out and called Howze.

'Dickey?' he asked pleadingly. 'Isn't there any way I can just come in bright and early tomorrow? I'm absolutely shagged out.'

'Benjamin, my good fellow.' That was a promising start. Howze sounded as though he'd sunk a few down at the pub. 'Life getting too much for you, is it?'

'No. I've just travelled halfway round Europe to get you a cracking good story. And I think I deserve some rest now.'

'Benjamin, how could I resist such a heartfelt plea? We've all left the office anyway. It's Aziz's birthday. We're having a bit of a shindig down here in the Coach and Horses. Why don't you come and join us once you're back on the island?'

'Thanks but no thanks, Dickey. When I get back I'm crashing out.'

'If you insist, Benjamin. Nine o'clock sharp tomorrow morning, mind. Don't be late.'

Hogan felt relieved that he didn't have to rush back to the office straight away, despite what – in Bucharest – had seemed like an urgent need for him to return. Typical of Howze. Urgent enough that Hogan had to cut short his trip – but not so urgent as to prevent Dickey Howze enjoying himself down the pub. Tosser!

Clara could tell Maria was scared. And had a secret. But she hadn't been willing to tell – at least so far.

'What's wrong, sweetheart?' Clara tenderly smoothed a strand of Maria's hair away from her face. They'd gone to bed early, at Maria's request, ostensibly to read their books. But Clara could tell Maria wanted to talk.

'S . . . s . . . so much has happened,' Maria stammered. 'I sometimes feel we're no longer in control.'

Clara started stroking her sister's forehead. 'Don't worry. Emma's on our side. She'll make sure we're all right.'

'But *is* she? Is she *really* on our side? I'm not so sure. I get the impression she's in it just for herself.'

Clara took her hand away from Maria and sat up in bed on her elbows, staring at her sister intently.

'You're wrong, you know. Who protected us over the first cliff fall?'

'Emma,' admitted Maria reluctant.

'That's right. So perhaps we owe her something, too.'

'B . . . b. . . but what about Romana?'

'What about her?' Clara was surprised by the cold tone of her own voice. But it was true. Romana had been useful, fun, while she'd been here. Just like her predecessor. But that was it. Clara felt no emotional attachment to her.

'She's d . . . d . . . dead.' Maria could hardly bring herself to say the word.

'Perhaps that's a blessing,' said Clara flatly.

'No . . . no . . . no!' Maria had begun shouting, tears welling up in her eyes. She drummed her fist against Clara's chest.

Clara caught Maria's arm in her own hand. 'Calm down. You know what I mean. A dead girl cannot tell her secrets.'

'But now there are *two* dead girls.'

'What?' Clara was confused. What was Maria talking about?

'Two. Francesca died today. In hospital. During my shift.'

'Oh my God!' Clara exclaimed. 'Now I know why you're so upset. My poor baby.'

She bent forward, trying to kiss her sister.

But Maria brushed her off. 'You *don't* know.'

'What?'

'Why I'm so upset. You don't know – and you can never know.'

'Maria,' Clara said sternly, 'if there's something you're not telling me, maybe we should get it out into the open. Now.'

'No. I'm sorry. You can never know.'

'Maria,' pleaded Clara. She tried to make her voice sound soothing, less harsh. Persuading rather than controlling. 'Darling, we've never had any secrets before.'

'How do I know you've never kept any secrets from me?' asked Maria.

'What are you trying to say?'

'How about Romana? She disappeared when all three of us were out of the house. Maybe you did it.'

'What?'

'Killed her. Maybe you killed her.'

'Maria, don't. You know I went to Freshwater. What about you? It seemed to take you a long time to get to Cowes and back?'

'So?' asked Maria, petulantly.

'So you would have had time to kill her too.'

Clara could see the rage in Maria's face. The fine balance of hatred and love between the two sisters seemed to have tipped – perhaps permanently.

117

10

'Thanks for putting in an appearance, Benjamin,' said Howze as he began the morning editorial meeting. 'What did Bucharest throw up?'

Hogan had already briefed Howze privately, but for the benefit of the others – Ed Sutcliffe and the Beast – he went through it again. When he had finished, Howze folded his arms, met Hogan's gaze and began to speak.

'You realise we'll have to tell the police now, don't you?'

Hogan had been expecting his boss to say something like this. 'I still think we should wait, just a little while longer. Just until I've had chance to check out this address for the adoption agency in Ryde.'

Ed Sutcliffe leaned forward, about to interrupt. Hogan feared the worst. Whatever the news editor said, Howze was liable to go along with it.

'I think he's right,' said Sutcliffe. Hogan sighed with relief. 'The police only help us when they want to. I don't think we have to go running to them when we've got only half the story.'

Howze looked worried. He glanced at the Beast, but the Beast just shrugged as though to say it was nothing to do with him. Hogan got the impression Howze didn't want to sanction any law-breaking on his own.

'I've a proposition for you, Benjamin,' he said at last. 'We might not have had this conversation . . .'

Hogan swore under his breath. Why couldn't the man just make a decision and stand by it?

'. . . What I propose is that you carry on. For a week at most. You haven't told me, or anyone else here, what you know. Perhaps you didn't find out anything in Bucharest. Do you get my drift?'

Hogan nodded. He got the drift all right.

Howze was engaging in a classic bit of fence-sitting. Not wanting to spoil the story, but not wanting to break the law either. Hogan was on his own on this one.

Hogan pulled the Peugeot over to the side of the road. He was in Colwell Street, Ryde, a mish-mash of burger bars, pubs and amusement arcades. But he couldn't for the life of him see number 36b, the address on the letter given to him by Nadia Popescu. The even numbers seemed to jump from 34, a kebab take-away, to 38, a betting shop. Just as he was about to give up, he saw a scrappy sign on the kebab-shop wall pointing the way to number 36. It seemed to be up a small alleyway between two terraces of buildings.

He found a meter and parked the car.

The entrance to 36 had a battered brown wooden door with an entryphone at the side. There was a button for 36b, but no mention anywhere of the Families for Teens agency.

Puzzled, Hogan rang the bell. No reply. He kept on ringing but couldn't get any answer.

Then he hammered on the door.

Still no one opened it.

Finally he turned and walked back towards the main part of Colwell Street. He'd have to ask someone if they knew who was based at 36b and how he could get into the building.

With the migraine that had started in on him this morning, he didn't fancy the bookies – too much smoke, and the deafening racket of race commentary. So he tried the Orpheus take-away.

The owner was busy cutting slices of doner kebab from a huge cone of minced lamb that was slowly revolving in front of an upright grill. The grease dripped down into a tray. It looked disgusting, but the smell of the cooked meat made Hogan's mouth water. It was only mid-morning, but he realised he was famished – the two-hour time difference from Bucharest was catching up with him.

He tried to attract the take-away owner's attention.

'Excuse me.'

The owner didn't take any notice. Hogan tried again.

'Excuse me, I was wondering if you could help me.'

The man turned angrily towards him. 'What do you want?'

'I'm looking for the people who run the agency at 36b, round the corner.'

'And why do you think I can help?'

'Well, you're next door. I thought you might know who they are.'

The man sighed. 'Try the bookies. You can't miss him. Never seems to do any work, the idle sod. He's a fat so-and-so, and always seems to be wearing the same filthy red jacket. Me, I mind my own business. Can't stand the guy.'

Hogan waved his hand furiously as he entered the bookies. The smoke made his eyes sting. He tried to waft the fug away, but as fast as he did so the smoke clouds rolled back at him. His head was pounding from his migraine, and the frantic horse-race commentary blaring through the loudspeakers didn't help.

Bookmakers' shops always made him feel queasy. And this one was no exception.

Hogan spotted the man in the dirty red top right away. He was sitting to the side of the room, pencil in hand, studying a crumpled copy of *Sporting Life*, talking to himself as he urged his horse home.

The commentary was reaching its climax and the man was caught up in the excitement.

'It's Spud Monkey by less than a length from Golden Flame on the near side as they approach the second last. Spud Monkey hit that one heavily and Golden Flame takes it up on the near side, with Tiger Feet making good progress . . .'

The man in red was suddenly shouting along with the commentary. Hogan didn't think it was the time to interrupt him.

'Come on, my beauty! Come on!' Red Jacket was thumping his paper against the table as though actually whipping the horse along.

'And now Tiger Feet takes up the running, coming up to the last, with Spud Monkey falling back and Tiger Feet's hit that one, and he's down . . .'

'Fucking stitch-up!' the man exclaimed. 'The bloody nag had it in the bag!'

He stood, ripped up his betting slip, and stormed outside. Hogan followed him and caught him as he rounded the corner to the alley that led to number 36.

Hogan tapped the man's shoulder. 'Excuse me, mate. Do you work for Families for Teens?'

The man stopped and glowered at him. 'You what?'

'Families for Teens? 36b Colwell Street – isn't that where you work?'

'What's it to you?'

'Hogan. *Wight Evening Star.*' Hogan held out his hand but the man ignored it.

'Why should I talk to you? Fucking reporters! What's it to you where I work?'

'OK, OK. No need to get shirty. I just want a bit of info, that's all.'

'What's in it for me?'

'I'll make it worth your while.' As he said the words Hogan wondered to himself how he would actually act on them. He was strapped for cash, and Howze would be angry enough about his claim for expenses for the Bucharest trip; he'd be unlikely to stump up any more.

Red Jacket thought for a moment. Then got a bunch of keys out of his pocket. 'Follow me. We'll go to the office.'

He opened the brown door and Hogan followed him into a dusty hallway. It was all pretty shabby – no carpets or flooring, just bare floorboards, many of them cracked and loose. On the floor were piles and piles of letters.

'Mind your frigging feet,' the man shouted as Hogan tried and failed to step around the heaps of unopened mail. 'There's valuable stuff in some of them packages.'

Hogan followed him up the creaking stairs to the first floor, where he unlocked another door. Inside the office were more piles of letters, sorted into a rudimentary filing system.

'Sorry. Bit of a mess. I'm halfway through sorting the latest delivery.'

Hogan was amazed. 'Is all this for Families for Teens? It must be a bigger operation than I thought.'

The man snorted. 'What's all this 'Families for Teens' lark? I don't what you're on about.'

Hogan pulled out the letter to Nadia Popescu with the address on

121

it. 'That's this address, isn't it?'

'Yup.'

'So this must be Families for Teens.'

'Nope.'

Hogan was utterly confused now. The man was sitting back in the chair at his desk, arms folded, smirking at him.

'I suppose I'd better put you out of your misery. We're an accommodation address – nothing more, nothing less. There's hundreds of people use us.'

He was scrolling through a computer list. Hogan looked over his shoulder and could see the list had reached the Fs. Red Jacket tried to shield the screen from Hogan by putting his body in the way.

'Like I said, nothing for Families for Teens.'

'What about Templeman Adams?' asked Hogan.

He saw the man scroll on through to the Ts.

'Nope, nothing,' he said finally.

'It could be under A,' said Hogan. He was beginning to feel desperate.

The man scrolled up through the list towards the beginning.

'Nope. I think you're wasting your time, mate.'

The journalist dropped heavily into a chair opposite Red Jacket, surrounded by piles of mailbags. This was it. All the good work in Bucharest coming to nothing in some cesspit of an office in Ryde.

But Red Jacket was looking thoughtful.

'Hang on a minute, though. That name does sound familiar. Quite posh, isn't it?'

Hogan watched him leafing through letters on his desk.

At last Red Jacket picked up a sheet of paper and examined it closely. 'Got it! Told you it sounded familiar. Look!'

Hogan got to his feet. The man thrust the bit of paper towards him, and now the reporter was closer he could tell it was a cheque.

'The posh bird. Ugly old crow. Looked a right old lezzie if you ask me. Anyhow, she normally paid her account in cash. But last week she said she wanted to close it there and then. All of a sudden, like. Well, I don't normally accept cheques. I don't like the rubber ones.'

The man paused, laughing at his own feeble joke. Hogan smiled just to humour him.

'But she said she didn't have any cash. Seemed to have a kosher bankcard, so I took pity on her. That's why her name didn't show up on the computer. The account's closed.'

Hogan checked the amount. Hardly a fortune. Just thirty pounds. He got out his wallet and counted out fifty.

'What you doing?' the man asked.

'Here's fifty quid,' said Hogan. 'Twenty for you, and thirty in lieu of the cheque. But I get to keep it.'

The man nodded his agreement. Hogan had a fair idea that the money would probably go straight onto some nag in the next race at Kempton Park.

He shook hands with Red Jacket and made his way back down to street level.

In the open air he held the cheque up and examined it closely. The signature was just a scrawl – he couldn't make it out. But the name was printed clearly underneath, and he recognised it instantly.

Clara Forbes.

Clara was watching from the bedroom window when the reporter came up the front path. She ducked out of the way, and was fairly confident he hadn't seen her. But before she did she'd been able to see his face clearly. It was Iain Hogan from the *Wight Evening Star*, the new newspaper. Each of the main stories on the paper's pages was now accompanied by a picture by-line. Clara thought this a bit tacky and tabloid – it was something the island's weekly paper would never do – but now it had turned out useful in identifying him. And, now that she came to think about it, she recognised the face from somewhere else as well. She dug through her memory for a few moments and then – *That's it!* He'd been at the ramblers' meeting when Maria had embarrassed them all by fainting in public.

The front doorbell rang. Clara ignored it. She looked down at her hands. They were shaking. She clasped them together to keep them under control.

Then she remembered Maria, asleep in the other room. She was in such a state these days, ever since the incident at the hospital, that she got very little sleep at night. She'd taken to napping in the afternoon, helped by a sleeping pill. Clara was getting more and more concerned about her sister. She wasn't sure she could be trusted any more to keep her mouth shut. Emma would have to be warned.

The bell rang again. More insistently this time. Even once it had stopped the echo bounced around inside Clara's head. It was a sign things were closing in, imploding.

Clara ran to the other bedroom to make sure Maria was still sleeping. She opened the door quietly, so as not to wake her sister.

But then the reporter rang the bell once more.

Maria, dishevelled, sat up.

'What . . . what is it?'

Clara leapt forward, and forced her hand onto her sister's mouth to shut her up.

Maria struggled. Clara could tell she was petrified, disoriented. But she couldn't afford for Maria to make any noise. If they had to talk to the reporter, it ought to be once they had checked their story through with Emma. Emma was experienced at dealing with the press. She would know what to do.

Then the phone rang. The sisters left the answering machine on constantly now, to screen calls. From here in the bedroom the sound was muffled, but Clara could make out her own recorded message being played.

And, despite Maria's whimpering, the caller's words were clearly audible. 'Hi. It's Iain Hogan here from the *Wight Evening Star*. We spoke a few weeks ago about the closure of the cliff path. Something's cropped up and I want to talk to you again. I'd like to do it face-to-face, please. Can you ring me back at the *Star* to arrange a time? If I don't hear from you, I'll pop round again tomorrow. Look forward to your call.'

Clara wanted to peek out of the window. Hogan must be using his mobile. He's still outside, she thought. What does he know? How *much* does he know?

She had to tell Emma about this, and quickly.

Maria was still struggling in her grip. Clara waited until she heard the garden gate slam shut as the reporter finally went away. Then she released her sister.

'W. . . w . . . who was that on the phone?' Maria stammered.

'You heard!' snapped Clara.

'Not clearly, no. Sounded like a man's voice. You had your arm round my head. How could you expect me to hear it properly?' Maria sounded hurt.

'It was nothing important,' Clara lied. 'Just the newsagents about the papers. I was thinking perhaps we should start taking the evening paper, now it's more established.'

'And w . . . w . . . why were you h . . . h . . . holding my mouth?' Maria asked.

'I was just trying to calm you down.' Clara knew she couldn't tell Maria the truth. Her sister was already in too much of a state. Discovering that the reporter had started sniffing around could send her over the edge.

Even though the doorbell had penetrated Maria's sleep, it was obvious that the pill had not fully worn off. She was struggling to keep her eyes open. Clara gently laid her sister's head back on the pillow and stroked her forehead.

'You just rest and get some more sleep. You had a disturbed night. It's all got a bit too much for you, you poor thing.'

'S'pose so . . .' mumbled Maria.

Clara waited until her sister had drifted off again, then got up and went downstairs to the phone. She replayed Hogan's message, just to make sure she had heard it correctly, then dialled Emma Thomas's number.

Since he'd returned from Romania, Hogan felt that Emma seemed distant, distracted. But he wondered if his attitude to her, too, had changed. His friendship with Antoaneta had been refreshing: it was rare for Hogan to actually maintain a relationship with a woman which didn't revolve around sex. Was that all his liaison with Emma was – an opportunity for both parties to sate their lust? He felt he had to find out. He owed it to himself; maybe he owed it to Lynn too –

despite what had happened. Before he'd gone to Romania, he and Emma had had their rows. He had questioned her over the arrest of Hughes, raised doubts about the arrest of an autistic man. Now he needed to ask questions of their relationship itself.

Driving from Bonchurch through Ventnor back towards Reeth, Hogan suddenly saw a poster at the side of the road outside the Winter Gardens that caused him to brake sharply. He looked at it twice to make sure his eyes weren't playing tricks. But it was there in black-and-white. The Rick Griffin lettering caught his eye first, and there were just three letters: 'MAN' – a.k.a. the Manband. One of his favourite groups from school, re-formed and playing on the island that very night at the Winter Gardens venue.

Man? How could they still be going after all these years? They'd never been very famous to start with – and when punk had arrived in the mid- to late 'seventies Man had been brushed aside. As far as Hogan had known, the band had split up for good back in the 'eighties sometime.

He got out of the Peugeot and studied the poster more closely. Nostalgia engulfed him as he read the names of the group – three of the 'seventies stalwarts still playing together, including the twin guitar spearhead of Micky Jones and – Hogan's old favourite – Deke Leonard.

He checked at the box office. They didn't have any advance tickets; it was just pay on the door. And, no, Hogan shouldn't have any problem getting in, the box office assistant informed him. The last time the band had played here, about a year earlier, only sixty or so hardy souls had turned up.

He got on the mobile and rang Emma. 'Hi there. It's me.'

'Hi, Hogan. Bit busy at the moment. Can I ring you back?' He was surprised at how cold and off-hand she sounded.

'It won't take a mo . . .'

Hogan heard her sigh, then a muffled sound on the line, as though she'd put her hand over the end of the receiver to stop him hearing something.

'OK, go on . . .' she said finally.

'I just wondered if you fancied going out tonight?'

'Iain, I'm not sure we should be seeing . . .' Then she paused, as

126

though having second thoughts. Finally she continued: 'OK, where?'

'There's a band on at Ventnor Winter Gardens. I thought we could go and see them. Then maybe you could come back to my place. For the night.'

'Not sure about staying the night. It's busy at the moment, and I need to get in early. And have we got the same taste in music?' She sounded distinctly unenthusiastic.

'Oh, go on. Give it a go – come to the gig at least. I promise you they're good.'

Hogan heard her sigh again.

'OK. But we need to talk. Where shall we meet?'

'I could pick you up . . .'

'No. I'll come in my car and meet you there.'

Hogan arranged for her to arrive a little before the start of the concert, so they could have a drink and the 'talk' she seemed to want. Hogan thought it sounded ominous. She sounded to be in a difficult mood.

The scene inside the Winter Gardens was slightly surreal. There was a strong smell of dope. Man had always been a psychedelic, drug-influenced band – a side of them Hogan had never been particularly into. He liked the music, period. Or, at least, he'd liked it when he'd last heard it, about twenty years ago. The vinyl records were festering in the cellar back in Twickenham – he hadn't even got a turntable any more. He reminded himself, not for the first time, that he really ought to buy one. It would be good to give his old Man records a spin.

Going to the Winter Gardens was a bit like going back in time. Everyone in the bar looked like a refugee from the 'seventies, as though they'd all swallowed an ageing pill and got about twenty-five years older overnight. A Buffalo Bill-type figure with a ponytail, sitting at the bar, chatting with a few other men, looked vaguely familiar. After a while Hogan suddenly realised who it was. Deke Leonard. Deke, the leather-clad, hard-edged rocker with the black-and-white Gibson SG, transformed into a slightly trendy-looking grandad, complete with white hair drawn tightly back into a ponytail.

Hogan looked at his watch. Emma was late. He wondered if she'd turn up at all. She hadn't sounded exactly thrilled about the evening. But then he saw Deke and his companions turn away from the bar, their eyes drawn to something or someone. Hogan shifted his own gaze to see what they were looking at and saw it was Emma, standing in front of him, smiling cheekily, looking something like her old self.

'You didn't tell me you were luring me into a drugs den,' she laughed.

'Yeah, it stinks of dope, doesn't it?' Hogan looked around. He could see people smoking joints openly. 'They were one of the biggest druggie bands in England – well, Wales actually.'

'Were?'

'Nearly thirty years ago.'

'Shit, you haven't brought me all this way to see some 'seventies has-beens, have you?'

'Not has-beens,' said Hogan. 'I can't believe they'd still be going if they couldn't still play.' He grinned.

He saw Emma looked around the sparsely attended bar. 'It's not exactly heaving, is it?' she said thoughtfully.

'It'll fill up.' He was aware he sounded more hopeful than he actually was.

'So are you going to offer me something to drink? Or maybe something to smoke?'

Hogan laughed. 'Not my scene, I'm afraid. I'll get the drinks in, though.'

About an hour later the lights went down and Hogan and Emma moved to the front for Man's set. They had passed the time pleasantly, if a little warily, avoiding the cliff case as a topic of conversation. Emma had made it clear she didn't want to talk shop. She hadn't broached any difficult subjects, though. The thing she'd said during the phone call that she wanted to talk about hadn't seemed to crop up. Hogan still had no idea what it was.

The stage had gone completely dark. He couldn't see if there was anyone on it or not.

And then the lights blazed on. His one-time heroes were there, bathed in spotlights, the twin electric guitars of Jones and Leonard ripping through the riff of a Leonard classic: '7171 551.' Hogan had read once that the title came from the phone number of Mike Nesmith of the Monkees. It sounded just like it had more than a quarter of a century ago at Man's gig at London's Chalk Farm Roundhouse – a three-night sell-out Hogan had attended as a schoolboy. The sound was crisp; the riff bit through the air. And then Deke was at the microphone growling out the verse.

Hogan was in heaven, but as he tried to put his arms round Emma she twisted away, giving him an annoyed stare. She mouthed something at him that he couldn't hear. He indicated as much.

Frowning, she shouted in his ear. 'This is too loud. And boring. I'm going back to the bar.'

He wondered about following her, but selfishness got the better of him. The slide-guitar riff heralded the next song, 'Day and Night', his favourite Man number and another Deke Leonard composition.

Leonard started to roar out the opening lines. At the full-to-overflowing Roundhouse all those years ago the words – talking about singing to an empty room – would have sounded strange and inappropriate. But Hogan couldn't clearly remember whether they'd even played it then. Here, in the twenty-first century, playing to just a hundred or so people – a mixture of die-hard fans, returnees like Hogan, and the just plain curious – the song took on new meaning.

A couple of songs later and Emma was back at his side. But not for long. She was shouting in his ear again. 'Thanks for inviting me, Iain, but it's really not my thing. I've got to get to work early tomorrow. I'm heading off back to Yarwater.'

He tried to persuade her to stay, but she was adamant. He bent forward to kiss her goodbye, but Emma moved her head aside at the last moment. What should have been a lovers' kiss became a chaste peck on the cheek.

As Emma went out towards the back of the hall, Hogan turned to watch her go. She's slipping away from me, he thought. Did he care? Yes – but he wasn't sure he cared *enough*. The heavy bass riff of 'Many Are Called but Few Get Up' fought for his attention, and won.

129

He had never been too impressed by the lyrics of this song. Its music, though: that was something else. He surged to the front and reached out to touch Deke Leonard's boots. For a few minutes Hogan felt like a teenager again.

Then the song was over. He stood back and realised he wasn't fifteen any more. He was a rather sad forty-something. Perhaps he ought to start acting like his age.

Another pint of Wight Spirit, that's what he needed.

He put his hand in his leather jacket pocket to pull out his wallet. A piece of paper fell out and fluttered to the floor. As he picked it up he saw it was a letter, handwritten on one of the paper napkins from the bar.

Dear Iain

By the time you read this I shall have long got back to Yarwater, and you will be back at the Chalet in Reeth.

Maybe I shouldn't have come tonight. I've been meaning to try to have a chat with you for some time, but I've been very busy.

You're a lovely man, very sweet, but tonight was an example of why we're not suited. Being here, being leched at by all these middle-aged men listening to their too-loud rock music, made me realise that perhaps age differences can't be bridged as easily as I'd thought.

Anyway, I'm sure you'll find someone else. We met when you were still getting over the split with your wife. Maybe it wasn't the most sensible time to start a new relationship.

Obviously we will still be talking from time to time about the cliff case. I'd ask you to try to keep these chats as professional as possible.

Best wishes
Emma (Thomas)
xxx

Hogan studied the three kisses at the end. Why did people do that? At the end of a letter like this they were meaningless, just rubbed salt in the wound. He wouldn't be kissing her again. And why put her surname in brackets? That was truly bizarre. How many other Emmas was he having a relationship with?

Even as he was thinking all this he realised he shouldn't be. He should simply be mourning a lost love. But he didn't feel particularly sad or upset. Just . . . empty.

The cheers of the crowd made him look up. Man had finished their set and were leaving the stage.

Then Hogan recognised a face at the front, by the stage. The man joining in the cheering was Kavanagh.

Hogan was tempted to confront him again – to demand recompense for the four slashed tyres – but thought better of it. What proof did he have? None. He'd just make a fool of himself.

What worried him more was that he had something – anything – in common with the revolting little man. They were both fans of the same rock group. It wasn't surprising, in a way – they were both about the same age – but still he didn't like it. With that creep in the hall, he wasn't hanging round for the band's encore.

Hogan felt utterly depressed as he walked back towards the Peugeot. It wasn't just Emma's letter. It wasn't just seeing Kavanagh again. Perhaps it was seeing his former boyhood heroes looking so old. To be honest, it was amazing they were still playing together – and playing so well – but it brought home to him how time had passed. How he had to start living for the *now*.

As he reached the car he bent down to examine the tyres. Surely even Kavanagh didn't hate him enough to play the same trick again. He checked all four. They were fine. Maybe Kavanagh hadn't even seen him – although he doubted that.

He'd parked some way away from the Winter Gardens, but decided to take the detour past them again as he drove back to Reeth. The route would take him along Ventnor's pretty Victorian seafront.

As the hill started he tried to drop down into a low gear, but the clutch seemed to be playing up again and he couldn't force the gear-change.

Never mind. He could freewheel down using the brakes to slow the car.

As he entered the first Z-bend, Hogan pressed the brake pedal. His foot just hit the floor.

Nothing.

Shit! The brakes've gone!

He heard the screech of rubber as he forced the car round the bend, gathering speed all the time.

The next bend was hurtling towards him. He thought for a moment about ploughing straight on into the Winter Gardens complex, deliberately crashing into the building to stop himself, but he couldn't do that. People were already coming out of the concert hall. The speeding car could cause carnage.

He yanked the steering wheel to the right with all his strength, just missing a pedestrian.

Now the car was flying down the hill towards the Esplanade. Hogan had no choice but to stay on the road and fight for control. A steep drop on one side, a high bank on the other. He gripped the wheel ever more tightly. He could see now where the road flattened out near the beach. There was hope. His speed would drop.

But then someone was stepping onto the crossing, expecting him to stop. He couldn't.

He swerved to the left to try to avoid them, and lost control.

The car crashed through the barrier between the road and the beach.

He raised his arms to cover his face as the windscreen shattered, and felt himself being thrown upwards, his head smashing against the roof, as the car jarred, nose-first, into the sand.

Then silence.

Just the roar of the sea as the waves crashed against the shore.

Sergeant Warren Dudfield had agreed to take the call from Central Control just for something to do. For a Friday night on the island, it was unusually quiet. At pub chucking-out time most Fridays you could rely on there being a ruckus outside some drinking hole or another, but not tonight.

Some pisshead had careered off the road at Ventnor seafront and ended up on the beach, narrowly missing a pedestrian. The ambulance was on its way.

Dudfield and his number two, Pete Birkitt, had been sitting in the squad car in Shanklin town centre when the call came through. Somebody was playing games with him, Dudfield was sure of that. He'd been moved back to uniform by Hale simply because he hadn't declared he knew Lee Hughes's family personally. And now he was being given shitty little jobs like the town-centre drunk watch. At least this trip to Ventnor would lift the tedium.

He changed down a gear as they descended the steep hill into the town. Dudfield glanced across at Birkitt. He liked Pete Birkitt – a local lad like himself – but at the moment Pete was getting on his nerves. The PC was full of himself because he'd been helping out that jumped-up Thomas woman on the cliffs case. And now someone had put Birkitt and Dudfield together on the same watch. Some fuckwit at HQ was just trying to rub Dudfield's nose in it. Probably Hale's little plan to get back at him.

As they drove down the hill past the Winter Gardens, Dudfield could see a small crowd gathered on the shore, surrounding a small red car. The blue flashing light of an ambulance gave the scene added drama.

They parked and got out of the squad car.

Dudfield shouted at the crowd to let him and Birkitt through. 'OK, mind out the way, please. You're not watching a fucking football match.'

Birkitt looked over at him disapprovingly. A directive had recently gone out from HQ instructing officers to mind their language when dealing with the public, so as to give a more professional appearance. Dudfield took great delight in ignoring it at every possible opportunity.

Dudfield stood at the smashed barrier and looked down the ten-foot drop to the beach, where the car was quarter-buried in the sand. The driver's door was open – but there was no sign of the driver.

'Right, where's the prat who did this, then?' asked Dudfield of no one in particular.

Someone pointed to the ambulance. A man was being treated there for what looked like fairly minor head wounds.

'Pete – you take a look at the car. I'll get this git to blow into our little black box.'

Dudfield opened the boot of the squad car and pulled out the breathalyser kit. He marched over to the man.

'Had one too many have we, sir?' he asked. 'Not very thoughtful, that, is it? In fact, a bit fuckwitted, I'd say. Sir.'

He looked properly at the man for the first time, and realised he knew him. It was the reporter, the one working on the cliff murders. Last time they'd met, Dudfield had nearly arrested him for impersonating a police officer.

'Oh, it's you,' Dudfield said. 'Didn't recognise you at first. What the fuck have you been up to?'

Hogan was holding his head and grimacing. 'Dunno,' he said, looking puzzled. 'The brakes just seemed to go. They haven't been giving me any trouble, but when I put my foot on the brake pedal there was nothing there. Nothing.'

'Didn't you see the signs to drop down into a low gear? That should have slowed you.'

'Clutch is a bit dodgy,' said Hogan, apologetically.

'Yeah. Likely story. Well, look' – Dudfield dropped his voice to a whisper – 'I'm going to have to get you to blow into our little box, 'cos all these people are watching and it's what the fuckers expect. Scuse my French.' He shot his eyes towards the onlookers, who were still gathered round. 'But don't worry about it, I'm sure it will turn out negative.'

He winked at Hogan and gestured at the tube into which Hogan should blow. He was careful to keep his hands over the lights and reading meters.

Hogan blew.

Dudfield could smell the alcohol on his breath.

He raised his voice to make sure the crowd could hear. 'That's a negative, sir. Just under the limit. You've passed – but only just. Be more careful next time. Never a good idea to drink and drive.'

He raised his hand slightly from the box, just enough for Hogan to see that the red light was lit. Hogan raised his eyebrows and mouthed a thanks.

Dudfield whispered to him, 'I'm doing you a little favour here, mate. Just remember it. I may need it returned one day.'

He winked again, then put the breathalyser apparatus back in the

134

squad car.

There was a shout from the beach. 'Sarge! Sarge! Come and have a look at this, quick!'

Birkitt had found something. Dudfield leapt down from the Esplanade onto the shore and went round to the front of the car, where Birkitt was busy beneath the bonnet.

'Look at this, Sarge.'

He was holding up two bits of rubber hose. Dudfield didn't understand the significance – motor engineering was not his strong point.

'Yeah – so what?'

'The brake pipes.'

'What about them?'

'Cut! They've been cut. This was no accident, Sarge. This was deliberate.'

Dudfield straightened, his brow furrowing. He turned, and realised the reporter was now standing next to them. As Dudfield looked into his face, he realised Hogan must have heard the whole exchange.

The reporter had gone a deathly shade of pale.

His eyes were those of a frightened man.

11

Hogan phoned in sick the next day. He did feel physically unwell after the crash, but the main reason for staying away from work was that he had so much to do if he wanted to get his life back on an even keel. Insurers had to be contacted, and Dudfield was coming round to take a statement. He also wanted to phone Emma; last night's date, and their relationship, had ended in such an unsatisfactory manner.

The insurance company was fairly unhelpful. Hogan had been hoping to get a hire car on the insurance, but they made it clear that wasn't going to happen. It was now a question of whether the Peugeot was a write-off. The insurers would pay for it to be recovered to a garage, but if it turned out that the repairs would be more expensive than the value of the car he would simply be given a cheque. Which probably wouldn't be large enough to buy him another car.

He picked up the mobile and tried calling Emma at Yarwater CID. Someone else answered.

'I'm sorry. She's not due in today,' said the detective.

'Strange,' said Hogan. 'She specifically told me she would be in early.'

'Hang on . . . I'll just check with the boss.'

Hogan heard the muffled sound of people talking in the background, and then the detective was back on the phone.

'No, it's definitely her day off. Can I take a message?'

'Yes. Can you tell her Iain Hogan rang? She's got my number.'

'OK, sir. Will do. Bye.'

Hogan sat down with a cup of tea and gazed out of the chalet window. The leaves had dropped now winter had arrived, and for the first time he could see distant glimpses of the English Channel through the trees. It was a peaceful scene – in complete contrast to his mind, which was in turmoil.

Who had cut the brake pipes? The obvious suspect was Kavanagh.

He held me responsible for the court case going in the papers, thought Hogan. He almost certainly was the one who slashed the tyres the other week at Steephill. But cutting his brake pipes? That was something much more serious – tantamount to attempted murder. Hogan had his doubts that Kavanagh hated him enough to want him dead. Unless he was involved in something more serious than simply looking at porn on the internet? Maybe that was it.

There was a rap on the chalet door. Through the obscured glass he saw the blurred shapes of two policemen in their blue uniforms. Dudfield had obviously come to question him.

Hogan got up to let him in. Dudfield was with the same constable who had attended the crash the previous night. Now he could see the man's face in a better light he recognised him as one of the two constables who'd first discovered the injured girl's body at the foot of the cliff back in September.

'Morning, mate,' said Dudfield, smiling. 'How's the head today? Bet it hurts.'

Hogan just grunted.

'That's what happens when you drink too much at your age. I bet the bang you got on it didn't do you much good either.'

Hogan still didn't speak. He wasn't in the mood for the sergeant's wisecracks.

Now Dudfield's colleague was speaking. Hogan suddenly remembered his name from that first day. Pete. Pete Birkitt.

'Not much of a gaff you got here, is it? I thought you reporters lived a life of glamour?'

'Yeah,' said Dudfield. 'But he works for the frigging local rag, not the bloody *Sun*, dumbo. If you pay peanuts you get monkeys – that's probably why I've got you helping me today.'

'Fuck off,' said the constable.

Hogan finally found his voice. 'Do I get a chance to say anything in all this, or are you two just going to continue your double-act all the time? If so, I'm off out. My head hurts.'

'Now, now,' said Dudfield. 'No need to be like that. We're best of mates really, aren't we, Pete?'

Birkitt didn't say anything. He just looked daggers at Dudfield, who hitched up his trousers and sat down in the best easy chair next to Hogan's cup of tea. Birkitt took the other armchair, leaving nowhere for Hogan.

Dudfield eyed Hogan's still steaming drink. 'Ah. A cup of tea. That would go down a treat, wouldn't it, Pete?'

'Yeah. Very nice. Milk and two sugars, please, mate.'

'Just the one for me,' said Dudfield. 'And then once you've made us a cup of tea we can get down to business.'

Hogan brewed up the tea with ill grace and banged the mugs down on the table in front of the two policemen.

'You do seem a bit the worse for wear this morning, if you don't mind me saying so,' said Dudfield, as if he'd only just realised it.

'Wouldn't you be?' Hogan retorted grumpily. 'I've got a huge lump on top of my head. I'm not going to have a fucking car for weeks. Someone seems to be trying to kill me. And I've just split up with my girlfriend.'

'Not much to worry about, then,' said Birkitt with a snigger.

Hogan shot him an angry glance.

'Of course, it could have been worse,' said Dudfield.

'Oh yeah? How, exactly?' asked Hogan.

'Well, we could have done you for drunk-driving.'

Dudfield and Birkitt both burst out laughing, but Hogan wasn't in the mood for their jokes.

'Look, let's just get on with this, can we?' he shouted. 'And cut the comedy routine.'

Dudfield and Birkitt finally got out their notebooks and asked Hogan about the background to the crash. They looked bored, but perked up as he told them about the previous incident when his tyres had been slashed.

'It's obviously that Kavanagh geezer,' said Birkitt.

'Ah, that's it, then,' said Dudfield sarcastically. 'Our budding Hercule Poirot's just solved it for us. We can all go home now.'

'What do you mean?' asked Hogan.

'He's just taking the mickey,' said Birkitt. 'Old Dudders here's a bit pissed off because I've been helping out on the cliff-murders case. But he's been moved back to uniform.'

Hogan could see Dudfield's face darken. He looked livid. 'Shut it, Pete,' he spat.

Hogan was intrigued by the mention of the cliffs case.

'So you know Emma Thomas?' he asked Birkitt.

'Yeah. She's a good detective.'

Dudfield snorted. 'Good detective my arse. She just brown-noses Hale all the time – that's how she's got on so quickly.'

Hogan thought he'd better intervene before the tiff between Dudfield and Birkitt got out of hand.

'I was out with her last night, actually,' he said.

Dudfield suddenly looked alert. 'Really? She was at the Winter Gardens with you? You didn't mention that before.'

'It didn't seem relevant,' said Hogan. 'She left well before the end of the show.'

'Why?' asked Dudfield.

'Didn't like it.'

'You two didn't have a row, did you?'

'No. Not particularly. Why do you ask?'

'Not *particularly*?' Dudfield emphasised the word. 'What does that mean? Did you row or didn't you?'

Hogan couldn't see why this was relevant or what Dudfield was driving at. 'We didn't have a row. I just said. But I guess we've been having an on-off kind of relationship.'

Dudfield and Birkitt looked intrigued.

'No wonder she got so many of her crackpot theories into the paper,' said Dudfield. 'That explains a lot.'

Hogan bristled. 'What are you fucking trying to say? That she's been using me?'

Dudfield smirked. 'I wouldn't put it past her.'

'Credit me with some sense,' said Hogan angrily. 'The only stuff that's gone into the *Star* has been reports that I've been one-hundred percent happy with. No way has she used me. No fucking way.'

Birkitt interrupted. 'OK, OK, sir. Calm down. We're just trying to establish whether anyone might have had a grudge against you. If you rowed with Sergeant Thomas before leaving in your car, that might be relevant.'

139

Hogan sighed wearily. 'I've told you. We didn't row. We've been seeing each other – I guess you could say we've been boyfriend and girlfriend.'

'And now you're not?' asked Dudfield.

'That's right. But she initiated the split, so I don't think you've got your motive there. She left because she was bored with the music. And she said she didn't want to see me any more . . .'

'Because she was bored with you, too.' Dudfield completed the sentence for him.

Hogan slumped. He wasn't angry with the sergeant. What he'd said was basically true.

The policemen were putting their notebooks away.

'What are you going to do now?' he asked them.

'Have a little chat to our friend Mr Kavanagh, I think,' said Dudfield. 'I expect he's got all our answers. He's not exactly unknown to us – and he's a nasty piece of work.'

'So you won't be speaking to Emma?'

'Acting DS Thomas? Nah! Wouldn't waste my time. She's not my favourite person, I'll give you that. But I can't for the life of me think why she'd want to do you any harm. You're her little stool pigeon in the local press.'

Hogan saw Dudfield narrow his eyes at him, as if he were trying to rile him into making a response. But Hogan let the insult pass without the dignity of a comment.

Dudfield continued, 'In any case, she hasn't got a motive here. Sounds like she'd already said her goodbyes to you, mate. She's too concerned with her own career to put it in jeopardy by playing silly buggers with someone's car. Especially a reporter's.'

Dudfield and Birkitt stood up to go. Hogan felt even more fed up. He'd half-hoped they might reassure him that the crash could have been an accident after all. But Dudfield at least seemed convinced that Kavanagh was out to get him.

If it was true, Hogan knew he had better watch his back.

Hogan felt less than one hundred per cent. Considerably less. But there was no use moping about at the chalet. Maybe he'd catch the bus to the eastern edge of Reeth, then go for a walk. If it cleared his head then perhaps he'd feel in a fit state to go on to Bonchurch and question Clara Forbes.

He prepared himself a picnic lunch, packed it in a small rucksack, and put on walking clothes and boots.

Immediately he opened the chalet door, a blast of cold, crisp air tightened the skin around his face. His head throbbed, and he decided to duck back inside again to get a woollen hat. There was beautiful hoarfrost covering the grass and trees in the communal gardens. The fronds of the palm trees looked as though they had been dipped in icing sugar, the reflected sun sparkling so brightly off them that Hogan had to shield his eyes.

He waited at the village bus stop for the round-island bus that linked the coastal towns and villages. Just as he was beginning to lose all feeling in his feet, despite the thick walking socks, a bus finally turned up. Hogan scanned the passengers' faces. He didn't want to come face-to-face with Kavanagh again.

He decided to check out the old railway station at Reeth East. Trains and railways had been a passion since boyhood. Not in a trainspotterish way. What he was interested in was railway history – how the railways had developed, declined and affected communities. The island was a good case in point. Its once-extensive network had shrunk to one passenger line linking the main easterly seaside towns, with second-hand rolling stock salvaged from the London Underground.

An old black-and-white photo of the station in its heyday which he'd seen in a shop had pricked his curiosity: he wanted to know what it was like now. There was some talk of trying to re-open the line.

From the top deck of the bus he gazed out across the Channel towards France. The sea shimmered in the sunlight. There was what looked to be a Channel Ferry in the distance, plying its way between France and Portsmouth. A couple of yachts were also out – their crews braving the freezing weather. Inside the bus, Hogan hunched himself down into his anorak. At least it was warm in here.

In the event, the station site was not as interesting as he had hoped. It was given over to light industry now, and there was little trace of the railway left. He took a short scout round. He could make out where the track had once been, and some of the warehousing looked as though it could once have been engine sheds.

Then he saw what looked like a path to the side. It wasn't signposted and therefore probably wasn't an official public right of way, but it looked well used. He decided to follow it and see what happened.

The path rose steeply. Part of it was stepped, with a handrail, which Hogan was glad of in the frosty, slippery conditions. At first he thought it might just be a shortcut. A path used by the people of Reeth to get from one part of the sprawling village to another. But then it turned sharply away from the scrub and undergrowth surrounding the disused station site, and headed out towards the Downs.

He was climbing steeply now, at a diagonal to the cliff face, winding up it. After a few minutes, his breath coming in rasps, he was at the top. He turned and saw the eastern edges of Reeth clinging to the Undercliff below him, and the sea beyond that. In the other direction, inland, the rolling Downs, the highest points on the island, were covered in glistening white frost.

He decided to trace the route of the tunnel above ground, and scanned the horizon for one of its airshafts. At first he couldn't spot any, just the occasional tree, permanently distorted into perverse shapes by the prevailing southwest wind that whipped the clifftops. Then at last he made out an airshaft, and started to walk towards it.

When he reached the top of the shaft, he was surprised to find it was simply fenced off. He'd been expecting some sort of solid brick or stone wall. Maybe that was why it had been so difficult to pick it out against the white of the frost-covered hills.

He looked north towards the next shaft, some five hundred yards or so away, and was startled to see another figure there. At this distance he couldn't make out whether it was a man or a woman. In fact the only reason he could see the figure at all was that the person was wearing red upper-body clothing which stood out against the white background.

He walked in the direction of the second shaft. There were no footprints in the frosty grass, so whoever it was up ahead hadn't come this way. He looked up again and saw the figure had moved away from the shaft, towards the west and Whitwell village. After a few moments, the red shape disappeared from view behind the brow of a hill.

Once he reached the airshaft, Hogan decided he'd had enough. It was an interesting walk, and it had helped to clear his head of the negative thoughts that had been filling it – and to clear his hangover as well. He felt much better. He leaned back against the wooden fence surrounding the shaft.

As he did so, it gave way. He fell onto his back – he was slipping towards the airshaft. He tried to dig his feet in to stop the slide, but couldn't. His leg kicked out at thin air. He clawed at the ground, but the slide continued. Just as he felt his centre of gravity tipping, sucking him down into the shaft, he managed to grab a tree root.

Slowly, using every ounce of muscle in his body, he tried to lever himself back up to safety. Then his leg gave way on the ice and he was hanging onto the root for dear life.

He felt it slithering out of his grasp.

But as his leg kicked the side of the shaft he suddenly found a foothold. With his right leg pushing and his arms pulling, he hauled himself back up to safety.

He lay panting on the ground for a few moments. Two near-death experiences in less then twenty-four hours. His blood pressure couldn't put up with much more like this.

He stood up finally and examined the fencing. One panel was completely loose. Hogan lifted the timber beams and fitted them back in position, but they were still loose and dangerous. Maybe that was why the figure had been at this airshaft. Maybe it was another walker who had noticed something wrong with the fencing. Hogan made a mental note to report the danger. Hopefully, if the other person did the same too, something would actually get done.

'Where the heck is he, Ed?' Howze was pacing angrily round the office.

'How should I know?' said Sutcliffe. 'You're the one who talked to him last. Anyway, I thought you said he'd had a crash and hasn't got a car. Maybe the bus is late.'

Howze checked his watch again. It was 10am. Hogan was an hour late, and hadn't bothered to ring in.

He sauntered over to the desk occupied by the *Star*'s newest recruit, Scarlett Reynolds. She was the daughter of the managing director of one of the biggest employers on the island, George Reynolds. Howze liked to keep in with the island's leading lights, and this was his way of getting in her father's good books.

'How's it going, Scarlett?' Howze leaned over her desk and wrapped an arm round her shoulder.

The girl flinched.

'OK, thanks, Mr Howze. Any stories that need doing?'

'Well, I was thinking it might be a good idea to help our chief reporter out on the cliff murders case. How would you fancy that?'

Howze could see the genuine enthusiasm on the girl's face. He squeezed her shoulder again, and moved his hand slightly down the side of her body. She moved away from the touch.

'That would be great experience. Are you sure? I don't want to muck anything up.'

'Don't you worry about that. And I understand from Ed that you've got your own car?'

'Well, yes. It's my mum's. I'm borrowing it at the moment to get to work and back.'

'OK, well, you'd better make sure you get it insured for business purposes. That is, if it's OK with you if you drive Hogan round for the story?'

Howze saw the girl's face fall. The penny had dropped. She was going to be nothing more than a glorified chauffeur, but Howze would take great delight in telling her father how he'd assigned her to the most important story on the island.

'Of course, Mr Howze. I'll ring my dad right away. He'll sort it out.'

'Good girl,' said Howze, squeezing her arm again. 'You'll go far.'

Just then he noticed a commotion by the entrance. It was Hogan – dramatically puffing and panting as though he'd been running.

'Just stroll in any time, why don't you?' said Howze sarcastically. 'Don't worry about the rest of us.'

'Sorry, Dickey. I set off before eight but one of the buses had broken down.'

'Hmm. I gave you frigging Saturday morning off because of your car troubles – the only Saturday you've been rota'd for so far. And then you still can't turn up on time today.'

Howze could see Hogan starting to lose his temper. "Car troubles'? Is that what you call it? Someone tries to kill me and you call it 'car troubles'!'

'Oh, don't be so dramatic! Why would anyone want to kill you?'

'Ask the cops if you don't believe me.'

'All right, all right. No need to get a strop on. I've done you a favour actually, Benjamin.'

Yet again Howze was using Hogan's hated first name to wind him up.

'What?' grunted Hogan.

'Sorted you out some transport, actually.'

'Oh, great. Thanks, Dickey.' Hogan sounded genuinely grateful. 'When do I pick it up?'

'Erm . . . not it. Her.'

Howze saw Hogan's puzzled expression. He was enjoying teasing the reporter.

'Come again?'

'Her. I think you were introduced the other day.' Howze grabbed Scarlett and made her stand up. 'Scarlett Reynolds. Daughter of a dear friend of mine.' Howze was aware that both Scarlett and Hogan were scowling. 'She's your set of wheels. She's going to join you as your assistant on the cliff-murders story, and she's got her own car.'

Howze saw Hogan force a smile. His chief reporter was too polite to risk upsetting the girl.

'Great,' Hogan said, without conviction. 'Get your notebook ready, then, Scarlett. We're off to Bonchurch to interview someone.'

'You're off out again?' queried Howze. 'No chance of all this research actually giving us some stories is there, Benjamin?'

'You've had plenty of stories,' growled Hogan. 'Now get off my back. Some of us have work to do.'

Hogan sat back in the passenger seat and enjoyed the luxury of being able to examine the island's landscape closely from the road for once, rather than having to keep his eyes peeled for oncoming traffic. He glanced across at Scarlett. She seemed bright enough. After just a few days, Ed Sutcliffe already held her in high regard. And if Ed thought she was good that was enough for Hogan.

'So where are we off to?' she was saying.

'Ventnor. Well, Bonchurch, actually. Next-door village. Whoops, watch it!'

Hogan slammed his foot down onto where the brake pedal would have been, forgetting for a moment that he was the passenger. A dog dashed across the road in front of them.

Scarlett seemed unflustered.

'Any particular reason?' she asked.

'For what?'

'Duh! Going to Bonchurch, of course.'

Hogan reddened. He wasn't used to a nineteen-year-old getting the better of him. 'Yeah. We're off to interview the chairwoman of the Wight Women's Ramblers.'

'Sounds fascinating.' Scarlett made no attempt to hide her boredom.

'Actually, it is,' said Hogan, irked now. 'She was one of the main opponents of the closure of the cliff path after the first girl fell. And she seems to be caught up in some dodgy adoption-agency racket.'

Scarlett still looked disinterested.

'Fancy some music?' she asked. Hogan nodded.

She turned a tape on. It was some sort of rap or dance track. Hogan wasn't very sure. His attempts to keep up with musical fashion had ended in the early nineteen-eighties. This stuff, with its heavy bass line and lack of tune, just gave him a headache.

'Got anything else?' he asked her.

She pouted at him, then switched the cassette off petulantly.

'Mind if I smoke?' she asked him.

'Well, it's your car, of course . . .' Hogan knew he sounded judgmental, but he couldn't help it. He'd rather have the incessant rap track on than face cigarette fumes.

'But you'd prefer me not to,' said Scarlett. 'God! You sound just like my fucking dad. Maybe this isn't going to work out. Maybe I ought to just drop you off in Bonchurch and then head back to the office.'

'As you wish.' Hogan hoped she wouldn't leave him marooned on the south of the island, but he wasn't going to give her the satisfaction of pleading.

They lapsed into silence. Hogan was pissed off. He wanted to be able to think clearly for his upcoming confrontation with Clara Forbes. Instead he seemed to be having an adolescent spat with a work-experience girl.

Maybe she was right. Maybe it wasn't going to work.

Clara was frantic. Maria had been missing now for nearly eighteen hours. At first Clara hadn't worried unduly. Maria hadn't been around when she'd set off for the regional Women's Ramblers meeting in Bath – but Clara had just assumed that maybe she was feeling better and had just popped out to the shops. Her fears had grown when she'd tried to ring her on the mobile phone from Bath itself – there was no answer. Yet she and her sister always carried their mobiles with them. Clara was so concerned she'd returned to the island, without actually ever getting to the meeting.

What made Clara particularly worried was that Maria had been acting even more strangely than usual over the past few days. In fact she hadn't been right since Francesca finally died during Maria's shift at the hospital. It was as if Maria blamed herself somehow.

Clara was reluctant to call Emma. She knew Emma was busy doing overtime. But who else could she call? If she went direct through the police control room, another police officer would almost certainly come around asking questions, bringing the danger of everything unravelling. Clara was already dreading the damn journalist from the *Wight Evening Star* appearing again – she hadn't responded to his answerphone message and was certain he would be calling round in person imminently. In fact, she was surprised he hadn't already.

Maria had gone off before on unexplained trips. About five years earlier, Clara had received a panic-stricken call from Mother. Maria had disappeared without warning, and her elderly parent had summoned Clara back to the island from London. Maria had turned up again a couple of days later. Things had got too much, she'd explained. She'd needed to get away for a while. But Clara had a nagging feeling that this time something was different. Most of the time recently Maria was in a semi-drugged state. Clara had initially encouraged the Valium tablets, but over the past few days Maria had come to rely on them.

What should Clara do?

Finally, giving in to the inevitable, she dialled the number of Emma's mobile phone.

Hogan went first along the path to the detached limestone house. He looked up at the walls briefly. Wouldn't mind something like this myself, he thought. Better than a bloody chalet.

He rang the bell. No answer. This had been happening a lot to him lately.

Scarlett, behind him, whispered, 'There's someone in. Deffo. Saw them ducking down beneath the upstairs window ledge as we came up the path.'

Hogan tried the bell again and still got no response. Then Scarlett shoved him aside and opened the letterbox.

'Hello!' she shouted. 'We know you're in there. We saw you trying to hide upstairs. We're not going away till you let us in.'

Hogan groaned. 'Did you have to do that?' he asked. 'I don't want her getting all worked up. I want to wheedle stuff out of her gently.'

'Softly, softly, eh?' sneered Scarlett. 'Well that's not my style.'

He found it hard to believe this was the same seemingly meek and mild trainee who'd been keeping out of everyone's way at the office all week.

The door finally opened, and Clara Forbes stood on the doorstep.

She didn't invite them in.

'S . . . sorry,' she stammered. 'I was upstairs. Didn't hear the bell at first. I think I'll have to get it looked at.'

'It rang loudly enough,' said Scarlett stroppily. 'I should think the whole village heard it.'

'Mind if we come in, Ms Forbes?' asked Hogan politely. 'There's just a few more questions I want to ask you.'

Clara Forbes still didn't move aside. Hogan watched in horror as Scarlett brushed past her and marched into the house.

'Hang on a minute . . .' Clara tried to stop the girl but to no avail.

Scarlett turned. 'Look, I'm not hanging around outside. It's cold. Let's all go inside and get it over and done with.'

Hogan and Clara trooped after her into the drawing room. Hogan caught up and hissed at her, 'Just leave this to me, please. You're going at things like a bull in a china shop. It's not helping.'

'Suit yourself,' said Scarlett with a shrug.

Clara sat in the two-seater sofa. Scarlett and Hogan drew up high-backed chairs opposite her.

'So,' said Hogan finally, 'Is your sister here? It might be better if we spoke to both of you together.'

'My s. . .s. . .sister?'

'That's right.' Hogan wondered why she seemed so flustered by the question.

'Er. . .N. . .n. . .no. Would you like me to ring her?'

'If you don't mind,' said Hogan.

Hogan thought it slightly strange that Clara reached into her jacket pocket and brought out a mobile phone, rather than using the normal one in her hall. She seemed to be fumbling with it.

'What's wrong?' he asked.

'The P . . . P . . . PIN number. It doesn't seem to want to accept it.'

'PIN number?'

'Personal Identification Number.'

Scarlett sighed ostentatiously. 'We *do* know what a PIN number is, Ms Forbes. But why do you need one?'

Clara Forbes shrugged. 'Both Maria and I use PIN numbers with our phones. It's so that if they're stolen, someone can't rack up big bills on our account. We don't even know each other's. Ah! There! It's working now.'

Hogan and Scarlett looked on expectantly.

Finally Clara shut down the phone.

'It's no good. Can't get a reply. She must be somewhere out of range.'

This time it was Hogan who sighed. 'We'd better get on without her then,' he said. 'What can you tell me about the Families for Teens Agency?'

The woman's face fell as soon as he mentioned the name.

She tried to recover herself.

'What do you mean?'

'Families for Teens. Tell me about it.'

'It's a business of mine.'

The answer momentarily threw Hogan. He'd been expecting some sort of denial.

'A legitimate business?'

'Well . . . yes. But, if I'm honest, I don't declare my earnings from it for tax. That's why I use the accommodation agency in Ryde for all correspondence.'

Clara Forbes's answers seemed plausible. But Hogan, looking at her wringing her hands, could sense her fear. 'And what about Francesca?'

'Sorry?' said Clara. He noted the querulousness of her voice.

'Francesca,' he repeated. 'Tell me about her.'

'She, er, stayed with us a while, until we found her a family in Devon. Lovely girl.'

'Devon? So how did she end up falling off a cliff on the Isle of Wight?'

'W-what?'

'You heard me! You must have seen the papers. Francesca died last week in Yarwater General after several weeks in a coma, remember? There was a mysterious cliff fall. Don't try to make out you don't know anything about it! I'm not that stupid, and neither are you!'

'Oh my god!' cried Clara. 'We don't get the local papers. I had

150

no idea.'

Hogan, watching her face, wondered what she was trying to pull. Of course Clara knew about Francesca's death – why was she trying to pretend she didn't?

As he started to ask his next question, the doorbell rang. Clara rushed to her feet, grateful of the interruption. A few moments later Hogan was shocked when she re-entered the room accompanied by Emma Thomas.

'Emma!' he gasped. 'What are you doing here?'

She looked angry, and sounded it too. 'I've come here to interview Ms Forbes.'

Hogan noted a look of relief on Clara Forbes's face. An odd reaction, he thought.

'More to the point,' continued Emma, 'what are *you* doing here? Not interfering with this case, are you?'

'No,' said Hogan.

'Well, you'd better be off now anyway. You and your new sidekick.' She threw a sneering look towards Scarlett.

'It's OK,' said Scarlett. 'We were just going anyway. We've found out what we wanted.'

Emma and Clara stood side by side as Hogan and Scarlett got up to leave. As he passed her, Emma muttered softly in his ear, 'Next time you want to stick your nose into my business and my case, ask me first. OK?'

Hogan turned away from her without answering, and followed Scarlett out of the door.

'So what do you make of that?' Hogan asked Scarlett as they drove out of Bonchurch and back towards Yarwater.

'Well, she's not telling us everything, that's for sure. And didn't you think it rather convenient the way that detective turned up when she did?'

Hogan thought about it. Scarlett was right. Just as they'd started to pin Forbes down, Emma had arrived. Coincidence? Unfortunately, it probably was.

He grabbed the passenger's handhold as Scarlett took a corner too fast, making the tyres screech.

'Careful,' he warned.

Scarlett shot him a withering look. He could read in her eyes the unequivocal message that he was a complete wimp. 'So what are we going to write about? This dodgy Families for Teens Agency?'

Hogan wondered about this. They had no proof at all that Clara Forbes had done anything wrong or underhand. The only link was that a girl brought over from Romania by her agency had ended up dead. It was enough for a story, but there were plenty of potential legal pitfalls. Hogan didn't want to land the *Star* with a huge libel suit. There was also the question of whether, if they published now, the trail would go cold.

'I don't think we write anything at the moment,' he said finally.

'Shouldn't we tell the police?'

'Probably,' admitted Hogan. 'But Emma Thomas is questioning Forbes at this very moment. Maybe we should let her do her own legwork.'

Scarlett glanced over at him. She was smirking. 'There seemed, shall we say, a certain prickliness between you two.'

'Mmm.' Hogan didn't particularly want to elaborate.

'And she didn't seem too happy to see me. Why would that be?'

'Dunno,' said Hogan. He was determined not to be drawn on it.

'Maybe she's got the hots for you, and sees me as a rival?'

'I doubt that. She could see you're young enough to be my daughter.'

'Yes, but *she's* young enough to be your daughter, too. And quite a looker – for a policewoman.'

Hogan could feel his face flush.

Scarlett laughed. 'Nice to know that old duffers like you can still . . . you know.'

'Just keep your eyes on the road,' he said, grumpily. 'This is a dangerous stretch here.'

* * *

152

'Ah. You two are back finally, then,' said Ed Sutcliffe. 'I hope you've got a story for me. We need something for tomorrow's page-three lead.'

Hogan shrugged. 'Sorry, Ed. We're not there yet.'

'How did the interview go, then?'

'It *was* going fine. Then we were interrupted by the police.'

'Shit. We're not in trouble, are we? Howze is on the warpath today already. Can't you sweet-talk your way out of it with that woman detective you've been seeing?'

Hogan shot an angry look at his news editor. 'Who told you about that?'

'Oh, it's all the talk at Yarwater nick. You forget, I've got some good contacts in this town. Quite the loverboy, aren't you?'

'Fuck off, Ed.'

Hogan sat down at his desk, and Scarlett took the place opposite him. She was grinning. 'So I was right! There *is* something between you and that detective. I thought as much.'

'Was,' growled Hogan. 'Was.'

'Aahh. Chuck you, did she? Poor lamb.'

'What is it with everyone today?' he moaned. 'What gives you the right to start prying into my love life? It's not as though it's even that exciting.'

Scarlett looked hurt. Maybe he had been a bit too harsh. But she was quite happy to dish it out, so she should be prepared to take it back.

'Watch out,' she murmured. 'Here comes trouble.'

He saw her looking at the other side of the office, at the advancing bulk of Dickey Howze. Hogan started tapping away furiously at his computer, trying to look busy.

'You two,' Howze thundered. 'You've been away far too long.'

'Stories don't just grow on trees, Dickey.' Hogan continued typing into the computer.

'You can cut out that 'Dickey' crap, too. There's a job that needs doing. Now. In fact, fifteen minutes ago, so you'd better get your skates on. Press facility trip. Site visit to see the plans for re-opening the rail line to Reeth East.'

Hogan began to take more interest.

'Here are the details.' Howze slammed a press pack down on the desk. 'You're supposed to meet the others at Godshill car park in ten minutes' time. So get a move on.'

Hogan and Scarlett gathered up their notebooks again.

As they were leaving, Scarlett said quietly, 'He's a creep. Why do you put up with him? He was trying to touch me up the other day – but if he thinks he'll get away with that with me he's got another thing coming.'

Hogan looked over at her. Her face and neck were hot with anger.

'So why have we been put on trainspotter watch?' Scarlett asked. They'd set off from Godshill and were following the rest of the group in convoy to another car park at the start of the walk along the disused track.

'Railway history's one of my interests,' admitted Hogan shamefacedly. He knew it sounded a bit limp.

Scarlett turned up her nose. 'Yuk. Dullsville. I don't mind acting as your personal chauffeur on a murder story, but this is boring with a capital 'B'.'

Hogan didn't answer. He looked out of the car window. All the surrounding hills still had their dusting of frost.

Scarlett indicated, and turned into the car park. 'Here we are. Oh God. Look at that bunch of anoraks!'

Hogan had to admit that the group of people gathered in the car park didn't look exactly thrilling. When they'd met in Godshill it had transpired that Hogan and Scarlett were the only members of the press who'd turned up. The others were experts from Yarwater college, a rail users' group, and a collection of local worthies.

'Couldn't we just have picked this one up over the phone?' asked Scarlett as they got out of the car and the freezing air hit them.

'Guess so,' said Hogan. 'But I think one of these committee men is a mate of Howze's. So it's a case of keeping up appearances.'

'Look out. One of them's coming this way,' warned Scarlett.

A bespectacled man with a professorial beard was approaching.

He grabbed Hogan's hand and shook it firmly. 'Ah, glad you could make it, Mr Hogan. Richard said he'd try to send you along because of your interest in railways. Is this your photographer?'

Before Hogan could explain that, no, Scarlett was on work experience from a journalism course, the girl had started to speak: 'Yes, that's right. Would it be OK to take your picture?'

Hogan noticed she had a small digital camera in her hand.

'Well, it's not really all about me,' the man replied in a pompous tone. 'But if you insist . . .'

'Ooh, please, yes!'

Scarlett's fake enthusiasm was lost on the man, but not on Hogan, who raised his eyes skywards.

'I didn't know press photographers used digital cameras nowadays,' the bearded man said. 'How times change, eh, Mr Hogan?'

'Yes, quite,' said Hogan. Just because Scarlett was bored with the story didn't give her the right to be taking the piss like this. He would have to exchange a few words with her, but not now.

They all set off along the disused track. The bearded man was explaining his plans to raise the finance to re-open the line between Shanklin and Reeth, and so link the south coast of the island once more with Ryde Pier and the ferry services to the mainland. Hogan knew the plan had little chance of success. Another group was involved in a similar scheme to try to get the rail line re-opened to Ventnor, a bigger resort. If either scheme had any chance, it was the Ventnor one.

Once the others were out of earshot, Hogan turned on Scarlett. 'What the hell do you think you're doing? And where did you get that camera?'

She grinned cheekily at him. 'It's mine. It's not suddenly a crime to carry a camera, is it?'

'No, but why did you go and tell him you were the photographer? It's totally out of order.'

'Oh, dear. What are you going to do about it? Put me over your knee and spank me? I've told you – you sound just like my dad.'

Hogan lapsed into silence. Despite the convenience of being driven around, he was beginning to think Howze's idea of pairing him with this girl hadn't been such a good one.

They trudged on. He was wishing now they hadn't come on this story. They could have sat in a café, claimed their car had broken down, and then got all the details from the bearded professor over the phone. He kicked out at a loose stone on the cinder track. Scarlett ran after it and passed it back to him. Hogan steadied himself and launched the stone with his foot, as though taking a penalty with a football. It whistled past the man with the beard at about waist-height.

Scarlett burst out laughing. The man didn't notice.

'You missed,' she whispered to Hogan. 'Shame.'

The group had reached the entrance to the tunnel under Reeth Down. This was more interesting. The professor explained that the tunnel extended nearly two miles and emerged where Hogan had been two days earlier, at the old site of Reeth East Station.

Hogan asked about the airshafts.

'Yes, there are airshafts,' the professor said. Hogan knew this already. He had just wanted to show an interest. 'They're about every five hundred yards or so.'

'And are they in good nick?' asked Hogan.

'I think so,' said the professor. He frowned. 'Why do you ask?'

'It's just I was walking on top of the Down the other day. I came across one of the shafts. Some of the timber fencing was loose. I very nearly fell down it.'

The professor looked slightly annoyed. 'Can't believe that,' he blustered.

'Well, I'm sorry,' said Hogan, 'but it's true.'

'That's most peculiar. Only last week we had contractors up there checking them out. They gave them all a clean bill of health.'

'Well, I'd get back onto them if I were you,' said Hogan, 'before somebody falls down one.'

The professor was going red in the face but trying to retain his composure. 'Let's get on with this. We're going to go into the tunnel now, everyone. We've got torches for those who want them.'

Hogan and Scarlett took a torch each. The professor unlocked the timber door to the tunnel and they all climbed in.

Scarlett tapped Hogan on the shoulder. 'Are you sure we have to do this? This place is creepy.'

'You can stay outside if you want. But this is the best bit. It's what I've been waiting for.'

After a few hundred yards, Hogan noticed the group in front stop. They were craning their necks upwards, bathed in a column of natural light from the airshaft.

'This is the first of the shafts,' said the professor. 'As you can see, it's in excellent condition.' He stared pointedly at Hogan.

They carried on walking down the tunnel.

'Can you tell me exactly what all this is for?' said Scarlett to Hogan. 'I'm beginning to feel claustrophobic, thinking about the weight of rock above us.'

'You can turn back if you want to,' said Hogan. 'I think it's fascinating.'

In the dim light, Hogan saw her pull a face at him. 'Ooh, 'I think it's fascinating'.' She repeated his words in a mocking tone. 'La di da di da.'

'Piss off,' he hissed.

At the second airshaft the professor stopped. 'This is as far as we can go,' he said. 'The rest of the tunnel hasn't been checked for safety, so you're not covered by insurance if you carry on.'

'Can we take the risk, though?' asked Hogan.

'As I say, I wouldn't advise it because you're not insured. But at the end of the day I can't stop you,' said the professor.

'I'd like to. I want to retrace my route below ground – the walk I took the other day.'

The professor threw Hogan an angry look as the remainder of the group turned to go.

Hogan pushed down the barbed wire blocking the rest of the tunnel and clambered over it.

He turned back to Scarlett.

'Are you coming?' he asked. 'If you'd prefer you could always go back with the others.'

'Great option,' she said sarcastically, moving over the wire fence. 'They're even more boring than you.'

'Even though it's claustrophobic down here?'

157

'Yeah,' she said, putting her hands to her opposite shoulders and looking around her with a shiver. 'I can hack it,' she added in an uncertain voice.

'Nice to know youngsters like you can still . . . you know.'

'Piss off, grandad.'

They walked on to the next airshaft. Hogan calculated they were about halfway through the tunnel. He noticed that up ahead some track had been left down. Beyond that were the shapes of what looked like trucks. He shone the torch on them.

'Come on. Looks interesting. Just as far as the next shaft, then we can turn back.'

The trucks were still loaded, full of limestone and chalk.

'Uh, creepy,' said Scarlett. 'To think this hasn't been moved in decades. The guys who loaded it up are probably dead now.'

Hogan could see, further along the tunnel, the light from the second-to-last airshaft, the one with the loose fencing that the professor claimed wasn't loose at all. Hogan wanted to check it out, even though he knew he wouldn't be able to see anything from down here.

Walking was more difficult now. The trucks filled most of the width of the single-track tunnel. Hogan and Scarlett squeezed their way along the sides of them.

They finally got to the bottom of the shaft.

'What's that?' said Scarlett, shining her torch at the top of one of the trucks.

Hogan peered. It looked as if a bundle of clothes or something had been dumped on the quarrystone.

'Hang on. I'll get up and take a look.'

The truck had a metal ladder at the end. Hogan climbed up it as Scarlett kept her torch beam trained on the bundle.

As he got to the top, Hogan froze.

It wasn't just a bundle of clothes.

He saw a walking boot on a leg sticking out at a crazy angle. Broken. He looked up the length of the body. In the uncertain light he could make out an arm, again unnaturally contorted. Then the head. Covered in dried blood. Face-down.

He heard Scarlett gasp. She had just realised what the bundle was.

He didn't know what to do next. He knew he shouldn't really disturb the body. But half of him hoped that, maybe, whoever it was, was still alive. He turned the shoulders over. The crushed face lolled madly backwards, the neck bones shattered. It was a woman. About his age, he guessed. But he couldn't really tell. Her face had been smashed into a chalky, bloody mess. The skin grey. All sign of life completely expunged.

The police arrived en masse at the car park. Hogan counted three squad cars, sirens wailing and lights flashing, as well as two unmarked cars. An ambulance, too, although Hogan knew it was too late for this. Most of the railway-feasibility group had dispersed; the professor had stayed on to watch. Hogan got the impression the man was slightly put out that his tour of the abandoned tunnel had been overshadowed by something far more dramatic.

'It's that woman detective again,' said Scarlett as Emma Thomas emerged from one of the unmarked cars. 'Little Miss Bitch on Wheels.'

Emma acknowledged them with a cursory nod. 'So who discovered the body?' she asked.

'I did,' said Hogan.

Scarlett corrected him. 'We both did.'

Emma glanced witheringly at Scarlett, and then addressed Hogan again. 'I hope you didn't touch it?'

Hogan felt his ears redden. 'Well, I wasn't sure she was dead. I had to check . . .'

Emma sighed and raised her eyebrows.

Another policewoman joined them. 'Problems?'

'I hope not, ma'am,' said Emma. 'Unfortunately, the body's been disturbed.' She looked angrily at Hogan, then introduced him grudgingly to her colleague. 'This is Iain Hogan, ma'am – reporter from the *Star*. He found the body and moved it when he checked for signs of life. Hogan, this is Detective Chief Inspector Jane Hale.'

'Ah, yes,' said Hale with a smile, shaking his hand. 'We spoke over the phone about the photograph of the girl. Poor thing. Still, you gave it a good spread as promised, so: thanks.'

Hogan nodded in acknowledgement, feeling guilty that he'd kept the identity of the girl to himself.

'And you are . . .?' Hale was looking at Scarlett.

'Scarlett Reynolds. I work for the *Star* too. Hogan and I found the body. Together.'

Hogan noticed Emma grimace as Scarlett said this.

'OK,' said Hale. 'We'd better get things moving. Mr Hogan, you'd better lead the way. Emma will make sure you're kitted out with sterile clothing – although it may be too late for that.'

Hogan was handed sterile overalls together with overshoes, hood and gloves. He watched as the police team dressed similarly. It looked like they were at the scene of a nuclear accident rather than a murder.

The group finally set off, leaving Scarlett and the professor in the car park, neither looking terribly pleased about this. The professor had tried to introduce himself to Hale but Emma had ushered him away.

When the party arrived at the line of trucks, Hogan went to the front and squeezed along the side of the tunnel, between the trucks and the wall. It was more difficult than last time, thanks to the bulky sterile clothing.

At one point his overall caught on one of the trucks. Emma was directly behind him. 'Come on,' she said impatiently. 'We need to get a move on.'

They finally reached the fourth airshaft, and Hogan pointed to the shape on top of the quarry truck. From below it still looked like a bundle of clothes.

'You stay here,' said Emma.

Hogan watched her climb onto the top of the truck together with DCI Hale and a man similarly kitted out in sterile clothing, carrying some kind of kit bag. The man approached the body and pulled a piece of apparatus out of his bag. Hogan assumed this must be the police surgeon, checking to make sure the woman was indeed dead – and possibly, too, checking the body temperature to try to find out when she'd died.

At last the doctor moved away from the body, climbed down the truck's iron steps, and shuffled off to one side. Another man climbed up – the police photographer, it became obvious as a series of flashes lit the scene with an unnatural brightness, highlighting the corpse against the white of the chalkstone.

Hale and Emma were deep in conversation. Hogan saw Emma look his way. When she spoke, however, it was not to Hogan but to a policeman who'd come up behind him. 'Pete, can you take Mr Hogan back to the car park? I'm sure he doesn't want to stay and watch us at work. Then get above ground and seal off the area around the airshaft opening.' She turned to Hogan. 'We'll be in touch. We'll need a statement.'

'Hello, Mr Hogan.'

The voice was familiar. Hogan peered through the gloom and realised it was the ubiquitous Pete Birkitt again.

'Hi, Pete. How's it going?'

'So so. Can't complain.'

They walked back down the tunnel together. Birkitt showed the way with a torch, but every few seconds flashes of brilliant light filled the tunnel as the police photographer continued his work.

'Nasty business, this, mind,' said Birkitt. 'I can't remember so many unnatural deaths on the island for a long while. You've been having a rough time of it too, sir.'

'How do you mean?'

'Well, with your car and everything. And now this. What do you reckon's happened?'

'Fallen down the airshaft,' said Hogan.

'By accident?'

'I don't know.'

'You want to watch your step, though, sir.'

Hogan turned to him. His eyes widened in alarm. 'Why do you say that?'

'Oh, nothing, not really. It's just there's a few strange things going on. And you seem to be at the centre of them all.'

Hogan didn't answer. He wasn't sure what Birkitt was trying to imply.

As they got towards the end of the tunnel, another man in sterile overalls passed them. Birkitt nodded a greeting.

161

'Who's that?' asked Hogan.

'Home Office pathologist,' said Birkitt. 'We're keeping him pretty busy on the island at the moment.'

Hogan was glad when they finally emerged into the daylight. He had to screw up his eyes until he got used to it. Then he noticed Scarlett standing there beside the professor.

She had a set face and looked to be in a foul mood.

As they drove back to the office to write up the story, Hogan could tell that Scarlett was still seething. She wouldn't look at him, just kept her eyes fixed on the road as they went along in silence.

At last he couldn't stand it any more. 'What's pissed you off? You don't seem in a terribly good mood.'

'Would you be?'

'How do you mean?'

'Left with that dull old geezer – the professor. Boring on about his bloody railway plans, as if I was more interested in that than the mystery death of an unknown woman.'

'Sorry, but it wasn't me who said you couldn't come with us.'

'No, but you didn't stick up for me, did you? I'm supposed to be a trainee, getting experience. The only experience I ended up with was experience of total boredom. If you're so interested in railways maybe you should have stayed with him.'

Scarlett was flushed. If she gripped the steering wheel any harder it would break.

'OK, I'm sorry,' he said. 'But you can come to the press conference with me. That should be most interesting.'

'Oh, yeah, right! What you mean is that you don't want to catch the bus to Yarwater nick, so can I give you a lift? That's all I am, your little personal assistant.'

'It's not true. It's good working with you. I like you.'

Their eyes met. Hogan noticed Scarlett's grimace soften. Then it turned into a smile. 'Hmm. . .well, I suppose you're not too bad for a living dinosaur.' Then she put on her angry face again. 'But just don't ever leave me out of things like that again, OK?'

162

'OK,' said Hogan. 'You've got your point across.'

He liked her feistiness. She was a fighter. It could prove useful.

12

Hale, Emma and another man filed into the room and sat at the table on the raised stage.

The man spoke first. Hogan didn't recognise his face, but he knew the voice. It was the Isle of Wight Police's press officer; Hogan had talked to him several times over the phone.

Hogan looked around. The room was pretty crowded. He nodded a greeting at the reporter from the weekly paper. There were also radio reporters and even cameramen and journalists from the regional television stations.

The press officer introduced Detective Chief Inspector Hale, who began to speak.

'Thanks for coming, everyone. I'll make a short statement, and then DS Thomas and myself will be happy to take your questions. As many of you probably know, at 3pm this afternoon the body of a woman thought to be aged about forty was found on top of a disused railway truck in Reeth Down tunnel. An initial examination of the body and the scene by the Home Office pathologist suggests she died in a fall down one of the tunnel's airshafts. We cannot release the woman's name until she has been formally identified and her next of kin informed. Forensic scientists will be doing a number of tests that may tell us more. We're appealing to anyone who was walking on Reeth Down on either Saturday or Sunday to make themselves known to us, particularly if they were anywhere near the tunnel's airshafts or saw anyone acting suspiciously. The phone number is on a printed press release which we'll give you at the end of this briefing.

'That's it. Any questions?'

Hogan turned as he heard the voice of the TV reporter. 'You say you can't release the woman's name. Does that mean you know who she is?'

'Yes,' said Hale. 'We've a pretty good idea through documents found on her. But we can't say anything until the formal identification.'

'When will that be?' asked the TV reporter.

Hale raised her eyebrows at Emma Thomas, who answered: 'The closest relative is very upset at the moment and under sedation. Once she is in a fit state we will ask her to formally identify the body.'

Scarlett, sitting next to Hogan, raised her hand. 'Are you treating this as a suicide?' she asked. 'Or an accident? Or murder?'

'It's too early to say,' said Hale. 'Various samples have been taken away for forensic analysis. Once we get those results then we may have a clearer picture.'

'What type of samples?' asked Hogan, pricked into action by Scarlett's question.

'The usual body samples, and also soil samples from her shoes. We found fibres on her clothing and on the fencing surrounding the airshaft, and we're looking at those, too.'

'From someone else's clothes?' asked Hogan.

He watched Emma look questioningly at Hale, who shook her head. 'We're not in a position to say at the moment,' said Emma.

'But if it's from someone else's clothes, that would imply foul play is involved, wouldn't it?' asked Hogan.

Emma glowered at him. 'As I've said, we're not prepared to go into that at the moment. We're keeping an open mind.'

Hale got to her feet. 'OK, well, if there are no more questions . . .'

'Just one more.' Hogan swivelled in his seat to look behind him again. The speaker was a reporter from local radio. 'Was the pathologist able to tell anything from the position of the body about the cause of death?'

Hogan tried to shrink down into his seat. Scarlett glanced across at him sympathetically. But he saw Emma look pointedly at him as she answered.

'Unfortunately the person who discovered the body disturbed it.' She shot Hogan an angry glance. 'So there is a limit to what we can deduce.'

'Disturbed it? Why?' asked the radio reporter.

Hale intervened and smiled at Hogan. 'Because the person wasn't certain she was dead. She was lying face-down, and he moved her head and shoulders to check in case she was still alive. It was a perfectly

165

natural reaction and obviously the right thing to do under the circumstances. Unfortunate for us. But perfectly natural.'

The radio reporter was like a dog with a bone, and wouldn't let go. 'So can you tell us who this person was, so that we can interview them?'

Emma answered this time. 'Yes . . .'

Hogan groaned to himself. Scarlett reached out to touch his hand in commiseration. But Hale intervened again.

'No. I don't think so. I don't think that would be appropriate.' She looked around the room once more. 'OK? Well, we'll hold another briefing when we know any more. We'll let you know when that'll be.'

The press conference broke up. Hale and Emma were ushered to one side by the police press officer, who gestured to the TV reporters to come forward. They wanted to do their own on-camera face-to-face interviews.

'Phew,' Hogan whispered to Scarlett. 'That was close.'

'Yeah. You nearly ended up as a TV and radio star. It would have been quite fun.'

Hogan helped her on with her coat.

'Fun? No, I don't think so. I can do without all that. I've still got to give a statement to the police in any case. I fit into the bracket of people who were walking on Reeth Down at the weekend.'

'And you fiddled with the fence. didn't you?'

'Shhh,' Hogan hissed at her. 'I don't want the whole world knowing about it.'

Hogan looked across the desk at Emma Thomas as she studied her notes. Outwardly she hadn't changed much since he'd first met her. He had to admit she did have a certain film-star quality – beautiful face, snub nose and blonde bob. But the looks had become – even in just a few weeks – more careworn. Her forehead was lined in concentration. And the tinkling, cheeky laugh seemed to have been locked away.

She looked up at him.

166

'So why exactly were you walking on Reeth Down?'

'I needed to clear my head, get some fresh air.'

'OK. I can buy that bit of it. You must have needed it after listening to that crap band the night before.'

Hogan grinned at her. 'There was a car crash as well, remember?'

She remained serious. 'But why over at Reeth East? There's plenty of walks nearer to you.'

Hogan didn't have a good answer for that. 'I guess partly I just wanted to try the bus. I knew I'd have to be using it regularly. And I'm interested in old railways – I wanted to see the site of Reeth East Station.'

'Fascinating,' said Emma with a sarcastic twist of her mouth.

'Well, it wasn't really. So I looked around, saw this path, and basically all I did was follow it. It took me up to the top of the Downs.'

'And?'

'I was interested in checking out the airshafts.'

'Why?' Emma's brow became even more wrinkled.

'That sort of thing just interests me. Can't really say why.'

'And so what happened next?'

'I saw someone by the next shaft.'

Hogan met Emma's gaze. A strange expression passed across her face. What was it? It looked almost like fear. "Someone'? Man or woman?'

Hogan thought she seemed worried now.

She'd started biting her fingernails. It was almost as if she was the one being questioned, not him.

'I couldn't tell. Too far away. And the sun was quite strong, reflecting off the frosty ground.'

He studied Emma's face again. She seemed suddenly to have relaxed.

'So, other than seeing that someone was there, you couldn't tell anything about them?'

'One thing. Red. He or she was wearing red.'

'All over?'

'No. It looked like just a red top. Or it could have been a coat or anorak, I suppose. Too far away to tell.'

167

There was a knowing look on Emma's face now. Hogan couldn't help thinking her reactions seemed strange.

'So what did you do next?'

'I walked towards the second airshaft, where the person was.'

'Why?'

Hogan shrugged. 'Dunno. Curiosity, I guess.'

'So did you see the person more clearly?' asked Emma. He felt her staring at him intensely.

'No,' he answered. And again he noticed a strange look pass across her face. 'Whoever it was had moved off, towards Whitwell. And then they disappeared from view.'

'But you carried on walking towards the shaft?'

'Yes. And when I got there I sat down and had my packed lunch. After that I set off back home.'

'And you didn't notice anything strange about the fence around the airshaft?'

Hogan paused. He knew he ought to tell the truth. But if he admitted to tampering with the fence – even though he'd been simply trying to put it back into place – things weren't going to look good.

'No,' he lied.

Emma raised her eyebrows. 'You sure?'

'Quite sure,' he said firmly.

She sighed and stretched her arms above her head.

'Tired?' he asked.

'What's it to you?' she said, her eyes narrowing. 'I told you in my letter the other night, we've got to just keep things professional now. Anyway I see you've got yourself another girlfriend already.'

'What?'

'The pretty dark-haired girl. I'd have thought she was a bit young – even for you.' Her mouth had turned down in distaste.

How quickly things change, thought Hogan.

'She's not my girlfriend in any way, shape or form. She's just a trainee helping me out with the story.'

Emma snorted in disbelief and got up from the table. 'She seems a bit confident for a trainee. She made sure she got in with her question at the presser before you did.'

'Nothing wrong with confidence,' said Hogan. 'It's not as though you're short of it yourself.'

Emma smiled unpleasantly at him.

Hogan got up too. 'So that's it, is it?'

She nodded. 'For now. Oh, there was one thing, though,' she added as an afterthought.

'What?'

'Your fingerprints. We'd better take them.'

'Why?'

'To rule you out, of course.'

'Eh? I'm not a suspect, am I?'

'No. Not at the moment.'

'Well, I don't think you have any right to take my fingerprints then, do you?'

'Suit yourself. Of course, if we arrest you, then we can take your prints without permission.'

The insolent smile was back on her face. Although this time it conveyed a sense of evil to Hogan. It sent a chill through him. There didn't seem to be any real choice, and Emma seemed to be enjoying his discomfort.

'OK, then,' he mumbled.

'Sorry?'

He spoke up louder.

'I said OK! You can have my frigging fingerprints. But I want you to do something for me.'

'Depends what it is.'

'Give me a clue who the dead woman is.'

'We told you at the presser yesterday. We can't say until she's been identified. And that hasn't happened yet.'

'But couldn't you tell me off the record?' Hogan could see the look of distaste on Emma's face. As though he was some sort of low-life. He wanted to wipe it off her.

She relented. 'All right. But it's strictly off the record. You haven't learned it from me, or from anyone here at Yarwater police. Got that?'

'Agreed.'

'The dead woman is Maria Forbes. Clara Forbes's sister.'

Hogan felt his jaw fall open in shock. He saw that Emma had noticed it. The cheeky smile was back. Hogan thought it seemed so strangely inappropriate when talking about a woman's death.

Clara thought the image would always stay with her. The mortuary assistant pulled the sheet back from her sister's face. It was grossly distorted, the nose completely squashed up towards the forehead, the chin shattered and pushed in, the lips puckered inwards because of the broken teeth. Like an old woman at night, with false teeth in a jar on the bedside table. Only here there was no bedside table, just a metal box in a freezer for a bed. And no blood. After seeing the dogs, Clara had expected blood. But the flesh was grey, strangely antiseptic. The injuries appeared to have been cleaned. There was no doubting that it was Maria, despite the facial contortions.

Clara just nodded at Emma, and the mortuary assistant laid the sheet back over Maria's face.

Oh God! Maria gone. The last line of flesh and blood. Now Clara was alone.

Alone except for Emma.

She turned to look at the policewoman. Emma seemed so different now. There had been a certain naivety when they had first met. Now it had been replaced by a cold, hard professionalism.

How much comfort would Emma be?

Clara had her doubts.

She had never felt so alone. In London, living by herself, there had always been friends, always been lovers. Now she was on her own. No one to cuddle at night. No warmth. And her dogs – they had gone too. Clara knew she had done wrong. So had Maria. And now it was as though someone were trying to punish them.

At home the workmen were just putting the finishing touches to the bell by the front gate. It would ring every time it was opened. Warning Clara when her solitude was about to be broken. She didn't want to be alone. But she didn't want anyone to interrupt her loneliness.

*   *   *

Now the bell at the front gate clanged.

Clara opened the bedroom curtains a crack. She felt herself break out in a cold sweat at what she saw. Emma was walking up the front garden path. That was nothing unusual. But behind her followed a number of uniformed police officers.

The doorbell rang. Clara didn't know what to do. Should she hide, pretend she wasn't there? But now someone was rapping hard at the door. She would have to confront them. There was no choice.

She felt her whole body shake as she opened the door. Emma was on the doorstep, with a piece of paper in her hand.

'Clara Forbes?'

The formal question made Clara realise that her worst fears were being realised.

She nodded.

'I have in my possession a warrant to search these premises for evidence in connection with the death of one Maria Forbes of this address. Do you understand?'

Clara nodded again. Why hadn't Emma warned her? She appeared so cold and professional now, as though she were an enemy. Clara had believed her to be a friend.

Emma listed the officers who would be involved in the search.

Clara went into the drawing room and Emma followed.

'You don't have to be here with me. you know,' said Emma. 'You can follow the officers and check what they're doing, if you wish.'

Clara dabbed at her cheek. It was moist. She realised for the first time she was crying. It was a strange feeling. The tears were forming almost without her realising it. As though her eyes were simply watering.

Emma put her arm round Clara's shoulder. Clara tried to shrug her off, but Emma was insistent and started to whisper to her in a soothing voice. 'Don't worry. This will be over soon. It's just a matter of routine. I will protect you. You know that. And you know why, don't you?'

Just then, there was a yell from the hall. 'Sarge – got something!'

The constable came into the drawing room. In his hands, which were protected by sterile gloves, was a red fleece. Clara's red fleece.

'Where did you find that?' she asked, puzzled. 'I lost it weeks ago.'

Clara saw the constable give Emma a questioning look, as though silently asking her permission to divulge the information. Emma nodded. The constable told Clara he'd discovered it in the space under the telephone cupboard seat.

'But I checked there just the other day,' said Clara. 'You must be mistaken.'

'No, madam. That's where I found it.'

The constable put the fleece into a sterile plastic bag.

Emma looked at Clara. 'We'll have to take it away for analysis,' she said. 'You realise that?'

'But I don't understand,' said Clara. 'How could it disappear and then re-appear. Unless. . .'

Her voice trailed off.

'Unless what?' asked Emma.

'Unless Maria was secretly wearing it, and put it back there after I checked.'

'It's possible, I suppose,' said Emma.

'So why do you need it?'

'We just want to check something. Don't worry. You'll get it back.' She shifted her gaze to the constable. 'Pete, can you give us a moment, please? Alone.'

Birkitt left the room and closed the door behind him.

'As I said before, don't worry. I'll look after you. If you're involved in any way in Maria's death . . .'

'What?' Clara half-shouted. 'You don't think I did it, surely? She was my own sister.'

'Calm down. Calm down.' Emma lowered her voice so that Birkitt and the others outside couldn't hear. 'I'm just hypothesising. If you were involved, I will make sure you get the best possible deal.'

'Listen,' said Clara. She was calmer now. But angry too. 'You were involved with Romana. An underage girl. Don't forget that. I certainly haven't.'

Emma flashed her an angry look. 'Don't try to threaten me,' she said. 'I'm only doing my job. There is no evidence against me in relation to Romana – it would just be your word against mine.'

'Yes, but the others saw . . .' Clara took a sharp breath and stopped herself. Realisation hit her like a hammer blow. They were all dead. The only other witnesses were all dead. The hold she had over Emma – now it was just, as Emma had said, her word against the word of a police officer. And a highly regarded police officer at that. Clara sank in her chair and held her head in her hands.

'I can see you understand now,' said Emma. Her voice was icy calm. 'But, as I say, I will do my best to protect you.'

She turned and left the room. Clara bit her tongue to try to stop herself crying.

Hogan took a mouthful of chicken and leek pie and washed it down with a swig of mineral water. He was off the beer again. Can't handle the hangovers, he thought to himself. He looked over at Scarlett on the opposite side of the table. She was stuffing scampi and chips into her mouth as though she hadn't eaten in weeks. How the hell does she stay so slim? he wondered.

They were in the Buddle Inn. Hogan had persuaded her to give him a lift home by bribing her with a pub meal – he couldn't stand the thought of trying to catch the bus in this weather. It was freezing. All that gumph about the southern coast of the island being like the Mediterranean seemed just plain bollocks today. On top of that he was knackered – emotionally and physically drained.

He yawned.

'Didn't your mother tell you to cover your mouth when you do that?' said Scarlett, smiling sweetly and chewing another mouthful of scampi.

'And didn't your mother tell you not to talk with your mouth full?'

'Ooh. Touché! So where do we go from here?'

'I guess we try to do what our mothers told us.'

'Oh, ha bloody ha. I meant with the murders.'

Hogan shrugged. 'I dunno. Being fingerprinted has spooked me a bit.'

'I think that the Thomas woman is just trying to warn you off.

She obviously doesn't like your meddling.'

'But it's got to be all linked, hasn't it? The connection to Clara Forbes is too strong. Her sister's death . . .'

'Or murder . . .'

'Or murder,' Hogan corrected himself, 'It has to be connected to the two cliff deaths.'

'Yes. That seems pretty obvious.' Scarlett sighed.

'Well,' said Hogan, 'surely everything points to Clara Forbes, doesn't it?'

'Agreed,' said Scarlett, this time through a mouthful of chips. Hogan chomped his own empty mouth, mocking her. Scarlett gave him a V sign. 'So what's your point?' she asked.

'We need to find something to pin on her. Something to place her where the murders were committed.'

'Isn't that the police's job?' asked Scarlett.

'Yes, but we're journalists. It doesn't stop us investigating too.'

'So where do we start?'

'Maybe tomorrow you could try to find out if she has a mobile phone.'

'Why?' asked Scarlett.

'Just a hunch,' said Hogan. He dropped his eyes back to his plate, and took a mouthful of the pie. He wiped his lips. It was delicious.

'Swap a bit of scampi for a mouthful of pie?' he asked her.

'OK.'

Hogan speared a piece of the pie with his fork and held it out to her. She swallowed it in one, and then licked her tongue around the inside of her open lips, suggestively.

Hogan blushed.

'So where's my scampi?' he asked.

'Here. You can have the rest.'

She pushed the basket over to his side of the table. He looked inside. It was empty.

He pulled a face at her.

She blew him a kiss.

*   *   *

Before he could catch the bus the next morning, Hogan received a call from Dudfield on his mobile. The police sergeant wanted to pop round to discuss how inquiries were going into Hogan's incident with his car. 'I've got something else which may be of interest, too,' he told Hogan mysteriously. He wouldn't say anything more over the phone.

Hogan braced himself for a call to Howze. His editor had become grumpier and grumpier, and Hogan wasn't sure why. He finally dialled the *Star*'s number.

'Sorry, Dickey. I'm going to be late again. The police want to talk to me again about my car.'

Howze, to his surprise, was full of bonhomie. 'Don't worry about it, Benjamin, old mate. You take as long as you want. It's important you get it sorted out.'

'You're full of the joys of spring this morning, aren't you? And it's the middle of winter. What's brought this on?'

'It's that assistant of yours, Scarlett. Good, isn't she? Her father was very pleased with the joint by-line she had with you yesterday. Excellent stuff.'

Hogan groaned to himself. A bigwig on the island was happy with him, so it had made Howze's day. How pathetic could you get?

He headed back to the chalet to wait for Dudfield.

Dudfield came on his own this time.

'Where's your number two?'

'Who? Pete Birkitt?'

Hogan nodded.

'Working with Acting DS Thomas full-time now,' Dudfield explained. 'Full of his own self-importance, too, the tosser. He acts like her little puppy.'

Hogan laughed.

'A bit like you used to,' added Dudfield, bitterly.

Hogan gave him a snarl. 'So what brings you round? Here to take the piss out of me again?'

'No, just thought I'd bring you up to date with the car. We went round to see Kavanagh.'

'And?'

Dudfield shrugged. 'He's a horrible little git. But I've got a hunch it wasn't him. He claimed he'd forgotten all about your little spat.'

'And you believed him?'

Dudfield straightened his body and looked Hogan in the eye. 'Kavanagh is a greasy little pervert. Nasty piece of work. Wouldn't trust him round any kids of mine. But he's also a coward. He was scared stiff when we went round. He's had one recent brush with the law. There's no way he'd take the risk of having another so soon.'

'But that's not proof he wasn't involved.'

'No, but he's got a pretty good alibi. And it seems to check out.'

Hogan leant forward. 'Alibi? What kind of alibi?'

'Well, he's a bit of a techie. That much you know. He's always playing round with computers and stuff.'

Hogan was puzzled. 'Yeah. So what?'

'Well, he's also a bit of a sound and lighting expert. The reason he was at the concert was to help with the sound system. He often helps out at the Winter Gardens for a few quid.'

'But surely the band have their own sound people?'

'Yeah. But Kavanagh was assisting them with the peculiarities of the venue's electrics. He was up on the mixing desk all the time. Right from the sound check onwards.'

Dudfield sat back on Hogan's favourite chair, which he'd managed to steal again, looking pleased with himself.

Hogan still didn't get it. 'But when I saw him he was at the front. Cheering with all the other fans.'

'Yup. He was enjoying himself so much he moved up to the front for the last song and the encores. That's what he says and it's what the band's sound people say, too.'

Hogan wasn't sure whether to be relieved or not. He paced up and down the chalet and fiddled with his hair.

'OK, so Kavanagh didn't do it. But *someone* did.'

'Yup. 'Fraid so,' said Dudfield.

Shit! Hogan felt worse now.

At least when Kavanagh was in the frame he'd had someone to look out for, a face to pin everything on.

But now there was an unknown still out there, trying to get him. And he hadn't a clue who it could be.

He sat down, slumping disconsolately opposite Dudfield.

'There *was* something else,' Dudfield said.

'What?' asked Hogan, disinterested.

'Lee Hughes.'

'Is he still a suspect? So much has happened since he was released on police bail.'

'Never *was* a bleeding suspect, in my book. Never should have been pulled in. But yes – officially he's still on police bail. He hasn't been told we won't be proceeding against him.'

'So what's new, then?' asked Hogan. He was more interested now, his fears put to one side for a few moments.

'I did a bit of digging with Lee's family,' said Dudfield.

'And?'

'Turns out the farmer who identified him as being involved in a fight on the cliff has a grudge against him.'

Hogan's eyes widened.

'Michael Alexander?' he said.

'Yeah. That's him. Well, a few years ago, Lee's dog worried some of his cows. Lee used to let her off the leash at the top of the cliff path, and she got into the cowfield. Only problem was one of the cows was pregnant.'

'Oh God,' said Hogan.

'Gave birth early. The calf died. So did the cow. And it was a prize one. Alexander had paid a tidy sum to have it artificially inseminated by an equally prize bull. Worse than that, he'd already got a buyer lined up for the calf.'

'So he's not a fan of Lee Hughes?'

'Nope. He filed an application to get Lee's dog put down, but it failed. It was ruled that he hadn't secured the fence to the field properly, so no action was taken.'

Hogan was perplexed. If the police knew all this, why hadn't they revisited Alexander and quizzed him further about his statement? To Hogan the man sounded like a tainted witness.

'I know what you're thinking,' Dudfield said. 'Why haven't I been round to see Alexander? Well, I can't do that, can I? I'm off the case. Officially. If Hale ever found out I'd done that my career would be over.'

'So what do we do about it?' asked Hogan.

'Well, there's nothing to stop *you* going to see him. When he knows you've got all that background info on him, it might shake him up a bit.'

Dudfield was right, thought Hogan. And it might help take his mind off whoever was out to get him.

Constable Pete Birkitt rushed into Emma Thomas's office.

'Sarge! Sarge!' he said. 'The Forensic Science Services report's come through.'

'You haven't been peeking at it before me, have you, Pete?' Thomas asked.

Birkitt looked like a schoolboy caught cheating in a test. 'Well, I just had a little look at the conclusion,' he admitted.

'And?' asked Thomas.

'Read it for yourself. I don't want to spoil it for you.'

Thomas could tell from Birkitt's excited expression that it must contain something pretty important. She started to read the report.

The first part concentrated on fibres found on the clothing of the two girls involved in the cliff falls, the fibres found on Maria Forbes's clothing, and the fibres collected from the fencing around the airshaft at the bottom of which Maria had been found dead. Fibres from all four places had been viewed under a comparison microscope to check for a match with control fibres from Clara Forbes's red fleece.

'OK,' said Thomas, pointing out the passage to Birkitt. 'At a very basic level, this says there was a match for colour and diameter.'

Thomas read on. The cross-sectional shape of the fibres, too, matched under the microscope. The forensic scientists had also performed a more sophisticated comparison with an infrared spectrophotometer. The infrared spectrum of the fibres – their chemical composition – matched as well.

'Wow!' exclaimed Thomas. 'I was expecting to get a result, but not one this good. So what's the conclusion say?' she asked Birkitt.

The constable bent over her desk and turned a couple of pages. 'There,' he said. 'Read it for yourself.'

The chief scientist's conclusion was that, given the exact match of the fibres found at the scene of the various incidents, the chance that they did not come from the same source was close to one in a billion.

'Bingo!' cried Thomas, and punched the air in delight.

'So what do we do now?' asked Birkitt. 'Pull her in?'

'Yup.'

'But she was adamant that she'd lost the top.'

'Oh, come on, Pete. A jury isn't going to believe that. However, there might be a way to fudge things so we don't have to go to trial.'

'How do you mean?'

'We do some sort of deal.'

Thomas saw the corners of Birkitt's mouth turn down. He didn't look too happy with the idea.

'But surely this is pretty much copper-bottomed evidence, isn't it?'

'Yes – but what of?'

'That Clara Forbes's fleece was at the scene of all three incidents.'

'Not necessarily,' said Thomas.

Birkitt scratched his head and frowned. 'Sorry, I'm not with you, Sarge.'

'You're forgetting: all three women involved all lived at Forbes's house. What's to have stopped their clothing becoming contaminated with fibres from her fleece within the house itself? Before they even got to the scene of the crime, as it were. It could have happened in a wardrobe, a drawer, anywhere. A good defence team would rip the case to shreds.'

Birkitt's face dropped at the same time as the penny. 'But that still leaves the fibres around the fencing at the airshaft. Surely there were too many of those to have come from Maria's clothing if it had simply been contaminated before she put it on?'

'Exactly,' said Thomas. 'You're catching on fast. We'll make a detective of you yet.' She smiled at him.

'So someone wearing Clara Forbes's red fleece must have been at the top of the airshaft when Maria fell?'

'Or was pushed, as seems more likely.'

'So how do we sort this one out?' Birkitt asked.

Thomas tapped her pen on the table, then flicked away a paperclip with it.

'Don't worry about that. I've got it all carefully mapped out. You'll see. But the key to it was finding the fleece. Well done. You've done a good job.'

Thomas saw Birkitt smile at her. It was almost an adoring smile. The sort a young schoolgirl might give to a senior she had a crush on. But this was a washed-up constable grinning at a detective sergeant half his age.

What a pathetic creep, she thought. Makes me feel quite sick.

'Isn't this what you wanted?' said Scarlett.

She handed Hogan the mobile-phone details he'd asked for – not just for Clara Forbes but for Maria as well. The list showed their numbers and details of the company they subscribed to.

Hogan smiled at her. 'Good work. How did you get these?'

'Let's just say that my dad, for all his sins, is pretty well connected on the island. But I've never heard of this company here, Island Telecom.'

Hogan had. It was a small mobile-phone offshoot of the island's cable-television company, linked to a larger, UK-wide group.

He scratched his head and then rested his chin in his hands, his arms propped on the office desk.

'This is the start. The problem now is how we get the detailed information we need.'

'What sort of detail?' asked Scarlett, her brow knitting in concentration.

Hogan explained how the information concerning the base station used by a mobile-phone call is retained at the beginning and end of the call, whether it was outbound or inbound. Because of the Isle of Wight's topography – its hills and coves, and its sheltered areas, like the Undercliff – the island had a higher concentration of mobile-phone masts than many other areas of the country. Even then, for some companies, there were 'shadow' areas where reception was poor or nonexistent.

'So how does that help us?' asked Scarlett.

'Well, we're in luck that both their phones are contracted to Island Telecom. That's its *raison d'être* – it promises the best coverage on the island,' explained Hogan.

'And therefore has the most masts?'

Hogan nodded.

'So,' continued Scarlett, 'if we can find out the details of the calls they made, we can find out where they were when they made them?'

Hogan nodded again. 'We'll know the location of the base station. For some companies, that wouldn't tell us an awful lot because they don't have that many masts on the island.'

'But you're saying it's different for Island Telecom?'

'Yup. The location information should be pretty precise, both for the caller and the recipient of the call – assuming the call was made from one spot on the island to another, and not to somewhere on the mainland.'

Scarlett beamed at him. 'That's brilliant.' Then her face clouded. 'But would they give the information to us?'

Hogan shook his head. 'No. That's the problem. Just police officers, the intelligence services, customs and excise, and tax inspectors. That's it.'

Scarlett tutted and raised her eyebrows. 'So after all that we're no further forward?'

He shrugged and smiled. 'There are ways and means. I'm sure we can think of something. I'm not saying – even if we got the info – that it's completely infallible, or absolutely precise. Sometimes, if there's congestion, calls aren't routed through the absolute nearest cell.'

Scarlett's eyes lit up suddenly. 'Wait a minute! Couldn't I pretend to be Clara Forbes and get the information that way?'

'Maybe. We'd have to have a lot of personal information about her – date of birth . . .'

'That's easy enough to get,' said Scarlett.

'Mother's maiden name . . .'

181

'That too.'

'And maybe even her secret PIN number,' said Hogan.

'Ah – that would be more difficult.'

'And, even if we got all that info, we would then have to persuade Island Telecom to hand over the location details we want.'

'What about the Data Protection Act?' asked Scarlett.

Hogan turned down the corners of his mouth. 'Theoretically, yes. But in practice firms usually worm their way out of giving information, citing commercial sensitivity as an excuse.'

'So it's easier for, say, the police to get details about your mobile phone use than it is for you yourself?'

'Exactly,' said Hogan.

They lapsed into silence.

'What about your friend at the nick?' said Scarlett after a while.

'Who? Emma Thomas? She's hardly a friend any more. She just glares at me all the time.'

'No, not *her*, stupid!' He saw Scarlett tip her nose at him as though he were an imbecile. 'The other one, the one who's been helping you with your car. What's his name? Duffield or something.'

'Dudfield.' He pointed his finger at her. 'Dudfield. Exactly. You're brilliant.'

Scarlett flushed with pride.

Yes, Dudfield was possibly the answer. Dudfield wanted to show that Lee Hughes was not involved. Pinpointing Clara and Maria Forbes's movements might just do that.

And, as someone who'd been working recently in CID, Dudfield might know a way of getting the necessary information out of the telephone company.

13

Hogan had the Peugeot back and repaired – so for now the chauffeur service from Scarlett was at an end. Sutcliffe had sent her off on another job today, but Hogan hoped their partnership wasn't completely over. He'd been half-hoping the Peugeot would have been written off – it might have been enough to persuade the Beast or Howze to invest in a company car for him.

He winced as the car jolted on the rutted farm track, and rubbed his head and neck. The pain from the accident in Ventnor still hadn't gone away completely.

The farm looked a mess. An abandoned tractor lay rusting by the side of the track. Over in the distance, next to a barn, a muck-spreader was parked with manure still caked to its rear end. Near it Hogan noticed a rather battered old green four-by-four.

As he got out of the Peugeot a vicious-looking Alsatian barked at him repeatedly and then lunged towards him. He jumped out of the way, only to see that the dog was chained and had already stretched its chain to the limit.

Michael Alexander opened the farmhouse door. The dog must have announced my presence, thought Hogan.

Alexander held out his hand for Hogan to shake. Hogan took it. It was moist, and seemed to be trembling slightly. Then Hogan noticed the half-drunk whisky bottle on the kitchen table, and as Alexander began speaking he smelled the alcohol on the man's breath.

'I don't have a lot of time,' said Alexander. 'I've got an animal-feed rep coming round. So can we make this quick?'

Hogan looked him in the eye. Alexander met his gaze just for a second, then looked down at his own shaking hands.

'That rather depends on you,' said Hogan. 'What I want is the truth. If I get it I'm sure we won't take too long.'

Alexander showed him through to the sitting room, where a log fire was blazing away. Hogan stood with his back to it and rubbed his hands together.

'I can't ever seem to get this house warm,' said Alexander apologetically. 'Never really wanted to go into farming. Just fell into it when my dad died.'

Hogan found it difficult to listen to the man. Alexander's voice whined, full of self-pity.

Hogan waited. Silent.

'Aren't you supposed to ask me questions?' Alexander said. 'What was it exactly you wanted to talk to me about? You're the reporter on the cliff murders, aren't you?'

Still Hogan said nothing. But the man seemed so afraid of the silence it was as though he had to fill it. 'Come on! Come on! I haven't got all day. I suppose it's something about Lee Hughes, is it? Everyone round here seems to think he's innocent.'

Hogan got his notebook and pen out of his pocket, and tapped the end of the pen on the notebook's cover.

'Stop doing that,' Alexander spat.

There was another half-drunk whisky bottle here in the lounge. Alexander poured himself a shot, then downed it in one. Hogan noticed the bottle was a cheap blend, the sort winos might favour.

'Bit early in the day for that, isn't it?' Hogan finally asked.

'What's it to you?'

Hogan didn't reply.

'Look, I can't stand this silent treatment,' Alexander shouted. 'Do you want to talk about the statement I gave to the police or what?'

Hogan sighed. 'I've already told you what I want. The truth. Simple. You tell me the truth. I go and leave you alone to drown your sorrows in your cheap, shitty whisky.'

'The truth about what?'

'You know very well, Mr Alexander. The truth about what you saw on the cliff edge the day the first girl fell.'

Alexander sagged into an old brown leather armchair. He looked up at Hogan by the fire; his eyes had a pleading look to them.

'I did tell the truth. But it wasn't the whole story. It wasn't my fault, though.' He held Hogan's gaze now. 'You've got to believe me. The detective didn't seem to want to hear any more. She was like a dog with a bone as soon as I mentioned Lee Hughes.'

'And did you tell her about your previous problems with Lee, about his dog and your precious cow?'

Alexander slammed his whisky glass down on the table. 'You don't fucking understand do you? How hard it's been for me to make this farm pay its way. I can't sell it because it's so near the cliff and all the erosion. No one would take the risk. And all the time I'm having to pay out for new fencing as the land collapses bit by bit.'

Hogan sighed. 'Look, Mr Alexander, I'm sure you do have problems. Everyone does. But not everyone deals with them by lying and letting an innocent, vulnerable man risk jail.'

'I didn't lie,' Alexander repeated.

Hogan marched the few paces across the room, and jabbed his finger into Alexander's chest. 'You make me bloody sick,' he boomed. 'Lee Hughes couldn't defend himself, so you set him up, didn't you? Set him up for a fall. It suited you and it suited the police.'

Alexander's face fell. He backed even further into the chair and clutched his arms to his chest. 'I did tell the truth,' he repeated quietly. 'But not *all* the truth. After the argument I saw Lee grab something from the woman and then turn and leave with his dog, heading back to Reeth.'

'And the woman?'

'She continued to sit there. She couldn't have been the one who fell. She was older.'

'Yet in your statement you talked about a female. You couldn't be specific about her age, you said.'

Alexander just grunted.

'Well?' said Hogan.

'OK, that bit wasn't quite true. But, again, it seemed to be what the detective wanted. She typed up the statement. I just signed it. I was close enough to see that the woman on the cliff was an adult. Probably young-middle-age – your sort of age, maybe a bit younger.'

Hogan didn't particularly appreciate being thought of as middle-aged. 'So what happened next? Did you keep watching?'

'Sort of. Not all the time. I was mending a fence. Just glanced over now and then at her.'

185

'And what did she do?'

'Just waited there for about twenty minutes or so. Then another woman arrived, put her arms round her, and led her away.'

'Where to?'

'Near the radio mast. There was a car parked there.'

'Could you identify it?'

'Nah. Didn't get a close enough look. It was partly obscured by the wall of the lane.'

Hogan put the top back on his pen and placed it inside his jacket pocket.

Alexander looked at him quizzically. 'That's it, then, is it?'

'As far as I'm concerned, yes, Mr Alexander. But I'm just a journalist.'

'You won't be putting all that in the paper, though, will you?'

'Of course I will. That's the whole point, isn't it?'

Hogan turned and let himself out of the house.

After the reporter had gone, Alexander poured himself another whisky and drank it. Then, his hands still shaking, he picked up the phone and dialled a Yarwater number.

The bell clanged again, and Clara peeked out from behind the curtains. It was only 6pm, but already completely dark outside – except for the blue flashing lights of the police cars cutting through the night sky. Clara saw Emma again, followed by another, older woman. The two policewomen trooped up the garden path with a number of uniformed officers in tow.

Even before the front bell rang, Clara was halfway down the stairs on her way to open the door. She had been expecting this moment for a number of days, ever since the fleece had been taken away for analysis. For all Emma's protestations that she would look after her, Clara had her doubts.

As the bell rang she stopped at the mirror in the hall and adjusted her hair and smart green tweed suit. They could try to demean her, try to cut her down, but she still had her standards.

She opened the door. Emma was there. They stood face-to-face.

They both knew such a lot about each other. How much of that was now going to come out into the public domain? The game was nearly up.

'You know why we're here,' said Emma gently. It was a statement rather than a question.

Clara nodded. She didn't trust herself to speak. She didn't want to lose control.

Then Emma was talking again, this time in clipped, professional tones. Just two words. 'Clara Forbes.'

Two of the uniformed officers moved forward to grab Clara's arms. She didn't resist. Emma went through the formal procedure, telling her she was being arrested for the murder of her sister, Maria. That was all at the moment, which surprised Clara slightly. There was no mention of Francesca or Romana.

Emma continued, 'You do not have to say anything. But it may harm your defence if you do not mention, when questioned, something which you later rely on in court. Anything you do say may be given in evidence.'

The two uniformed officers now placed handcuffs on her. Clara gave Emma a vicious look. Why the handcuffs? There was no need. It was almost one indignity too far.

'Is there anything you want to say?' asked Emma.

'Yes,' said Clara. She was surprised by the firmness and clarity of her own voice. 'I didn't do it. And what's more' – Clara jabbed her handcuffed arms at Emma – 'you know perfectly well that I didn't.'

Emma appeared unruffled. But Clara noticed the other woman detective looked perplexed.

'You'll get your chance to say what you want . . . down at the station,' said Emma icily.

Clara felt the two uniformed policemen tug at her elbows, eager to guide her away down the garden path, towards the waiting police car for the journey to Yarwater police station.

'OK, I'm turning the tape on,' said Emma. 'In the room as well as myself, Acting Detective Sergeant Emma Thomas, there is Detective

187

Chief Inspector Jane Hale, Police Constable Peter Birkitt, and the suspect, Clara Forbes. Clara, I understand you do not want legal representation at this stage?'

'That's right,' said Clara. She tried to meet Emma's gaze, but the detective avoided looking directly at her.

DCI Jane Hale spoke out. 'We would strongly advise that you do have representation, Ms Forbes. We can easily get the duty solicitor.'

Clara shook her head.

'For the tape, the suspect shook her head,' said Emma.

Just then there was a knock on the door.

'Come in,' said Hale.

A uniformed constable stuck his head round the door. 'Guv, there's the press on the phone. Seems like they've got wind of the arrest.'

Hale sighed and got to her feet. 'I'd better go and deal with it, Emma. You and Pete carry on. I'll come back later.'

Hale followed the constable out of the room.

'For the tape, DCI Hale has now left the room,' said Emma into the microphone.

Clara saw Emma breathe in deeply, as though gathering her thoughts. The policewoman looked at her watch and then leaned towards the tape machine again. 'Interview suspended at six forty-seven p.m.'

Emma sighed and looked across at Birkitt. Clara recognised him as the officer who had found the red fleece.

'Pete, could you leave us alone a few moments? There's something I need to discuss with Ms Forbes, off the record. And keep a watch outside for Hale coming back.'

Birkitt looked slightly dubious about the propriety of this, but reluctantly nodded and got up to leave the room.

As soon as the door shut behind him, Emma reached across to stroke Clara's hand. Clara looked down. Emma's hand was so delicate, so perfectly formed. Half of her wanted to pull her own hand out from under it; the other half of her wanted to bring the hand to her lips and kiss it gently. Clara glanced up into Emma's eyes. They were such a pretty shade of blue – captivating, she'd always thought. How could Clara not trust her?

'There's something I want to show you. It's strictly against procedure, but I promised I would help you, and I want to keep that promise,' said Emma.

She bent down, removed a file from her briefcase and then came round to Clara's side of the desk. She put the file down on the desktop and opened it towards the end.

'Read that page,' she ordered. 'Just the conclusion. It tells you all you need to know.'

Clara read, with mounting dread. The fibres from her fleece. Found. At four locations connected with the series of deaths. Only a chance of one in a billion that they had not come from her clothing.

Emma sat down opposite her again. 'You understand what this means, don't you?'

Clara began to cry.

Emma reached out across the desk and touched her hand again. 'Don't cry. Please don't. We can sort this out. So that we both come out of this as well as possible.'

'What if I tell them about you?'

Emma shrugged. 'You can if you wish. It would be your word against mine, remember. I've told you that before. You have no evidence at all that I had sex with Romana. Would they believe your word, someone charged with murder, over that of a highly regarded police officer? And' – Emma tapped the forensic file – 'don't forget that I have the evidence. It's here in black and white.'

Clara realised she was trapped. 'So what can I do?' she said in a quiet voice.

'We do a deal. We've done deals before, remember?' Emma gave a cruel laugh.

Clara shuddered.

'First you get a brief – a lawyer. You tell him to insist on psychiatric reports. You admit that you pushed Maria, but only in anger. You started fighting at the top of the railway airshaft after she admitted killing Romana and Francesca.'

Clara gasped. 'But we don't *know* who killed them, do we?'

'But Maria admitted it to you, didn't she? She was wearing your fleece each time to try to frame you. She admitted that to you at the top of the railway shaft. She was laughing at you. You lost your temper. It's understandable. Any jury would sympathise.'

Clara's eyes widened. She found Emma's scheming hard to take in. But it had a ring of plausibility to it. It was feasible. Not only that, she could see how it could lead to a lighter sentence, possibly no sentence at all, and no disgrace.

But still she was puzzled.

'OK. That makes some sense. But what was Maria's motive for killing the girls?'

'She liked having sex with adolescent girls. That was another reason for you getting into a fight with her. You were disgusted by her actions. Just think how a judge or jury would react.'

'How?' asked Clara.

'They would sympathise with you. Who wouldn't, with a pervert like that for a sister?'

Emma started rocking with silent laughter now. Clara had to admit the plan was brilliant. It meant heaping shame on Maria's memory, but her sister was dead. Maria couldn't complain. And, anyway, Clara still suspected Maria had killed the dogs. Perhaps she deserved some opprobrium in death.

Clara sat upright, alert. 'But maybe that's what really happened? All except the bit about me killing Maria, of course. The rest could be true, couldn't it? It fits in with Lee Hughes seeing the woman by the cliff. That could have been Maria. After she had pushed Francesca over the edge.'

Emma giggled. 'That's my girl. You see, you're believing it yourself now.'

'But what about you? Surely for your career it would be better to nail someone for murder.'

Emma frowned. 'Maybe you're right.' She stroked Clara's hand again. 'But I couldn't do it to you, could I? I said I would look after you. You can show me your gratitude once this is all over.'

Emma met Clara's gaze and, with a lascivious smile, licked her lips.

There was a knock on the door. Birkitt.

'Hale just went past. Says she'll be back with us in a couple of minutes.' He sat down at the table. 'Everything go OK?'

'Yup,' said Emma. 'Everything is just hunky dory.'

She turned the tape machine back on and spoke into it. 'Interview resumed at 7.14pm with Ms Forbes, DS Thomas and PC Birkitt present. Now, Ms Forbes, I understand you would like to speak to the duty lawyer after all?'

Clara spoke up confidently. It was all going to be all right. Everything was going to be all right. 'Yes, please. I would.'

Ed Sutcliffe placed a letter on Hogan's desk.

'This came for you this morning, mate.'

Hogan held the envelope up to the light and examined the postmark closely. It was stamped 'Portsmouth and Isle of Wight'. Which told him very little. Every item sent through the island's mail got this all-embracing postmark. But, equally, the letter could have been posted on the mainland.

He slit open the envelope with his finger.

Then he shrieked in pain and surprise and dropped it.

'What's wrong?' cried Scarlett.

Hogan looked down at his finger. Blood poured from a clean, deep wound. The end of the finger was almost hanging off. He could see the bone.

'Yuk! Nasty,' said Scarlett. 'You'd better get down to Casualty.' She got out a clean handkerchief and wrapped it round the wound, then made Hogan hold his hand up above his heart to slow the flow of blood. With her scarf she made a makeshift sling.

Ed Sutcliffe rushed over.

'Can you drive him down to the hospital, Scarlett? I'll take a closer look at the letter.'

He picked a disposable knife up off the desk and, holding the envelope gingerly, continued to slit it open. He carefully tipped the contents out onto the desk as Hogan watched, his face screwed up in pain.

There was a razor blade, tipped with Hogan's blood. And the blade was attached to a plain white postcard that someone had stuck some letters on. They'd been cut out of newspaper headlines to form words. Hogan, shivering from the shock, read them aloud:

You're not wanted on this island. Why don't you go back to the mainland to your wife and children? They may need you to protect them.

The words sent a chill through him. 'What sort of sick fucker's sent this?'

Ed put his hand on Hogan's shoulder. Hogan winced – just the touch jarred his injured finger.

'It's probably nothing,' said Ed. 'Someone sees your by-line on the paper. They get jealous. There are a lot of sickos around.'

Scarlett ushered Hogan towards the office door. He stopped and turned back to Ed. 'If Scarlett and I both go down to Casualty, who's going to go to the presser? It's in less than an hour. There's no way we'll get back in time.'

'Shit,' said Ed. He reached inside his pockets and got his car keys out. 'I'll take you to the hospital. Scarlett, you'd better go to the presser. Think you can handle it?'

Scarlett smiled. 'Sure. Is that OK with you, Hogan?'

Hogan put his hand out to pat her back in congratulation. Then wished he hadn't as the pain pulsed down his arm. He recoiled, and touched his finger through the handkerchief gently.

'Youch! Sure it's OK.' He smiled at her. 'Give them hell from me.'

Scarlett sat in the front row of the press conference. There were fewer people here than last time – the nub of the story had already got out. One sister had pushed the other to her death while the balance of her mind was disturbed. It wasn't as exciting as a mysterious death.

Hale and Thomas were again the police representatives on the platform, together with the press officer.

After waiting for a few stragglers to enter the room, the press officer got to his feet.

'Morning, everybody. Thanks for coming. Same format as last time. DCI Hale will read a short statement and then she and DS Thomas will be available for questions.'

Scarlett was puzzled. She looked at Thomas, who avoided her gaze. Last time Thomas had been Acting Detective Sergeant. Had her title changed? Or was the press officer just not bothering with the 'Acting' bit?

Hale stood up to speak. 'As many of you already know, a woman was arrested last night in connection with the death of Maria Forbes. We can now confirm that the woman is her sister, Clara Forbes. She is co-operating fully with our inquiries. We are expecting to charge her this afternoon. As a result of information gleaned from these inquiries, we have also managed to clear up the cases involving the two girls who fell from the cliffs at Reeth. As you know, one died immediately and the other was seriously injured and died later in hospital.'

Hale paused, took a sip of water from the glass on the desk, and continued. 'Thanks to what Clara Forbes has told us, and corroborating forensic and witness evidence, we are satisfied that Maria Forbes was responsible for the death and injury sustained by the two girls.'

There was a collective gasp from the gathered reporters, including Scarlett. This was the sting in the tail. It was general knowledge that Clara Forbes had been arrested in connection with Maria's death, but the rest was new. The reporters from regional TV who had stayed away out of lack of interest had missed a trick, thought Scarlett.

Hale waited for the hubbub amongst the audience to die down, and then resumed. 'The inquiry is therefore closed, and we are looking for no one else.' She turned to Thomas now. 'I'd like to thank DS Thomas and her team for some excellent work.' Thomas smiled shyly. 'OK. So we'd be happy to answer your questions as far as the legal process allows,' Hale concluded.

Scarlett raised her arm immediately. She saw Thomas grimace, but Hale picked her out. 'Yes. You in the front row. Sorry, I recognise you but I don't know your name.'

'Scarlett Reynolds. *Wight Evening Star*. You say you expect to charge Clara Forbes. What exactly with? Murder?'

'We expect the charge to be manslaughter, on the grounds of

diminished responsibility,' said Hale.

'Why not murder?' asked Scarlett.

Hale and Thomas looked at each other. Thomas shrugged, as though leaving the decision to answer the question up to Hale.

'Clara Forbes had just been told some very disturbing things by her sister,' Hale replied.

'What, exactly?' asked Scarlett.

'Maria Forbes had admitted pushing the two girls off the cliffs. While wearing some of Clara's clothing to try to frame her.'

There was another gasp from the reporters, but it was still Scarlett asking all the questions.

'Forgive me, Chief Inspector. I still don't fully understand. What was Maria's motive?'

Hale and Thomas whispered to each other. Thomas shook her head. 'We don't want to go into that at the moment. Right, if there are no more questions . . .'

'Just one more,' said Scarlett. She saw both Hale and Thomas frown. She knew she was getting under their skin. 'Has DS Thomas been promoted? I noticed she wasn't introduced as *Acting* DS Thomas this time.'

Thomas stared at her furiously, but Hale remained calm. 'Not promoted, no. But I have confirmed her position as a Detective Sergeant in Yarwater CID as a result of her good work on this case. I'm glad you've mentioned it.'

Hale paused to take another sip of water, before continuing again. 'This means our force's Criminal Investigation Department is one of the few in the country which has now met its diversity targets for this year in terms of the number of women officers we have, and the positions they hold.'

Scarlett almost felt like puking as she saw Hale and Thomas smile simperingly at each other. All very cosy and neatly it had worked out. A bit too cosy for Scarlett's liking.

The wait in the Casualty department of Yarwater General was about two hours. Hogan wasn't going to die, said the duty nurse, so he could take his turn with everyone else.

Ed went back to the office, telling Hogan to ring him as soon as he was finished and he'd try to pick him up or arrange a cab.

So Hogan was left to wait and fret on his own. He was a bit hacked off, too, that Scarlett was ending up with the best job of the day – the presser at Yarwater nick on the Maria Forbes case.

The letter he'd received worried him. Personal threats to himself he could just about deal with. It was scary, but at least it was just him involved. But now there had been the hints about Lynn and the kids.

He leant down to get his mobile phone out of his bag. He winced from the pain of the finger – it was OK when he kept it still, but as soon as he moved it throbbed like hell.

He tried to press the mobile's buttons with his left hand. It took him ages. The first time he got it wrong and some old lady answered the phone. Finally he got through to Lynn.

'How goes it?' he asked.

'OK. The kids are quite excited with their school Christmas parties and everything. I can't say I'm looking forward to spending Christmas on my own.'

Hogan thought how comforting it was to hear her voice. Despite their rows, despite her affair, he'd missed her.

'Why don't you come over here? Bring the kids?'

He said it on the spur of the moment. The words were out of his mouth before he really thought about the consequences, and whether – given the threats he'd received – it was safer for the family back in Twickenham or on the island.

'Where would we stay? Tamara tells me there's not enough room at the chalet.'

'She's right. But there's loads of holiday accommodation here that only gets booked up in the summer. I'm sure there'd be some nice places at good prices.'

The line was silent for a moment as Lynn mulled over his proposal.

'Look,' she said finally. 'I'm not saying no. But I'd better talk it through with the kids and have a bit of a think myself. I'll ring you on the mobile tonight and let you know. OK?'

'OK. If I've got a spare half-hour I'll have a look through the property paper and see what there is to rent.'

'And Iain?'

'What?'

He heard Lynn begin to cry. 'I'm sorry. About Grant and everything. It was stupid, and selfish.'

'Oh, God, don't cry. Look, I was becoming a pain to live with, I know. I was unhappy in that job. The redundancy was a blessing in disguise, really. It can't have made things easy for you, though.'

He squeezed his legs under his chair as a child with a broken leg hobbled by on crutches.

'That's sweet of you,' said Lynn. 'But I still feel a heel.'

'Is everything else all right? No problems with the kids or anything?'

Hogan tried to make that last question sound as innocuous as he could. It was the real reason for the phone call, to try to find out if any threats had been made directly against the family. But he didn't want to frighten Lynn unnecessarily.

'They're fine. Why do you ask?'

'I'm their father. I guess I worry more when I don't see them. I hope we can all see each other more often.'

'OK, let's try,' said Lynn. 'I'll ring you tonight.'

They said their goodbyes. Tender but guarded. Hogan didn't want to be hurt again, but he knew there was still some hope that things could be repaired. If he could get Lynn over for the Christmas break, and everything went well, then maybe, just maybe, he could convince her that the island was where they should base the family home. All of them together.

He had one more call to make. Again he had to punch out the number left-handed. He was halfway through doing it when the person sitting next to him nudged his arm.

'Ouch. What the hell are you doing? Look!'

The finger started throbbing madly again. He brandished it at the old man who'd poked him.

'Sorry, mate.' The man looked sheepish. 'I was just going to point out the notice to you, before that dragon of a nurse comes round to give you an earful.'

'What notice?' asked Hogan.

The elderly patient pointed to the far wall. There was a large red ring with a black mobile phone in it. And a red diagonal line going through it.

Hogan grunted.

'Well, I'm ringing the police. So if the nurse wants to complain she can talk to them.'

This seemed to shut the man up, and he sulkily turned his head back to his newspaper.

Hogan started laboriously to tap out Dudfield's number with his good hand again, with the phone wedged between his legs.

Dudfield answered after a long wait. 'Oh, it's you,' he said. 'Thought you'd be down the presser. They did tell you about it, didn't they?'

'Yes. But I'm otherwise indisposed. Look, I need a favour.'

Dudfield sighed wearily at the other end of the line. 'Go on.'

Hogan asked him to hang on a moment. He asked the old man next to him to save his place, then moved off to find a quiet corner. He explained his idea to Dudfield of trying to trace Maria and Clara Forbes's movements through their mobile-phone company.

'Of course,' he added, 'there might not be a lot of point to it now. With Clara Forbes having been arrested.'

'I wouldn't trust anything hatched up by that Thomas woman,' said Dudfield grumpily. 'Word at the nick is that the Maria creature made some cock and bull confession to the other murders before her sister pushed her down the hole. All sounds a bit too smooth to me.'

'What are you trying to say?'

'Nothing, I suppose. Maybe I'm just jealous that she's sorted it out. But your idea sounds a good one. It's worth a try. Although if it ever gets back to Hale I'm for the high jump.'

Hogan gave him all the details of the phone numbers, and then told Dudfield to make sure he bought a copy of that day's *Star*, as there was something in it to interest him.

'What's that, then?' the policeman asked.

'The results of my interview with Michael Alexander. They'll make fascinating reading for you.'

'I bet they will,' said Dudfield enthusiastically. 'And it'll put the cat among the pigeons down here at HQ, too. Shouldn't think Hale will be as pleased with teacher's pet Thomas when she has a gander at it.'

'And another thing,' said Hogan.

'Make it quick. I've got to be getting back to work.'

'You've got good contacts with Lee Hughes's family, haven't you?'

'Yes. And?'

'I want to interview him. Now he's no longer in the frame. Could you sort that out for me?'

Dudfield chuckled. 'Sure can, mate. I'd be delighted to. I'll phone you once I've talked to them.'

Hogan returned to his seat. His finger still throbbed. But the conversation with Dudfield had made him feel a lot, lot better.

14

The meeting with Hughes was at his mother's house, a council semi on the edge of Ventnor. One of the conditions of the man's police bail had been that he should reside with his mother rather than at his own chalet. Now that he was free of the bail restrictions, he still hadn't moved back to full independent life.

Hogan saw the net curtains twitch as walked up the garden path, and a moment later Mrs Hughes opened the door. 'Thanks for coming, Mr Hogan,' she said, beckoning him into the living room, just off the hall. She appeared to be keeping her voice low so her son couldn't hear. 'It seems daft, doesn't it? Warren said you live on the same chalet site as Lee. But all this police stuff has really hit Lee's confidence hard. He isn't ready to go back to living on his own just yet.'

Hogan studied her as he sat down on the threadbare orange velvet sofa. A small, wiry woman. What was left of her thinning hair was dyed an unnaturally yellow blonde. Hogan thought her face looked worn out. Half a lifetime looking after a troubled son had put years on her.

'Lee!' she shouted up the stairs. 'It's the reporter from the paper come to see you.' Then she turned back to Hogan. 'He'll be in his room playing with his model trains. It's all he's done all day for the past few weeks.'

Mrs Hughes hovered by him, nervously drawing on a cigarette. Hogan noticed it hardly left her mouth, and the ashtray on the coffee table was filled with butts and ash.

'I'd given up before all this,' she said. Hogan realised his disapproving look must have been all too obvious. 'But it's hard to cope with on my own. His dad moved out years ago. Won't have anything to do with him.'

Then she turned to the stairs again.

'Lee! Get down here this instant! Otherwise no pocket money for that train you've been saving for.'

Hogan was surprised by the threat. It was the sort you might make to a five-year-old boy, not a man of thirty plus. But both the Beast and Dudfield had told him about the man's other-worldliness.

Mrs Hughes shrugged at Hogan and asked if he wanted a cup of tea.

'Love one,' said Hogan. 'Any Earl Grey?' He knew even before he said it that it was a doomed request.

'No, sorry, love. I don't go in for that fancy yuppie-type stuff. I've just got normal teabags.'

'That'll do fine,' said Hogan. 'Milk, no sugar, please.'

Lee's mother went off to the kitchen, and a few seconds later Hogan saw a man's legs coming down the open-plan stairway, followed by his body. His grossly overweight body.

Hogan stood up to shake his hand.

'Hello, Lee,' he said. 'Thanks for agreeing to meet me. It won't take long. Just a few questions.'

Lee gave a half-smile for a second, but then his features lapsed back into a morose frown. He wouldn't meet Hogan's gaze. He sat down to one side of Hogan in a battered brown velvet armchair.

The reporter began to question him. Just gently, trying to tease the information out, particularly about the circumstances of his arrest and his initial interview with Emma Thomas.

Then Hogan brought a file from his bag. He opened it and took some photographs out.

'You told the policewoman that a woman hit you on the clifftop when you tried to get your phone back, yes?'

Lee nodded, looking puzzled.

Hogan selected a picture of Francesca, the girl who had died in hospital after falling from the cliff.

'Is this a woman?' he asked.

'What do you mean?' asked Lee, frowning more heavily.

'Would you say this was a woman or a girl?'

'It's a woman, of course,' said Lee. He seemed to be getting agitated. 'She's got breasts.'

Hogan looked at the picture again. It had been taken from the website, but cropped so that it showed little more than Francesca's head and shoulders. But, yes, the upper swell of her breasts was just visible.

He showed Lee another photograph, this time of Clara Forbes. 'And what about this one. Woman or girl?'

'Woman, of course,' said Lee again, perplexed.

'So you would have described both of these as women?'

'Yes!' Lee was almost shouting now in anger. 'That's what I said, wasn't it?'

Hogan was surprised at the man's extreme reaction. Both the Beast and Dudfield had described him as a gentle giant. But at the moment the description didn't really fit.

Mrs Hughes was back, carrying two mugs of tea. 'Lee, don't raise your voice to the man. He's only trying to help you. Sorry, Mr Hogan. He's been a bit like this lately. Not his usual self.'

Hogan heard barking from the kitchen. 'His dog,' said Mrs Hughes somewhat unnecessarily. 'Lovely thing, but the hairs get up my nose. I have to keep it out of the lounge.'

Hogan held up another photograph, this time of Maria Forbes.

'That's her,' said Lee excitedly. 'That's the one, mum. I gave her the phone to ring you for help. But she was saying funny things. I tried to take it back 'cos I thought you'd be worried. I wasn't being naughty, honest!'

Lee started crying, and his mother moved over to comfort him.

'Sorry,' said Hogan. 'I didn't mean to upset him.'

Mrs Hughes turned, and mouthed a 'don't worry' to him while stroking her son's back, trying to calm him down.

His sobs subsided. Then he looked at Hogan. 'I saw her again, you know. With another woman. A few weeks later,' he said. 'But I hid from her. I didn't want to get into trouble again, and I wasn't supposed to be at Reeth.'

'Lee!' cried his mother in alarm.

'It's OK, Mrs Hughes,' said Hogan. 'Remember, I'm on your side.'

He looked at Lee.

'Did you tell the police this?'

'No. We decided to keep it a secret.'

201

'We?' asked Hogan, beginning now to share some of Mrs Hughes's fears.

'Lucy and me,' said Lee.

'Don't worry,' said Mrs Hughes to Hogan. She looked relieved. 'That's his dog – Lucy.'

'Ah,' said Hogan. 'So, Lee, are you sure it was the same woman?'

'I didn't see her face. I wasn't near enough. But I saw the red jacket she was wearing. It was the same one.'

Hogan nodded in understanding. Lee's story seemed to back up the police's case against Clara Forbes, and her story about her sister.

He put his notebook away, shook Lee's hand, and then let Mrs Hughes guide him to the door.

'Are you sure you won't finish your tea?' she asked.

'No, thank you. I'd better be off. Lots on at the moment.'

'I do worry about him, you know,' whispered Mrs Hughes. 'He's an innocent soul, the poor lamb. What'll happen when I'm gone?'

Hogan could hear the emotion in her voice, and see the distress etched in her wrinkled face.

'Look,' he said, 'we're going to do all we can to help. In my view the police were well out of order arresting Lee in the first place. His story backs that up.'

'It's kind of you, Mr Hogan, but I don't really see how you can help.'

'We're going to start a campaign, Mrs Hughes. I've already discussed it with my editor. A campaign for justice for your son. He deserves compensation – and we will make sure he gets it. Enough so that you won't have to worry about his future ever again.'

He shook hands with the woman. From the look in her eyes she didn't really believe him. But Hogan was determined. Emma Thomas had stitched Hughes up, of that he was sure. He just didn't know why. But he did know that, whatever the reason, the Isle of Wight Police had bungled, and would have to pay the price.

Hogan could tell that Howze was dubious about the merits of running a story questioning the decision to arrest Hughes. As he watched him

202

twist the hairs of his beard, Hogan wondered exactly what thoughts were going through his editor's mind. He'd already read Hogan's copy through once, and now he re-read it, and made notes on the draft.

'We're going to have to run it past a lawyer,' Howze said finally, placing Hogan's print-out on the desk in front of him. 'What worries me is that this story is very one-sided. You haven't given DS Thomas much chance to defend herself.'

Hogan sighed and moved round to Howze's side of the desk.

'Look,' he said, pointing to the print-out, 'it clearly says that DS Thomas was offered the chance to put her point of view, but referred the matter to the force's press office. And they declined to comment. What more can I do?'

Howze sat back, and then looked up again at Hogan. 'I appreciate your enthusiasm, Benjamin. But this is the local newspaper, not some campaigning national paper. We have to have a working relationship with the police.'

Hogan could feel himself starting to lose his temper. 'And that's more important than telling the truth is it?' He shook his head at Howze. 'What are you worried about? Your Freemason friends?'

Howze's face turned bright red. 'Don't give me any of that crap!' he shouted. 'That's got nothing to do with it.'

Hogan grabbed the copy from the table, and thrust it under the editor's nose. 'If you're too yellow to run this, then I'll take it to one of the nationals.'

He moved towards the door.

'Hang on a minute,' said Howze. Hogan stopped and turned. 'There's no need for anything hasty. You know as well as I do that if you did that you'd be in breach of contract.'

'So? Quite frankly, if you're not prepared to put this in print, we might just as well end my four-month trial contract here and now, rather than at the end of January.'

'Who said anything about you leaving at the end of January? I thought you liked it here and wanted to stay.' Howze had a hurt look on his face.

Hogan brandished his story in Howze's face again. 'Not if you won't print my stuff.'

Howze slumped forwards on his desk, and placed his head in his hands. 'Jesus. This is tantamount to blackmail.'

Hogan swivelled back towards the door.

'OK, OK,' said Howze grumpily. 'Give me it here. I'll take another look at it and see if I can knock it into shape. But I warn you, this story is probably more trouble than it's worth.'

Hogan fought back a smile. 'I don't think Lee Hughes's family would think it was more trouble than it's worth. Do you?'

Howze glanced up from the story, and grimaced. 'God, who do you think you are? Clark Kent in disguise? You'd better start wearing your underpants on the outside. Now fuck off before I change my mind.'

Hogan marched out of the door, and finally allowed a broad grin to fill his face.

There was a knock on the chalet door.

Hogan was wary. He didn't get many visitors, especially in the evening and, after the criminal damage to his car and the booby-trapped letter, he was on his guard.

He opened the curtain a crack and looked through the window. Emma Thomas. Hogan wasn't completely surprised. But if she'd come to try to sweet-talk him out of running the story about Hughes she was going to be out of luck.

As he opened the door he felt a blast of cold air on his face.

'Can I come in?' she asked. 'It's freezing out here.'

Hogan stood to one side to let her enter.

She looked around the small room. 'Wow. You've made a good job of this. It was a dump last time I saw it. And a real wood-burning stove. Great.'

Hogan apprehensively watched her move over to the stove, and warm her back by it. 'So what can I do for you?' he asked. His tone was neutral and professional, not friendly.

'I just wanted to ask a favour, really. Well, two favours, actually.' She turned her blue eyes on him, but her gaze didn't have the same hold on him as before. The spark had gone. Yes, she was still pretty.

But Hogan realised he no longer found her attractive. He wondered if she knew what he was thinking, or whether she was oblivious to it.

'The first was . . . I don't know how to say this really . . .'

'Lost for words? That's not like you.'

'No? Well, we all change, I guess. I've been feeling a bit lonely, to tell you the truth.'

Her eyes seemed to be pleading with him. Hogan turned his gaze away and switched on the kettle.

'Tea?' he asked.

'Got anything stronger?'

'Nope. Not drinking any more. And I don't want any temptation.'

'Coffee?'

'No,' he said, flatly. 'It's tea or tea.'

'I'd better have tea, then.' She laughed, but to Hogan the laugh sounded forced, and nervous.

'So you've been feeling lonely,' he said as he got the teabags out of the cupboard.

'Yes. Look, are you deliberately trying to make this hard for me?'

Hogan pretended to be puzzled. 'I'm not sure what you mean.'

'I want us to start . . . you know, going out again.'

Hogan sighed. 'We had sex a few times. I'm not sure we were ever going out together, were we? It was hardly the most intense love affair of my life.'

Her face dropped. 'So you're saying no?'

'Emma, it was you who ended it.' He shrugged. 'And it's over now. I want to try to rebuild things with my wife.'

'Oh,' she said.

'What was the other favour?'

Her expression changed now. Hogan noticed something else in her eyes. What was it? Hatred?

'Don't piss me about, Hogan. You know what I want.'

Hogan moved towards the door and opened it. 'Maybe the tea's not such a good idea. Maybe you ought to just go.'

She strode to the door angrily, but then, as she reached it, thrust her face into his.

'Don't think you're going to beat me,' she spat. 'I can do no wrong with Hale. She thinks the sun shines out of my arse. So print your petty little tale about Hughes if you want. Our lawyers are watching, and it'll give me great pleasure to see you in court.'

Hogan pulled his face back from hers as she spoke. He wiped her spittle off his cheek with the back of his hand as she slammed the door behind her.

How had he ever fancied her?

He wasn't sure of the answer.

Hogan slept fitfully. The same nightmare woke him twice. A black clock tower and a bell that tolled, again and again. He didn't know what it meant. Since childhood he'd had this dream, usually accompanied by a fever. It was as though something terrible were about to happen and the only escape was wakefulness, even though his body craved sleep. By morning he felt more tired than he had the night before.

To try to clear his head on the way to work, he took a detour along the Military Road, hoping the glorious view and the sea air would inspire him. But this morning there was no view – sea mist enveloped the coast road. And instead of bracing, fresh sea air, the atmosphere was cold, damp, and slightly eerie. He had his headlights on full, but still he didn't dare go too fast.

He swerved sharply as another set of car lights came towards him. His heart pounded: in jerking the car out of the way, he had gone frighteningly close to the cliff edge. Hogan readjusted and continued, driving even more slowly now. He tried to focus his eyes through the mist, looking for a familiar landmark, but there was just the road disappearing into the greyness and, to his left, he knew, a drop of several hundred feet over the cliff edge.

Then he noticed bright car lights in his rear-view mirror. The car behind was closing in on him, its lights on full beam. It seemed to be trying to overtake. Mad fool, Hogan thought. A moment later the car was almost alongside him. He could sense it in his blind spot. But the driver had stalled the overtaking manoeuvre.

Without warning the steering wheel jerked in his hands. He heard a groaning and splintering. The other car was pushing him to the left, toward the cliff edge.

He gripped the steering wheel harder, fought for control. But then the Peugeot lurched again as the other vehicle rammed sideways into it. Hogan felt the left front wheel leave the road surface. He couldn't turn it back.

The car was spinning. In a last desperate move, he threw his door open and launched himself out. He felt himself falling, the taste of earth in his mouth as his head dragged along the ground. For an instant, there was stillness. Then his ears thundered to the sounds of a crash and explosion far below him.

15

Hogan examined his bandage-covered finger. It throbbed like hell. But, other than jarring it during his fall, he'd had a remarkably lucky escape. If he'd been a cat he'd have used up three or four of his nine lives by now. But he wasn't a cat – he was a vulnerable, mortal human. Whoever was out to get him had failed with two serious attempts on his life. Maybe next time Hogan wouldn't be so lucky, and they would make sure they finished the job.

'You OK, mate?' The question came from PC Gavin Earnshaw, sitting opposite him in the chalet. The policeman lifted his head momentarily from his copy of the *Wight Evening Star* as he asked the question, then dropped his eyes and continued reading.

The police had finally begun to take the threats against him seriously. Hogan remembered Earnshaw as one of the two policemen who had discovered the first girl at the bottom of the cliff. He was now Hogan's personal twenty-four-hour guard. Earnshaw's ginger head was buried in Hogan's own story about Hughes. Every now and then he let out a little chuckle.

Hogan was pleased he'd filed the copy by e-mail after Emma Thomas had left the chalet the previous evening. He would have been in no fit state to write it today. Physically, he was pretty much OK, except for a few scratches and bruises. But mentally he was shot. His nerve had gone.

Earnshaw finally put the newspaper down on the coffee table. 'You really have laid into her, haven't you?' he said. Hogan noticed there appeared to be a certain amount of relish in his voice. 'I don't think the *Star's* going to be getting too much co-operation from us in the future. I heard DCI Hale and Superintendent Reilly were livid, and it's pretty obvious why.'

'With me?' asked Hogan.

'Well, with your paper, anyway.'

'What's going to happen to Emma Thomas?'

'Nothing's been said yet,' said Earnshaw. 'The thing is, Hale is the one with ultimate responsibility, and Reilly loves her. Won't hear a word against her. So if Hale backs Thomas then she's pretty much fireproof.'

Hogan grunted. This afternoon he didn't really care. He'd had enough. His mind was almost made up. Much as he liked the Isle of Wight, he couldn't put up with any more of this. He was going to tell Howze that he wanted out.

'So who do you think's got it in for you, then?' asked Earnshaw.

Hogan just shrugged. He had his theories, he had his suspicions, but he wasn't certain. And he certainly wasn't going to discuss them with the policeman.

There was a knock on the door. Earnshaw gestured to Hogan to stay seated as he went to open it.

It was Scarlett. Hogan felt slightly ashamed and embarrassed. He didn't really want her to see him like this, hiding away from the world in his tiny chalet. It all seemed so pathetic.

'All right?' she asked.

'You heard, then?' he said gruffly.

'Talk of the office, I'm afraid. Everyone's got their own theory about what's going on. Ed, Dickey and the Beast all wished you well.'

Hogan grunted, and let his eyes fall to the floor.

'He's feeling a bit sorry for himself,' said Earnshaw, smirking.

'Fuck off!' muttered Hogan. 'How would *you* frigging feel?'

'Ah, that's a bit better, sir. A bit more like your old self.'

Hogan allowed himself a small smile. 'So what brings you here?' he asked Scarlett.

'Aren't I allowed to just come and see how you are?'

'Yeah, sure. Thanks.' He could feel himself blushing.

'Actually, there *was* another reason. You know that info that someone was searching out for us? Well, they've got it.'

For a moment Hogan frowned in confusion. Then understanding dawned. Dudfield. He must have got the mobile-phone location details for Clara and Maria Forbes. He looked at Scarlett questioningly.

'And?'

Scarlett gestured with her eyes towards Earnshaw. 'I can't tell you

209

here, can I? Anyway, he didn't give me the full story. Just the top line. He wants to meet us in the pub.'

'When?'

'I said we'd see him in about ten minutes. That is, if you're up to it.'

Hogan suddenly felt two hundred per cent better. He got up and reached for his coat.

'Where are you going, sir?' asked Earnshaw, also getting to his feet, a worried expression on his face.

'You heard. Just down the pub. Don't worry – Scarlett will look after me.'

Earnshaw's expression of concern deepened. 'I really ought to come with you, sir.'

Hogan sighed in frustration. 'Look, you're here to protect me at my request. But I'm not under arrest or anything. If I want to go off to the pub without you, then I will. OK?'

Earnshaw sat down in his chair again and shrugged. 'Up to you, then, sir. But don't try to claim later on that I didn't offer to come. The lady's the witness to this.'

Scarlett reassured the policeman that she would indeed back him up if he got into trouble, then she led Hogan out of the door.

Hogan felt the dark clouds of self-pity lift as he glanced across at Scarlett in her car.

She smiled at him. 'Feeling better?'

'Yes,' he said. 'Much. I think I just needed to get away from the chalet and Earnshaw. It does my head in, him watching over me all the time. So what did Dudfield have to say?'

'He didn't go into the details. Just said that the search had turned up something interesting. Very interesting.'

'Look, he's here already.' Hogan pointed to Dudfield's squad car in the Buddle Inn's car park. Dudfield was standing by it, illuminated by a street lamp.

Scarlett parked alongside the police car, and Dudfield came round to Hogan's door to help him out.

'It's all right,' said Hogan, brushing Dudfield's arm away. 'I'm not a fucking invalid yet.'

Dudfield smiled across at Scarlett. 'He uses quite colourful language, your colleague, doesn't he? I get into trouble for saying things like that.'

Scarlett laughed and they moved towards the pub.

Just as they were about to enter, Dudfield grabbed Hogan by his good arm. 'Look, I'm going the back way into the barn. It looks pretty empty. I could murder a pint and I don't want anyone seeing me drinking on duty,' he said.

'What'll you have?' asked Hogan

'Do they do Wight Spirit here?'

'Sure do. Pint?'

Dudfield nodded. 'Sounds good.'

With Hogan's cut finger still out of action, Scarlett was left to carry the drinks. Hogan looked longingly at Dudfield's beer as it was pulled from the handpump, but just ordered a soft drink for himself.

They gathered round a large table in the barn area of the pub. This part was popular with families and children in the summer, but tonight they were the only customers.

Hogan watched Dudfield get various documents out of his briefcase. The policeman laid them out on the table. Hogan could see a list of mobile-phone numbers, dates and columns headed 'Cell Data'. It didn't make a lot of sense to him, but Dudfield started to explain what it all meant.

'These are Clara Forbes's records for December the first,' he said, using his hands to iron out the creases in the papers.

'The Cell Data indicate which mobile-phone transmitter the call was routed through. Now we know that the window for killing Romana was between 2pm and 3pm on the day in question. Clara made two calls during that time. One was routed through cell number 58032 at 2.14pm, the other through cell number 58031 at 2.37pm.'

Hogan could see Scarlett looking puzzled. He himself wasn't sure what Dudfield was driving at.

'That probably doesn't mean a lot to you,' said Dudfield with a grin, 'until I show you this.' He got out a guide to Island Telecom's base station numbers and pointed to 58032, Totland Bay, and 58031, Freshwater Bay.

'So that means her story about going to Freshwater to the caterers was true?' said Hogan

'Probably. It certainly gives her an alibi. But look who she was ringing,' said Dudfield.

He lined up the 'Number Receiving Call' column with Maria Forbes's mobile number. They matched. Clara had made the calls to her sister. The base-station numbers for the receiver's phone were also listed: 49021, Gurnard Bay, and 49022, Cowes Town Centre.

Hogan's eyes widened. 'So that gives Maria an alibi, too,' he said. 'And means she couldn't have been in Reeth when the second girl was pushed off the cliff.'

'Yes, pretty much. Her story was that she was getting wine for the party from Cowes. This would seem to back her up. Unless . . .'

Dudfield paused.

'Unless what?' asked Scarlett.

'Unless someone else was using their mobiles – in which case all this amounts to diddly squat,' said Dudfield.

Hogan leaned forward and jabbed the index finger of his good hand on the documents.

'Yes, but we know that's not possible,' he said.

'Why?' asked Dudfield.

'Well unless Clara Forbes was lying to us – and I don't think she had any reason to in this instance – she said both her and her sister's phones were locked with PIN numbers,' said Hogan.

'That's right,' said Scarlett. 'She did say that. And she said she didn't know Maria's PIN number and vice versa. They'd hardly be likely to give their PIN numbers to anyone else if they'd not even give them to each other, would they?'

Dudfield straightened, and smiled at them both. 'It doesn't surprise me,' he said. 'Emma Thomas's case against Hughes was full of holes, and this solution and alleged confession by Clara Forbes has always sounded a bit too neat, hasn't it? But that's not all.'

The policeman tugged yet another document out of the briefcase. 'These are Lee Hughes's phone records for October the thirty-first.'

Hogan nodded. 'The day Francesca fell – or was pushed off – the cliff.'

'That's right,' said Dudfield. 'They show that someone using Hughes's phone rang Clara Forbes's number at 5.41pm. The outgoing call went through St Rhadegund Cliff's transmitter, the incoming through Bonchurch Shore.'

'What does that tell us?' asked Scarlett, looking perplexed.

'Not a lot,' said Dudfield. 'But if, as Hughes said, he lent Maria Forbes his phone, this would seem to back his story up.'

Dudfield leafed through the sheaf of documents until suddenly he stopped. 'Finally, this one is probably the most interesting of the lot. Clara's records again, this time for December the tenth, the day Maria died.'

He paused and drained the rest of the beer from his glass.

'Now, from the pathologist, we have a pretty accurate time of death, to within one or two hours. Sometime between 1pm and 3pm that afternoon.'

Hogan and Scarlett both nodded.

'During that time, Clara made two calls, from base stations 39307 and 39308.'

Hogan tried to find the numbers on the Island Telecom transmitter list, but couldn't. 'They don't seem to be there,' he said.

Dudfield had a self-satisfied look on his face. 'That's because they're not Island Telecom base stations. They belong to Island's affiliate on the mainland.'

'The mainland?' said Scarlett.

'That's right. These numbers correspond with base stations in central Bath.' Dudfield banged his fist down on the table to emphasise his point. 'Clara Forbes couldn't have killed her sister, and never had a fight with her on Reeth Down. She wasn't even on the island at the time. She was in Bath.'

'Shit,' said Scarlett.

Hogan was slightly surprised. Scarlett hardly ever swore. He looked at Dudfield.

'But what about Clara's confession to Emma . . .?'

'Pack of lies,' spat Dudfield. 'It must have been.'

213

Hogan exhaled slowly. 'Jeesh! So the fuss about Hughes's arrest is the least of Emma's problems.'

Dudfield nodded slowly. 'The question is what we – or, rather, you – do about it.'

'Me?' asked Hogan.

'I can't do anything. I'm officially off the case. Hale would string me up for approaching the telephone company, and for interfering. It's down to you. I think you need to have another little chat with DS Thomas – and don't fucking mention anything about it being me that gave you this info.'

Hogan looked at Scarlett, and squirmed in his chair. She gave him a sympathetic look and reached over to touch his good hand.

Hogan was dreading the phone call, but knew it had to be made. Scarlett and Dudfield had gone back to Yarwater, and he was back in the chalet. He waited until Earnshaw excused himself to go to the toilet, giving him at last a few moments of privacy.

He lodged his mobile between his legs and tapped out Emma Thomas's personal mobile number with his good hand.

'Hi. Emma?'

There was a moment of silence on the other end of the line, even though the call had been answered.

'Emma, are you there?'

'Hogan. Yes, it's me. Nice hatchet job you did in the paper.' Her voice sounded cold, emotionless. But he wasn't going to apologise.

'It was the truth. You can't argue with that.'

'Mmm. Anyway, what do you want?'

'I've got some information. About the Forbes case. It may be useful.'

'I doubt it,' she said dismissively.

'I've nailed down Clara's whereabouts when Maria died. It couldn't have been her. She wasn't even on the island. She was in Bath.'

Hogan thought he heard a sharp intake of breath. But nothing else.

'Emma?' he said. 'Are you still there?'

'Yes, I'm still here. How do you know this?'

'Her mobile-phone records. And, what's more, Maria couldn't have killed Romana. She was in Cowes – her phone records prove it. She wouldn't have had time to get from there to St Rhadegund's Cliff and back, and commit a murder in between.'

There was a pause again. Hogan felt he could almost hear Emma's mind working.

'Who've you told?' she said finally.

This time Hogan paused. He didn't want to get Dudfield into trouble.

'No one. Just you,' he lied. 'I wanted to tell you first, especially after all the trouble with Hughes. I realise this could be a little awkward for you.'

'Awkward?' Emma cried. And then she started laughing. Hogan thought the laughter had a slightly manic edge to it.

'Are you OK, Emma?' he asked. He realised he still had some feelings for her, even though she had used him for her own ends, then discarded him when he was no longer useful.

'Yes, yes, I'm fine. Look, I can show you why Maria was guilty, and prove Clara's involvement. There must be something wrong with those phone records.'

'I don't think so,' said Hogan.

'There must be, and I can prove it.' She sounded excited now, as though she'd pulled herself together after the initial shock of his revelations. 'Meet me at the bottom of the cliff path in half an hour. I'll show you.'

And then the line was dead, before Hogan had had the chance to explain that his minder, Earnshaw, would almost certainly insist on coming too.

Hogan heard the toilet flush, and Earnshaw returned to the room.

'Sounded like you were on the phone to someone. Who was it?'

Hogan looked at him angrily. 'None of your fucking business.'

Earnshaw looked hurt. 'All right. Keep your hair on. I'm supposed to be protecting you, remember that? So I need to know what's going on.'

Hogan grudgingly apologised, and then explained that he had to go out.

215

'I'll have to come with you,' said the policeman. 'You know that, don't you?'

Hogan nodded, and then moved to the kitchen area to put the kettle on. 'We've just got time for a cup of tea to warm us up. Then we're going on a walk.'

They set off after about twenty minutes, and by the time they got to the entrance of the chalet park, and the start of the Coastal Path, Thomas was already waiting.

Hogan watched her face. She looked surprised that Earnshaw was with him, although she must have known he was now under police protection.

'No need for you to come too, Gav. I'm sure I can look after Mr Hogan well enough,' she said. 'We're just going for some fresh air up by the radio mast. Fresh air and . . . and a bit of a chat.'

Earnshaw looked at Hogan questioningly.

'It's OK. I'll be fine,' said Hogan. He reached into his pocket, pulled out the chalet keys, and tossed them to Earnshaw. The throw was a bit low, and the policeman had to stoop to make the catch.

'Well, if you insist, Mr Hogan. I really ought to stay with you, but I guess if DS Thomas is with you that should be all right.'

'It'll be fine,' said Hogan. 'Don't worry. Here – take my mobile number in case there's any problem. You could put the lunch on if you like. Give us a ring when it's ready.' Hogan winked at the constable.

Earnshaw pulled a face at him and then headed back to the chalet.

The two of them were alone now. Hogan studied Thomas's face. Her mascara was slightly smudged, and her hair looked like it hadn't been washed for weeks. Her face was drawn, lined. Still pretty, but the radiant beauty that had first attracted Hogan had evaporated.

'How's your hand?' she asked as they began to stride up the hill towards the cliff.

'How did you know about that?'

'Duh. It's covered in a bandage, thicko. Did you do it when you had the car accident?'

Hogan noticed she was smirking at him. As though she were trying to goad him.

'That wasn't an accident.'

'Yes. So you say. I read your report. Are you sure you haven't just got a fanciful imagination?'

Hogan lapsed into silence. She was still fitter than he was, and ahead of him already. He puffed and panted behind. He watched her bottom, still shapely, still in tight jeans, hardly standard police-wear – even for CID. But the jeans were dirty. And he noticed a strange lumpy shape in the right-hand pocket of her jacket.

They reached the fenced-off area of the path and the signs diverting walkers away from the dangerous part of the cliff. He watched as she reached into her jacket pocket, pulled something out, and then grabbed with her gloved hands at the barbed wire of the fence.

'Wire cutters,' she explained. 'I thought I'd better come prepared.'

She cut a hole in the wire, and they both climbed through and continued towards the cliff.

'That's criminal damage, isn't it?' joked Hogan.

She laughed. 'Ooh. Sorry, Mister Policeman.' She held out her arms. 'Handcuff me, please. Do anything you want with me.'

Hogan grinned. It was a small glimpse of the old Emma Thomas, cheeky and flirty, the way she had been just a few weeks earlier, when they had first met. Now, for the most part, that side of her stayed hidden.

The path opened up onto the Downs above the cliff edge. The heart-stopping view to the white cliffs near Freshwater Bay was there; the thick mist of the previous day had disappeared. The last time the two of them had been here, bright autumn light had picked out the cliffs; now there were ominous-looking grey clouds overhead. And it was so much colder. Hogan shivered, and drew the collar of his jacket up around his neck.

'We're nearly there,' she said. 'Here. Let's sit here.'

She was pointing to a worn area by the cliff edge. It stuck out slightly from the rest of the cliff – it looked as though it was a regular resting spot for walkers. There was a litter bin for people to put their picnic waste in.

'Come on, sit down.' She had already taken her place on the

ground, and was motioning him to sit in front of her. He was slightly wary of the cliff edge, but there still seemed plenty of space. She rested her arms on his shoulders.

'So where did we go wrong?' she asked him.

Hogan used his good hand to scratch idly in the earth, as though he were doodling on a piece of paper.

'Dunno,' he said glumly. 'But we've been over this before, haven't we?'

She didn't seem to be listening to him. It was as though she were lost in her own thoughts. 'You were a nice man. Most of the time.'

'Nice'? thought Hogan. What sort of a feeble word is that?

'And I think you always acted with the best intentions.'

Hogan shivered again. This was starting to get a bit creepy. And why was she using the past tense, almost as though he didn't exist any more.

'Look,' he said, 'I didn't really come to talk about us. You said you were bringing me here to prove Clara's and Maria's guilt.'

'Ah, yes,' she whispered dreamily. 'OK then. I'll explain.'

Earnshaw realised he must have dozed off in front of the chalet's wood-burning stove. Now an urgent rapping on the front door woke him with a start. He leapt up, alarmed. He could see the shapes of three or more figures through the frosted glass. Fuck! Was this the heavy mob come round to get Hogan?

He nervously opened the net curtains an inch and peeked out.

Dudfield shouted at him, 'Earnshaw, you dozy bugger. Let us in. Now!'

He opened the door to be confronted by not just Dudfield but also DCI Hale and Superintendent Reilly.

'Where's Hogan?' Dudfield barked.

Earnshaw's heart sank. This was trouble, big trouble. Dudfield wouldn't have brought the top brass if it wasn't deeply serious.

'Come on, lad, we haven't got all day. Where the fuck is he?'

Earnshaw noticed neither of the high-ups batted an eyelid at Dudfield's language. Deeply, deeply serious.

'Erm . . . He went for a walk.'

'A walk?' Dudfield sounded incredulous. 'You fuckwit! You've let him go out on his own, haven't you?'

'No . . .' Earnshaw looked at Hale and Reilly, hoping he might get some support against Dudfield's tirade. But they looked just as angry and concerned. 'No,' he repeated. 'DS Thomas was with him. They said they had something they wanted to talk about, so they were going for a stroll up by the radio mast.'

Dudfield's face went white. Earnshaw backed away as the sergeant seized him by his shirt lapels and slammed him against the chalet door.

'You berk! You didn't exactly have a lot to do, and you've fucked that up.'

Hale grabbed Dudfield's shoulder and pulled him off. 'Leave him, Warren! It's not helping. We've got to work out what to do.'

Dudfield seemed to pull himself together. 'Sorry, ma'am.' He began shouting orders into his police radio.

'We need back-up at St Rhadegund's Cliff. At the radio mast – no sirens or lights, mind, and unmarked cars if possible. Tell them to wait there for further orders. And we need the same at Reeth – tell 'em to wait by the end of the cliff path for further instructions. Better have some marksmen as well. Oh, and get an ambulance and paramedics on standby. Send them to Reeth – again, no sirens.'

Earnshaw was impressed by Dudfield's attempts to control the situation, although he still wasn't at all clear what was happening. Surely, if Hogan was with DS Thomas, then he had at least some protection.

He suddenly remembered Hogan giving him his mobile number. He scrabbled for the bit of paper in his pocket.

'Here,' he said, thrusting it at Dudfield. 'Hogan took his mobile with him. That's the number.'

Dudfield glanced at Hale.

'What do you think, ma'am?'

'The trouble is, if the mobile rings, it could just trigger everything,' she said, frowning.

Earnshaw could see Dudfield think about it for just a second.

219

Then he watched as the Sergeant got out his mobile and began to dial.

Hogan was conscious that Emma seemed to be rambling now. About the Forbes case. It was just a re-hash of the official police version – nothing new, certainly not the proof she'd promised.

Then his mobile rang. He felt her hands tighten on his shoulders. He got the phone out of his pocket with his left hand, and held it awkwardly to his ear.

'Hogan?' It was Dudfield. 'Is that you?'

'Yes,' said Hogan. He laughed. 'Who did you expect?'

'Listen. And listen carefully.' There was an urgent, almost frightened tone to Dudfield's voice. 'Are you with her?'

'Who?'

'Thomas, of course.'

'Yes.'

'Can she hear?'

'Dunno.'

'OK. Well, with a bit of luck, with the noise of the wind and the sea, she can't. So, as I say, listen very carefully to me. You're in great danger. From her.'

Hogan felt her hands on his shoulders. She had been acting oddly. But, even so, what Dudfield was saying didn't seem to make sense.

Dudfield was continuing. 'Alexander rang me. In a panic. He'd read in the paper about the car forcing you off the road. He believes it was his car.'

Hogan remembered the car. It had indeed looked like a green four-by-four. He'd seen a green four-by-four recently. Next to a manure-covered muck-spreader. Up by Alexander's place . . .

'He'd lent it to Thomas. She brought it back damaged. With scrapes of red paint on the side.'

Hogan swallowed. He tried to fight down the feeling of panic that seemed to be rising up from his stomach.

'You understand what that means, don't you?' Dudfield was asking. Hogan did. All too well. 'She wants you dead. It's her that's been after you. Keep her talking as long as you can. We'll try to . . .'

Without warning, the phone was wrenched from his hand and there was cold metal pressing against the right side of his forehead. Out of the corner of his eye he saw the gun barrel.

'I think this has gone on long enough, don't you?' Emma Thomas said.

He watched in sick fascination as her other hand threw the mobile over the cliff edge.

'You don't need that any more,' she said with a tight smile.

He could feel the blood pounding in his temples.

She was silent for a moment. All he could hear was the wind whistling in his ears and the roar of the sea far below.

'I suppose you want to know what happened, don't you?'

Hogan didn't trust himself to speak. The tightness in his throat was almost choking him. He didn't want to betray his fear to her. She'd moved the gun now, round to his back. He could feel it pressing in between his ribs.

'I didn't mean for it to turn out this way,' she said, her voice catching. 'They tricked me. Maria and Clara. Clara fancied me – you knew she was a lesbian, didn't you?'

Hogan didn't reply. He didn't need to – the question was rhetorical.

Thomas continued her monologue. 'Well, I used that to . . . you know . . . persuade her to drop her stupid walking group's opposition to closing the path. Why? I don't know. I guess I thought it would get me in HQ's good books. A gold star to help me with promotion.'

She laughed. With one hand she tousled Hogan's hair tenderly. The other still held the gun firmly against his back.

'And of course when Michael Alexander told me about Lee Hughes getting into a fight on the cliff edge, it seemed too good an opportunity to miss. We weren't getting anywhere quickly with the inquiry. If I could pin the crime on someone, anyone, that too would help my career.'

This didn't surprise Hogan. He'd always been convinced that Hughes was innocent.

'Then I discovered Clara's little adoption-agency scheme. It turned out that her sister liked young girls too.' Emma snorted in what

221

sounded to Hogan like disgust. 'But by then I'd got, well, *involved* myself. Unintentionally, sort of. I did think the girl, Romana, looked about seventeen or eighteen. Honestly.'

She paused. Hogan could hear her crying softly. Despite what she'd been telling him, he still felt some pity for her.

'But she wasn't. She was fifteen. Just fifteen. What had I become? I was ashamed of myself. The first girl who fell, Francesca, well, that was an accident. At least, that's what Maria said. There's no reason to disbelieve her. Clara liked to leave Francesca locked up in the house. But Maria took pity on her and took her for a walk on the cliff. They went a bit too near the edge. It was just by chance that Maria was wearing Clara's fleece – she couldn't find a jumper of her own and had just picked up Clara's fleece without thinking. But Maria was terrified in case the girl came out of her coma and revealed exactly what had been going on. Fucking perverts.'

Hogan had to bite his tongue. He didn't think now was the time to interrupt, despite the woman's hypocrisy. He heard her sniffling.

'Of course, by the time I learned all this they already had a hold on me. It was like blackmail. If I disclosed anything about what had really happened, they would make sure my career was ruined. Trouble was, Romana started threatening me too. So I had to do something about it. I knew about Maria wearing the fleece when she'd been with Francesca on the clifftop. So it seemed a good idea for me to wear it too.'

Hogan gasped. 'So you killed Romana?' He realised these were his first words since Thomas had begun her story.

'If you like. She fell, actually. But with the help of a little push.'

'What about the dogs?'

'Oh, that. A little embellishment. I couldn't stand the disgusting animals. I knew Maria couldn't either. I thought it might make Clara think Maria was responsible – which she did for a while. Then, of course, you started poking your nose into things. That started making life difficult for me.'

'Oh, I am so, so sorry,' said Hogan sarcastically.

Thomas jabbed the gun harder into his ribs. 'Don't push your luck. I'm telling you all this as a favour, because you aren't going to be around much longer and you've expended so much energy trying to work it all out. But don't get smart, otherwise I won't bother.'

Hogan felt a chill at Thomas's words. They were confirmation of what he had feared. She planned to kill him. If only he could keep her talking. His teeth were chattering now as the cold and fear invaded his body.

She continued, 'We read the story in that rag of yours about Francesca showing signs of coming out of her coma. We couldn't afford for that to happen, obviously. Luckily Maria occasionally worked shifts in the intensive care ward. I distracted the ward sister with some stupid questions while Maria did the necessary.'

Jesus, thought Hogan. This woman is *evil*. And to think that at one stage I was . . . well, if not in love with her, then at least in lust with her.

'But Maria wasn't terribly stable, to be honest. She started to have second thoughts. Wanted to blab. So I re-arranged the fencing around the airshaft, took her for a walk, and gave her a bit of a shove – just a little shove, you understand. A little, little one. While wearing the red fleece again, of course.'

'So it was you. Up on Reeth Down?'

'That's right. You shouldn't have been there. I thought my adjustments to your car's braking system might have done the trick.'

'So you've murdered three people, and tried to murder me as well – all just to protect your fucking career. Bit sick, don't you think?'

'*Just* to protect my career?' She made a strangled cry. 'Have you *any* idea what my life's been like. Dad leaves Mum and I – cuts me out of his life completely – when I'm just nine. Think about it. *Nine.* Then my stepfather abuses me. Then I keep seeing my real dad rising up the police ranks with his new, apparently perfect, family life. My career was my only weapon to one day get back at him. Rise up the ranks myself as quickly as possible, and then one day challenge him to his face.'

Hogan was silent. The self-piteous rant seemed to be over. It didn't cut any ice with him. He was desperately trying to think of a way to escape.

Then Emma poked the gun barrel against his back again.

'There's only one flaw in your story,' exclaimed Hogan. He'd remembered. In his wallet. His one last chance.

'What?' said Emma. She sounded genuinely alarmed.

'The girls. The girls you thought were underage.'

'What about them?'

'They weren't. They were sixteen.' He heard her gasp behind him. 'All your murders were for nothing. The Romanian woman who arranged their 'adoption' simply lied about their ages, because Clara and Maria wanted 'em young. They asked for underage girls, so that's what Nadia Popescu sent them, sort of. The girls were young, all right. But not too young, according to English law. When you had sex with them you weren't doing anything illegal.'

'No!' shouted Thomas.

Hogan reached into his pocket to bring out his wallet. It was just luck they were still there, that he'd never got round to transferring them to his file: the birth certificates Nadia Popescu had handed him in Bucharest. The birth certificates for the two girls she'd sent to Families for Teens Agency. Francesca and Romana.

He took them out and passed them back over his shoulder to Thomas. She wouldn't be able to understand the Romanian, of course, but the relevant dates were comprehensible in any language.

He heard her crying intensify, felt the pressure of the gun barrel ease. Calculating she was in shock from what he'd told her, he spun round and tried to grapple the gun away from her.

She was stronger than he'd expected.

He heard the gunshot, felt a sharp pain in his leg, and then, suddenly, they were no longer sitting at edge of the cliff, but tumbling down it amid a mass of earth and rocks.

Pain.

Darkness.

16

The first thing he felt was a cold, wet sensation on his cheek. He tried to open his eyes. No go. Then the pain jabbed up his body from his legs. He grimaced reflexively, and the movement opened his eyes an agonising crack.

But at least he found he'd not been blinded. Greyness above him. And flecks of white. It was snowing.

He could hear, too. Sirens, in the distance. Growing closer.

He turned his head towards the sound. He could make out a faint blue flashing light through the snow. It hurt him to turn his head, but he persisted, now trying to move it the other way.

And he saw her. Looking so peaceful. The pretty blonde face, the snub nose. Maybe she did look a bit like a younger version of Meg Ryan.

Whatever, she seemed contented.

A snowflake helicoptered down through the air and landed on her eyelid.

He looked up to her blonde hair. The bob had bounced back into place. But behind and to one side of her head . . .

He turned his eyes away. Didn't want to look. The blood. The flesh. The mess. One of the black rocks that had given their name to this beauty spot on the Undercliff had pierced her skull.

He didn't have any doubt she was dead. Not like Maria at the bottom of the airshaft. No need to turn her body over.

He eased his head back and stared at the grey sky.

'Fucking hell.' The curse, the voice. Familiar. A friendly voice. Something he needed to hear.

Dudfield.

He turned his head towards the approaching copper.

'Bloody Nora,' shouted Dudfield. 'He seems to be OK. But she . . .'

Hogan watched, as if on television,

Dudfield glanced across at Emma.

'. . . she isn't,' said Dudfield.

Then the policeman was bending over him. Hogan could feel the man's warm breath melting the snowflakes.

'It's all right, mate. Just take it easy. The paramedics are on their way. You're going to be all right.'

'My leg,' cried Hogan.

Dudfield quickly examined it. 'Yeah, well, it's still there. You might not be walking too well for a bit, but it looks like we're not quite shot of you yet.'

Hogan lay back, relieved, and drifted off into unconsciousness once more.

When he woke the next time the first thing he saw was William's face.

'Mum, mum!' he heard. 'Dad's awake! Quick!'

Then Lynn's face. God, but he was pleased to see her. And Tamara by her side.

'Hi, Iain.' Lynn was smiling. 'You've been in the wars a bit.'

'Is . . . is . . . my leg OK?'

'Of course it is, you big baby. Broken. But OK.'

'Why are you here?'

'Daaad!' said Tamara. 'We're your family. We *want* to be here.'

He reached out to his daughter and ruffled her hair.

'We've sorted out somewhere to stay. So you're stuck with us for Christmas now. That was what you wanted, wasn't it?' asked Lynn, tentatively.

'Yes. Yes. Of course.' He stroked her hand. 'How long was I unconscious?'

'A few hours. Enough time for them to get you settled here in hospital, get your leg set, and enough time for us to come down from London. And tie things up with that rental place you found.'

Hogan tried to wiggle his toes, and winced in pain.

* * *

226

Dudfield was the next visitor.

'Haven't they got you doing physio yet, then?'

'Give it a rest.'

'No. I'm serious. Some of the nurses are real crackers. I'd swap places with you any day.'

'Fuck off,' said Hogan. 'H . . . how's Emma?'

Dudfield snorted. 'She was never too concerned about *your* welfare, mate. I wouldn't worry too much about her. Anyway, I think you know the answer.'

'Dead?'

Dudfield nodded. 'Good riddance, I say. She was trouble from the word go. Hale wouldn't listen to me. She's had to now, though.'

'Why?'

'CID are stuffed, aren't they? Hale's just lost her favourite detective. And she's in huge trouble with the Super. He's utterly pissed off with the fuck-ups over Hughes and Clara Forbes. Says he's sick of her politically correct policing methods. She's got to go back to basics – or she's out.'

'And will she?'

'Well, she's asked me back onto CID for a start.'

'You'll go of course?'

Dudfield sat back, roaring with laughter. 'Yeah. But I'm going to make her sweat a bit first. And then demand that she considers me first for any openings at DI level.'

Hogan let out a chuckle. And then wished he hadn't. The vibrations made his leg hurt. 'What about Michael Alexander and Clara Forbes?'

'Alexander's in serious trouble. Turns out he'd been using explosives to deliberately loosen parts to the cliff face, the mad fucker.'

Hogan gasped. 'Why?'

'He was just determined to get the path closed. I don't think he really thought through his actions or believed someone might actually be standing there when the cliff collapsed.'

'So was that where we were, on one of the parts he'd booby-trapped?'

'That's it, spot on. He'd hoped he was just making it unsafe and the council would close the path. Which they did, of course. But then you two clowns went and cut the wire fence, and the vibrations of the gunshot were the last straw that broke the camel's back, as it were.'

'Jesus!' said Hogan.

'So a file's gone to the CPS. I expect they'll nail him for something. Maybe even manslaughter.'

'But what about Forbes?' asked Hogan.

'Released without charge,' said Dudfield, slightly apologetically.

'Eh?' Hogan couldn't believe what he was hearing.

'What do we do her for? Underage sex? Well, they weren't underage, you know that. Although some forty-something woman making out with a sixteen-year-old who she thinks is fifteen seems pretty effing sick to me.'

'Would it have made any difference if she'd been male – a man messing around with underage kids?'

Dudfield shook his head. 'Not if they were really sixteen it wouldn't. Just shows you though, it's not always men who are the sickos. It's been a bit of an eye-opener, this case.'

'Yeah, but come off it. How many cases like this have you come across involving women? This must be one of the few. More often that not it's an evil male – an evil heterosexual male - behind this sort of thing.' Hogan looked Dudfield in the eye. 'We've a lot to answer for.'

'Who?' Dudfield looked genuinely puzzled.

'The male gender.'

'You've lost me there mate. Don't go all philosophical on me. It's not my strong point.'

'No. That's painfully obvious. But surely there's something you can do Forbes for. What about the fake adoption agency? Trafficking in humans? Prostitution? – that's what it really was, you know.'

Dudfield shrugged. 'It's easier for Hale just to try to sweep things under the carpet as much as possible.'

'But surely she can't, can she? Not totally?'

Dudfield smiled at him. 'She and Reilly will have a good go. I guess there'll be an inquiry. But they'll just try to make it out it was one rogue cop, and you can't really legislate for that.'

'Turned out all right for you, though,' said Hogan, acting resentful.

Dudfield laughed again. It was good to see him laughing so much. A lot of the accustomed bitterness seemed to have gone out of his face. 'Yeah, I guess so. But really I'm back where I started. What about you? Will you stay on here on the island now, or have you had enough?'

Hogan tried to shrug but it hurt too much. He didn't know the answer to the question. A few weeks ago, it would have been an unequivocal yes. But so much had happened.

He wasn't sure.

After twenty-four hours in hospital while they ran various tests, Hogan was given a pair of crutches and released.

Lynn and the kids came to pick him up in the people-carrier. The remains of the Peugeot were washing around in the English Channel somewhere.

'Do you want to go back to the chalet, or come to ours first?' she asked. It looked like free nursing care wasn't on the agenda, then. He didn't fancy going back to the chalet on his own with a broken leg. He didn't think he'd be able to cope.

'Let me think about it,' he said as he eased himself awkwardly into the back of the car, laying his plaster-encased leg out across as much of both seats as he could. 'First, can you take me to the office? There's something I've got to sort out with the editor.'

It was just a short drive from the hospital to the trading estate. When they arrived, the kids turned up their noses.

'Ugh, Dad! You don't work here, do you? It's yukky!' said Tamara.

'Yeah. I must say I'm no great fan of the surroundings,' said Hogan.

'Can we come and look inside the office?' asked William.

'Maybe – in a mo,' said Hogan, easing himself out of the people-carrier. Lynn was at the car door, holding his crutches.

'Are you sure you'll be all right?' she asked.

He took the crutches and levered himself upright. 'Sure. I'm getting to be a dab hand with these. I'll give you a ring on the mobile in a few minutes, and you can bring the kids up.'

He hobbled round the back of the warehouse, and then paused and glared at the stairs. This bit posed problems. He took the easy option, sitting down on the stairs and hauling himself up on his backside, step by step, dragging the crutches along at the same time.

At the top he pushed himself to his feet, negotiated the crutches under his armpits, and entered the *Star*'s open-plan office.

He heard the song first. 'For He's a Jolly Good Fellow.' Then he noticed all the staff gathered round in a group, singing and pouring glasses of champagne.

Odd, he thought. I didn't tell them I was coming.

Then it dawned on him. They were gathered round Scarlett. The song was 'For *She's* a Jolly Good Fellow'. For her.

Hogan, unnoticed by the doorway, felt out of it.

Scarlett saw him first, and rushed to greet him.

'Hogan!' she shouted. She studied his crutches. 'Hey, they suit you . . .Grandad!' Then she stood on tiptoe to kiss him on the cheek.

Hogan let the crack about his age pass. He liked her. They made a good team.

Howze came over and slapped his back, almost toppling him.

'Benjamin, my good man, we heard you'd been in a bit of a scrape.' He winked, and whispered in Hogan's ear, 'Scarlett wrote it all up very well, you know – better than you'd have done.'

'Piss off,' hissed Hogan, but he was smiling. 'So what's the celebration for?'

'Scarlett,' beamed Howze, handing Hogan a glass after he'd propped himself against the desk. 'She's agreed to leave her course and join us full-time. Bit of a coup, that, I'd say. And with you saying you didn't want to carry on, we needed to fill the gap.'

'Eh?' said Hogan.

Howze frowned. 'That *is* what you said, Benjamin, isn't it?'

'Well . . .' Hogan didn't know what to say.

Then he saw Ed Sutcliffe failing to suppress a giggle. And now Howze was roaring with laughter too.

'Had you there, didn't we, you old sod. But, in all seriousness, what are you planning to do? Do you want to stay on?'

Hogan looked his editor up and down. Howze was a prat, but

quite a loveable prat. 'You haven't asked me yet, have you?'

'Well, I'm asking you now,' said Howze.

Hogan paused. He knew he ought to discuss it with Lynn and the kids. But it was his life, his new life. He had to take control of it.

'Yes. Yes, I would like to stay.'

'Good show, good show!'

Howze slapped him on the back again, spilling Hogan's drink all over his shirt. Hogan gritted his teeth and said nothing.

'Of course, you'll have to change your ways,' continued Howze. 'Stick to reporting rather than trying to save the world. No more of that Clark Kent stuff.' Howze looked down at Hogan's plastered leg. Scarlett was crouched on the floor, busily signing it. 'After all,' he sniggered, 'you've just proved to us you can't fly.'

Hogan gave him a V sign as Howze guffawed at his own joke.

'Oh, by the way,' said Scarlett, 'this arrived for you.'

She handed him an envelope.

Hogan looked at it sceptically. 'It's not full of razor blades again, is it?'

Scarlett giggled, 'No. Although we did run a magnet over it just to make sure. It's fine.'

Hogan examined the postmark. Bucuresti. From Romania. He opened it. It was a Christmas card, from Antoaneta, with a letter inside.

Dear Hogan

I guess I owe you an apology and an explanation. I'm so sorry for abandoning you at the villa near the Romexpo Centre. But, first, do you like my English better now! I've given up the hostessing, and have been taking an English course. I'm going back to English teaching.

So my apology. I followed you as you know to the back of the house. And we saw the woman there, in the photographic studio. For you, she was just any woman. But I have a confession. I was once a street girl too, and had to fight to survive – like the girl Marica we found, the one who died from the cold and malnutrition.

I was not particularly pretty. But I soon realised men liked me, liked me for my body. Anyway, the way I found to survive was by selling my body. And the woman who controlled me – that was the woman we saw in the studio, Nadia Popescu. I couldn't face her again. She revolts me. That is why I left you there.

Anyway, I know you are all right. I found the website for your newspaper and have been reading your stories.

So, Hogan, I wish you a Happy Christmas, and hope that someday we will meet again.

Love from
Antoaneta

Scarlett tried to peek over his shoulder. 'Ooh. Love from Antoaneta. How exciting. Is she your secret Balkan lover?'

Hogan folded the letter up and put the card in his pocket. No she wasn't his secret lover – maybe she could have been, but now he would never know. But he wasn't going to tell Scarlett that.

He tapped his finger on her nose, in time to the words.

'Mind – your – own – business.'

When Lynn saw him struggling up the steps to the chalet, she finally took pity on him. 'Look, OK, you win. You'd better come and stay with us. I can't be bothered having to haul myself over here to play nursemaid the whole time,' she said with a grin.

After all the upheavals of the year, Hogan would be able to spend Christmas with the kids. And with Lynn. It wouldn't be a white Christmas – the snow had already melted – but it would still be a special one.

The rental Lynn had chosen was in Bonchurch. A two-bed ground-floor flat just two doors along from the Forbes' house. As they approached, Hogan noticed that Clara had already put a To Let sign at the garden gate.

Lynn noticed it too.

'That looks a lovely house,' she said. 'If we're going to make our home here, then I want somewhere like that.'

It *was* a beautiful house. But Hogan was more interested in what Lynn had just said than in where she wanted to live. The key thing for him was the words she'd used: 'We' and 'our home'.

He looked across at her tenderly.

The kids were excited. Christmas on the island was something different. They looked through the guidebook Hogan had got from the tourist office, picking out things they wanted to do.

'Hang on, hang on,' he said. 'Most of these places are closed in the winter. Let's look in the paper and see what's actually open.'

He felt a bit guilty looking in the island's weekly, but it had a better What's On section than the *Star*.

'See here, dad!' shouted William. 'The model railway. It's got a special Christmas show.'

'Oh, no!' groaned Tamara. 'Not a model railway. That's boring stuff, *boys'* stuff. Look, what's this?' She pointed out another advert, for a Christmas exhibition at the waxworks. 'Dad, that looks much more fun,' she whined.

Hogan looked over at Lynn. She seemed unsympathetic.

'You can sort it out,' she said. 'I've had to put up with this sort of thing on my own for the last few months.'

'OK, then,' said Hogan. 'This is what we do. Model railway first, this morning. And then the waxworks this afternoon. OK?'

'Great, dad,' the kids said, almost in unison, and both kissed him on the cheek.

The model railway was at the far northwest of the island, beyond Yarmouth, at Fort Victoria. About as far as possible away from the waxworks at Brading, on the east coast. Hogan kept quiet about this in case Lynn kicked up a fuss about the driving.

The car journey took about thirty minutes. On arrival the kids rushed inside the exhibition hall before Hogan had managed to haul himself out of the car. He and Lynn finally followed, paying for the family ticket.

They turned the corner to the exhibits.

William and Tamara had already rushed down to the far end, where the Christmas show was signposted.

Lynn nudged Hogan.

'Who's that they're with? I don't like the look of it.'

A rather fat man was holding Tamara up to see the miniature mechanical Christmas grotto. Hogan could see why Lynn was alarmed, but he wasn't worried.

He approached the man and children from behind, moving quite quickly now on his crutches, overtaking Lynn with ease.

'Hello, Lee,' he said.

The man turned round, still holding Tamara carefully.

'Mr Hogan. What have you done to yourself?'

'I had a bit of an accident, Lee. But I'm coming along fine.'

Tamara grabbed him by the coat sleeve and tugged. Hogan had to move his crutch quickly to avoid staggering.

'Dad, look! All the little elves making the presents.'

'And, Dad,' said William, 'there's Santa's sleigh being pulled along by the reindeer.'

'It's all exactly to scale of course, Mr Hogan. I like the trains best, but the kids love this bit. Most of the year it's a fairground, but they put this Christmas show on once a year.'

'It's great, Lee. Fantastic.' Hogan said it like he meant it, and a moment later realised that he did. 'So how are you? Feeling better?'

'Yes, Mr Hogan. Thanks to your help. Sometimes I think I've been a bit naughty, though, getting the police into trouble.'

Lee was frowning.

'Don't worry about that,' said Hogan. 'They were in the wrong. It doesn't often happen but, when it does, they have a duty to put it right.'

Lee's worried expression was replaced by a big smile. 'Mummy's forgiven me, you know, Mr Hogan, for sneaking off back to the cliff the way I did. Says it's her best Christmas ever. *A hundred thousand*, she keeps saying to herself. The lawyers . . . what exactly are lawyers, Mr Hogan?'

'In this instance, Lee, they're people who help you. I wish that were always the case.'

Lee looked puzzled for a moment, then continued.

'Well these lawyers are saying she could get as much as a hundred thousand when it's all sorted. I don't know what they're on about, really. I never was much good at money. But she's bought me that train I was saving for.'

Hogan chuckled.

'And she says it's secured my future. For when she's gone. But she's not going anywhere, is she?'

'I hope not, Lee. I hope not.' Hogan looked into the man's eyes. They were twinkling with joy now. 'Not for a long time, anyway.'

Printed in the United Kingdom
by Lightning Source UK Ltd.
93149